BRAND
Brand, Max,
Iron dust :
33277003219461

D0209324

Iron Dust

OTHER FIVE STAR WESTERNS
BY MAX BRAND:

Men Beyond the Law (1997); *Beyond the Outposts* (1997); *The Fugitive's Mission* (1997); *In the Hills of Monterey* (1998); *The Lost Valley* (1998); *Chinook* (1998); *The Gauntlet* (1998); *The Survival of Juan Oro* (1999); *Stolen Gold* (1999); *The Geraldi Trail* (1999); *Timber Line* (1999); *The Gold Trail* (1999); *Gunman's Goal* (2000); *The Overland Kid* (2000); *The Masterman* (2000); *The Outlaw Redeemer* (2000); *The Peril Trek* (2000); *The Bright Face of Danger* (2000); *Don Diablo* (2001); *The Welding Quirt* (2001); *The Tyrant* (2001); *The House of Gold* (2001); *The Lone Rider* (2002); *Crusader* (2002); *Smoking Guns* (2002); *Jokers Extra Wild* (2002); *Flaming Fortune* (2003); *Blue Kingdom* (2003); *The Runaways* (2003); *Peter Blue* (2003); *The Golden Cat* (2004); *The Range Finder* (2004); *Mountain Storms* (2004); *Hawks and Eagles* (2004); *Trouble's Messenger* (2005); *Bad Man's Gulch* (2005); *Twisted Bars* (2005); *The Crystal Game* (2005); *Dogs of the Captain* (2006); *Red Rock's Secret* (2006); *Wheel of Fortune* (2006); *Treasure Well* (2006); *Acres of Unrest* (2007); *Rifle Pass* (2007); *Melody and Cordoba* (2007); *Outlaws From Afar* (2007); *Rancher's Legacy* (2008); *The Good Badman* (2008); *Love of Danger* (2008); *Nine Lives* (2008); *Silver Trail* (2009); *The Quest* (2009); *Mountain Made* (2009); *Black Thunder* (2009)

Iron Dust

A WESTERN STORY

Max Brand®

FIVE STAR

A part of Gale, Cengage Learning

GALE
CENGAGE Learning™

Detroit • New York • San Francisco • New Haven, Conn • Waterville, Maine • London

GALE
CENGAGE Learning

LIBRARY OF CONGRESS CATALOGING-IN-PUBLICATION DATA

Brand, Max, 1892–1944.
   Iron dust : a Western story / by Max Brand. — 1st ed.
     p. cm.
   Originally published under the name George Owen Baxter as an eight-part serial in Street & Smith's Western story magazine, (1/29/1921–3/19/1921).
   ISBN-13: 978-1-59414-836-1 (hardcover : alk. paper)
   ISBN-10: 1-59414-836-8 (hardcover : alk. paper)
   I. Baxter, George Owen, 1892–1944. Iron dust. II. Title.
PS3511.A87I68 2010
813'.52—dc22   2009046841

First Edition. First Printing: March 2010.

Published in 2010 in conjunction with Golden West Literary Agency.

Printed in the United States of America
1 2 3 4 5 6 7 14 13 12 11 10

EDITOR'S NOTE

Although the majority of Frederick Faust's many serials were generally published in six or seven installments, ten were somewhat longer, appearing in eight parts. One of these was "Iron Dust," which was published in Street & Smith's *Western Story Magazine* in 1921 in the issues dated from January 29th through March 21st. Since then it has never appeared as originally published. The task of rounding up the installments finally ended in 2008, thanks to the Special Collections of the University of Oklahoma Library, the Library of Congress Periodical Division, and William F. Nolan.

The sequel to "Iron Dust"—"When Iron Turns to Gold"— will be published in *The Black Muldoon* (Five Star Westerns, 2010).

CHAPTER ONE

Beside the rear window of the blacksmith shop Jasper Lanning held his withered arms folded against his chest. With the dispassionate eye and the aching heart of an artist he said to himself that his lifework was a failure. That lifework was the young fellow who swung the sledge at the forge, and truly it was a strange product for this seventy-year-old veteran with his slant Oriental eyes and his narrow beard of white. Andrew Lanning was not even his son, but it came about in this way that Andrew became the lifework of Jasper.

Fifteen years before the father of Andy died, and Jasper rode out of the mountain desert like a hawk dropping out of the pale-blue sky, for the clan spirit of the Lannings was as strong as the clan spirit of Campbells and Stewarts in the old days. Jasper buried his brother without a tear, and then sat down and looked at the slender child who bore his name. Andy was a beautiful boy. He had the black hair and eyes, the well-made jaw, and the bone of the Lannings, and if his mouth was rather soft and girlish, he laid the failing to the weakness of childhood. Jasper had no sympathy for tenderness in men. His own life was as littered with hard deeds as the side of a mountain with boulders. But the black, bright eyes and the well-made jaw of little Andy laid hold on him, and he said to himself: *I'm fifty-five. I'm about through with my saddle days. I'll settle down and turn out one piece of work that'll last after I'm gone, and last with my signature on it.*

That was fifteen years ago. And for fifteen years he had labored to make Andy a man according to a grim pattern that was known in the Lanning clan and elsewhere in the mountain desert. His program was as simple as the curriculum of a Persian youth. On the whole, it was even simpler, for Jasper concentrated on teaching the boy how to ride and shoot, and was not at all particular that he learn to speak the truth. But on the first two and greatest articles of his creed, how Jasper labored.

For fifteen years he poured his heart without stint into his work. He taught Andy to know a horse from hock to teeth, and to ride anything that wore hair. He taught him to know a gun as if it were a sentient thing. He taught him all the draws of old and new pattern, and labored to give him both precision and speed. That was the work of fifteen years, and now at the end of this time the old man pressed his bony shoulders against the wall of the blacksmith shop and knew that his work was a failure.

It came coldly and smoothly home to him as truths that we discover for ourselves are apt to do, or as a poniard point comes easily home to the heart. Jasper felt like that—there was death inside him—but he rolled his cigarette in Mexican style, thin and hard, and smoked it with a mask-like face. His lifework was a failure, for he had made the hand of Andrew Lanning cunning, had given his muscles strength, but the heart beneath was wrong.

It was hard to see Andy at the first glance. A film of smoke shifted and eddied through the shop, and Andy, working the bellows, was a black form against the square of the door, a square filled by the blinding white of the alkali dust in the road outside and the blinding white of the sun above. Andy turned from the forge, bearing in his tongs a great bar of iron, black at the ends but white in the middle. The white place was surrounded by a sparkling radiance. Andy caught up an eight-pound hammer, and it rose and fell lightly in his hand; the blows were a shower; there was strength for you. The sparks were flung to the farthest corners of the shop. On the floor they became little spots of darkening red; they rushed against the leather apron of the hammer wielder, and, as the blows fell, rapid waves of light were thrown against the face of Andrew.

Looking at that face one wondered how the lifework of Jasper was such a failure. For Andy was a handsome fellow with his blue-black hair and his black, rather slanting eyes, after the Lanning manner. Yet Jasper saw, and his heart was sick. The face was a little too full; the square bone of the chin was rounded with flesh, and, above all, the mouth had never changed. It was the mouth of the child, soft—too womanly soft. And Jasper blinked.

When he opened his eyes again, the white place on the iron had become a dull red, and the face of the blacksmith was again in shadow. All Jasper could see was the body of Andy, and that was much better. Red light glinted on the sinewy arms and the swaying shoulders, and the hammer swayed and fell tirelessly. For fifteen years Jasper had consoled himself with the strength of the boy, smooth as silk and as durable, the light form that would not tire a horse, but swelled above the waist into those formidable shoulders.

Now the bar was lifted from the anvil and plunged, hissing, into the bucket beside the forge. Above the bucket a cloud of steam rose and showed clearly against the brilliant square of the door, and the peculiar scent that came from the iron went sharply to the nostrils of Jasper. He got up and straightened his long, age-withered limbs as a horseman entered the shop. He came in a manner that pleased Jasper. There was a rush of hoof beats, a form darting through the door, and in the midst of the shop the rider leaped out of the saddle and the horse came to a halt with braced legs. It knocked up a cloud of dust that blew slowly over to Jasper in the rear of the shop.

"Hey, you!" called the rider as he tossed the reins over the head of his horse. "Here's a hoss that needs iron on his feet. Fix him up. And look here"—he lifted a forehoof and showed the scales on the frog and sole of the hoof—"last time you shoed this hoss you done a sloppy job, son. You left all this stuff hangin' on here. I want it trimmed off nice an' neat. You hear?"

The blacksmith shrugged his shoulders.

"Spoils the hoof to put the knife on the sole, Buck," said the smith. "That peels off natural."

"*Hmm,*" said Buck Heath. "How old are you, son?"

"Oh, old enough," answered Andy cheerily. "Old enough to know that this exfoliation is entirely natural."

The big word stuck in the craw of Buck Heath, who brought his thick eyebrows together. "I've rid horses off and on come twenty-five years," he declared, "and I've rid 'em long enough to know how I want 'em shod. This is my hoss, son, and you do it my way. That straight?"

The eye of old Jasper in the rear of the shop grew dim with wistfulness as he heard this talk. He knew Buck Heath; he knew his kind; in his day he would have eaten a dozen men of such rough words and such mild deeds as Buck. But searching the face of Andy, he saw no resentment. Merely a quiet resignation.

"Another thing," said Buck Heath, who seemed determined to press the thing to a disagreeable point. "I hear you don't fit your shoes on hot. Well?"

"I never touch a hoof with hot iron," replied Andy. "It's a rotten practice."

"Is it?" said Buck Heath coldly. "Well, son, you fit my hoss with hot shoes or I'll know the reason why."

"I've got to do the work my own way," protested Andy.

A spark of hope burned in the slant eyes of Jasper.

"Otherwise I can go find another gent to do my shoein'?" inquired Buck.

"It looks that way," replied the blacksmith with a nod.

"Well," said Buck, whose mildness of the last question had been merely the cover for a bursting wrath that now sent his voice booming, "maybe you know a whole pile, boy . . . I hear Jasper has give you consid'able education . . . but what you know is plumb wasted on me. Understand? As for lookin' up another blacksmith, you ought to know they ain't another shop in ten miles. You'll do this job, and you'll do it my way. Maybe you still got another way of thinkin'?"

There was a little pause.

"It's your horse," repeated Andy. "I suppose I can do him your own way."

Old Jasper closed his eyes and grinned in a silent agony. Looking again, he saw Buck Heath grinning with contempt, and for a single moment Jasper touched his gun. Then he remembered that he was seventy years old. He stood up. "Well, Buck?" he said, coming forward. For he felt that, if this scene continued, he would go mad with shame.

There was a great change in Buck as he heard this voice, a marked respect was in his manner as he turned to Jasper. "Hello, Jas," he said. "I didn't know you was here." He stretched out his hand, but Jasper brushed by as if he did not see it.

"Come over to the saloon, Buck, and have one on me," said Jasper. "I guess Andy'll have your hoss ready when we come back."

"Speakin' personal," said Buck Heath with much heartiness, "I don't pass up no chances with no man, and particular if he's Jasper Lanning." He hooked his arm through Jasper's elbow. "Besides, I'm all lined with alkali, Jas." Then he added: "And that boy of yours has got me all heated up. Where'd he learn them man-sized words, Jas?"

All of which Andy heard, and he knew that Buck Heath intended him to hear them. It made Andy frown, and for an instant he thought of calling Buck back. But he did not call. Instead he imagined what would happen. Buck would turn on his heel and stand, towering, in the door. He would ask what Andy wanted. Andy chose the careful insult that he would throw in Buck's face. He saw the blow given. He felt his own fist tingle as he returned the effort with interest. He saw Buck tumble back over the bucket of water. His thoughts roved on. He saw Buck drag himself up and away with a lump on his jaw. He saw the faces of other men as he passed them on the single street of the town. He felt their eyes on him—the man who beat up big Buck Heath.

By this time Andy was smiling gently to himself. His wrath had dissolved in that thinking, and he was humming pleasantly to himself as he began to pull off the worn shoes of Buck's horse.

CHAPTER TWO

Young Andrew Lanning lived in the small, hushed world of his own thoughts. Between him and the bitter necessities of a man's world stood the figure of Jasper, and Uncle Jasper's name was one to frighten off trouble from the most troublesome. Half a century ago he had done things that were now legend, and the awe of his past still surrounded him. It was pleasant for Andy to make things with his hands, and therefore the blacksmith shop contented him. As for the hard labor, his muscles made it play, and as to the future, for which every young man lives, the dreams of Andy made up that time to come.

In reality he neither loved nor hated the world and the people around him. He simply did not see them. His mother—it was from her that he inherited the softer qualities of his mind and his face—had lived long enough to temper his vocabulary; also, she had even left him a little stock of books. And although Andy was by no means a reader, he had at least picked up that dangerous equipment of fiction that enables a man to dodge reality and live in his dreams. Those dreams had as little as possible to do with the daily routine of his life, and certainly the handling of guns, which his uncle enforced upon him, was never a part of the future as Andy saw it.

It was now the late afternoon. The alkali dust in the road was still in a white light, but the temperature in the shop had dropped several degrees. The horse of Buck Heath was shod, and Andy was laying his tools away for the day when he heard the noise of an automobile with open muffler coming down the street. He stepped to the door to watch, and at that moment a big blue car trundled into view around the bend of the road. The rear wheels struck a slide of sand and dust, and skidded. A girl cried out, and then the big machine gathered out of the cloud of dust and came bowling toward Andy. It came with a crackling like musketry, and it was plain that it would leap through Martindale and away into the country beyond at a bound. Andy could see now that it was a roadster, low-hung, ponderous to keep the road. The ways through the mountains must be murderous to such a make of car.

Pat Gregg was leaving the saloon; he was on his horse, but he sat the saddle slanting, and his head was turned to give the farewell word to several figures that bulged through the door of the saloon. For that reason, as well as because of the fumes in his brain, he did not hear the coming of the automobile. His friends from the saloon saw, however. They yelled a warning, but he evidently thought it some jest, as he waved his hand with a grin of appreciation. The big car was coming, rocking with its speed; it was too late now to stop that flying mass of metal.

But the driver made the effort. His brakes shrieked, and still the car shot on with scarcely abated speed, for the wheels could secure no purchase in the thin sand of the roadway. Andy's heart stood still in sympathy as he saw the face of the driver whiten and grow tense. Charles Merchant, the son of rich John Merchant, was behind the wheel. Drunken Pat Gregg had taken the warning at last. He turned in the saddle and drove home his spurs, but even that would have been too late had not Charles Merchant taken the big chance. At the risk of overturning the machine, he veered it sharply to the left. It hung for a moment on two wheels. Andy could count a dozen heartbeats while the plunging car edged around the horse and shoved between Pat and the wall of the house—inches on either side. Yet it must have taken not more than the split part of a second.

There was a shout of applause from the saloon. Pat Gregg sat his horse, mouth open, his face pale, and then the heavy car rolled past the blacksmith shop. Andy, breathing freely and cold to his fingertips, saw young Charlie Merchant relax to a flickering smile as the girl beside him caught his arm and spoke to him.

And then Andy saw her for the first time. She wore a linen duster and a linen hat. All Andy could see was the white flash of her hand as she gestured, and her face. But that was enough. His eyes had been traveling with lightning speed as the car threatened the horse and Pat. Now, in the brief instant as the machine moved by, he not only saw her clearly, but he printed the picture to be seen again when she was gone. What was the hair? Red bronze and fiery where the sun caught at it, and the eyes were gray, or blue, or a gray green. But colors did not matter. It was all in her smile and the turning of her eyes, which were very wide open. She spoke, and it was in the sound of her voice.

"Wait!" shouted Andy Lanning as he made a step toward them. But the car went on, rocking over the bumps and the exhaust roaring. Andy became aware that his shout had been only a dry whisper. Besides, what would he say if they did stop?

And then the girl turned sharply about and looked back, not at the horse they had so nearly struck, but at Andy standing in the door of his shop. It seemed to him that that glance entered his eyes and reached his soul; he felt sure that she would remember his face; her smile had gone out while she stared, and now she turned her head suddenly to the front. Once more the sun flashed on her hair, and then the machine disappeared. In a moment even the roar of the engine was lost, but it came back again, flung in echoes from some hillside.

Not until all was silent, and the boys from the saloon were

shaking hands with Pat and laughing at him, did Andy turn back into the blacksmith shop. It confronted him like a piece of black night with shadows in it. Perhaps that was the effect of the sudden turning from bright daylight.

He sat down on the anvil with his heart beating, and began to recall the picture. Yes, it was all in the smile and the glint of the eyes. And something else—how should he say it?—of light shining through her.

Once, in the mountains, looking suddenly up, it had seemed to Andy that all the stars were looking at him, that he could hear the silence of the wilderness. And his heart had beat as it was beating now. He had never had that sensation again, but he knew the sky would always be there, waiting. And so with this girl. In the dusty street, in the sharp, hot sunshine, in the roar of the motor and the crackling of voices, she had fallen on the mind of Andy like a holy quiet. But having seen her once, he would never see her again.

He could have borne that loss; he could have retained the picture as something beautiful and beautifully impersonal if he had not heard her voice. As a touch of velvet will thrill all the nerves from the fingertips, so the sound of her voice had gone softly through him. And when her face was forgotten, the memory of that voice would keep tugging at his heartstrings.

Suppose one wakens from a dream of music. The music is gone; only the happiness remains, together with the bitter sense of loss. Andy sat on the anvil with closed eyes and put his hand over his heart, where the pain was.

He stood up presently, closed the shop, and went home. Afterward his uncle came in a fierce humor, slamming the door. He found Andy sitting in front of the table staring down at his hands.

"Buck Heath has been talkin' about you," said Jasper.

Andy raised his head. "Look at 'em," he said as he spread out his hands.

"Buck Heath has been sayin' things that would've got him shot when I was your age," said Jasper more pointedly than he had ever spoken before. And he sickened when he saw that Andy refused to hear.

"Look at 'em," repeated Andy. "I been scrubbin' 'em with sand soap for half an hour, and the oil and the iron dust won't come out."

Uncle Jasper, who had a quiet voice and gentle manners, now stood rigid. "I wisht to God that some iron dust would work its way into your soul," he said. He let his voice go big. "Oh, Lord, how I wisht you had some iron dust in your heart."

"What are you talking about?"

"Nothin' you could understand . . . you need a mother to explain things to you."

The other got up, white about the mouth. "I think I do," said Andy. "I'm sick inside."

"Where's supper?" demanded Jasper.

Andy sat down again, and began to consider his hands once more. "There's something wrong . . . something dirty about this life."

"Is there?" Uncle Jasper leaned across the table, and once again the old ghost of a hope was flickering behind his eyes. "Wash off the dirt with soap, then."

"Soap won't touch some kinds of dirt. Uncle Jas, I'm sick inside."

A picture often recurred to Jasper Lanning of the little boy he had first seen, straight, handsome—too handsome. It came home to him now, and he winked his eyes hard.

"Who's been talkin' to you?"

He thought of the grinning men of the saloon, the hidden words. Somebody might have gone out and insulted Andy to his face for the first time. There had been plenty of insults in the past two years, since Andy could pretend to manhood, but none that might not be overlooked. "Who's been talkin' to you?" repeated Uncle Jasper. "Confound that Buck Heath! He's the cause of all the trouble."

"Buck Heath? Who's he? Oh, I remember. What's he got to do with the rotten life we lead here, Uncle Jas?"

"So?" said the old man slowly. "He ain't nothin'?"

"*Bah!*" remarked Andy. "You want me to go out and fight him? I won't. I got no love for fighting. It doesn't buy me anything. I don't like to talk to people when they're mad. Makes me sort of sickish."

"Heaven above!" the older man invoked. "Ain't you got shame? My blood in you, too."

"Don't talk like that," said Andy with a certain amount of reserve that was not natural to him. "You bother me. I want a little silence and a chance to think things out. There's something wrong in the way I've been living."

"You're the last to find it out."

"If you keep this up, I'm going to take a walk so I can have quiet."

"You'll sit there, son, till I'm through with you. Now, Andrew, these years I've been savin' up for this moment when I was sure that. . . ."

To his unutterable astonishment Andy rose and stepped between him and the door. "Uncle Jas," he said, "mostly I got a lot of respect for you and what you think. Tonight I don't care what you or anybody else has to say. Just one thing matters. I feel I've been living in the dirt. I'm going out and see what's wrong. Good night."

CHAPTER THREE

Uncle Jas was completely bowled over. Over against the wall as the door closed he was saying to himself: "What's happened? What's happened?" As far as he could make out his nephew retained very little fear of the authority of Jasper Lanning.

One thing became clear to the old man. There had to be a decision between his nephew and some full-grown man, otherwise Andy was very apt to grow up into a sneaking coward. And in the matter of a contest Jasper could not imagine a better trial horse than Buck Heath. For Buck was known to be violent with his hands, but he was not likely to draw his gun, and, more than this, he might even be bluffed down without making a show of a fight. Uncle Jasper left his house, supperless, and struck down the street until he came to the saloon.

He found Buck Heath warming to his work, resting both elbows on the bar. Bill Dozier was with him—Bill who was the black sheep in the fine old Dozier family. His brother, Hal Dozier, was by many odds the most respected and the most feared man in the region, but of all the good Dozier qualities, Bill inherited only their fighting capacity. He fought; he loved trouble, and for that reason, and not because he needed the money, he was now acting as a deputy sheriff. He was jesting with Buck Heath in a rather superior manner, half contemptuous, half amused by Buck's alcoholic swaggerings. And Buck was just sober enough to perceive that he was being held lightly. He hated Dozier for that treatment, but he feared him too much to take open offense. It was at this opportune moment that old man Lanning, apparently half out of breath, touched Buck on the elbow.

As Buck turned with a surly—"What in tarnation?"—the other whispered: "Be on your way, Buck. Get out of town, and get out of trouble. My boy hears you been talkin' about him, and he allows as how he'll get you. He's out for you now."

The fumes cleared sufficiently from Buck Heath's mind to allow him to remember that Jasper Lanning's boy was no other than the milk-blooded Andy. He told Jasper to lead his boy on. There was a reception committee waiting for him there in the person of one Buck Heath.

"Don't be a fool, Buck," said Jasper, glancing over his shoulder. "Don't you know that Andy's a crazy, man-killin' fool when he gets started? And he's out for blood now. You just slide out of town and come back when his blood's cooled down."

Buck Heath took another drink from the bottle in his pocket, and then regarded Jasper moodily. "Partner," he declared gloomily, putting his hand on the shoulder of Jasper, "maybe Andy's a man-eater, but I'm a regular Andy-eater, and here's the place where I go and get my feed. Lemme loose!" The he turned and kicked open the door of the saloon. "Where is he?" demanded the roaring Andy-eater. Less savagely he went on: "I'm lookin' for my meat."

Jasper Lanning and Bill Dozier exchanged glances of understanding. "Partly drunk, but mostly yaller," observed Bill Dozier. "Soon as the air cools him off outside he'll mount his horse and get on his way. But, say, is your boy really out for his scalp?"

"Looks that way," declared Jasper with tolerable gravity.

"I didn't know he was that kind," said Bill Dozier.

And Jasper flushed, for the imputation was clear. They went together to the window and looked out.

It appeared that Bill Dozier was right. After standing in the middle of the street in the twilight for a moment, Buck Heath turned and went straight for his horse. A low murmur passed around the saloon, for other men were at the windows watching. They had heard Buck's talk earlier in the day, and they growled as they saw him turn tail. He would have no pleasant reception when he next returned to Martindale.

Two moments more and Buck would have been on his horse, but in those two moments luck took a hand. Around the corner came Andrew Lanning with his head bowed in thought.

At once a roar went up from every throat in the saloon: "There's your man! Go to him!"

Buck Heath turned from his horse; Andrew lifted his head. They were face to face, and it was hard to tell to which one of them the other was the least welcome. But Andrew spoke first. A thick silence had fallen in the saloon. Most of the onlookers wore careless smiles, for the caliber of these two was known, and no one expected violence. But Jasper Lanning, at the door, stood with a sick face. He was praying in the silence.

Everyone could hear Andrew say: "I hear you've been making a talk about me, Buck?"

It was a fair enough opening. The blood ran more freely in the veins of Jasper. Perhaps the quiet of his boy had not been altogether the quiet of cowardice.

"*Aw,*" answered Buck Heath, "don't you be takin' everything you hear for gospel. What kind of talk do you mean?"

"He's layin' down," said Bill Dozier, and his voice was soft but audible in the saloon. "The skunk."

"I was about to say," said Andrew, "that I think you had no cause for talk. I've done you no harm, Buck."

The hush in the saloon became thicker; eyes of pity turned on that proved man, Jasper Lanning. He had bowed his head. And the words of the younger man had an instant effect on

Buck Heath. They seemed to infuriate him.

"You've done me no harm?" he echoed. He let his voice out; he even glanced back and took pleasurable note of the crowded faces behind the dim windows of the saloon. Just then Geary, the saloonkeeper, lighted one of the big lamps, and at once all the faces at the windows became black silhouettes. "You done me no harm?" repeated Buck Heath. "Ain't you been goin' about makin' talk that you was after me? Well, son, here I am. Now let's see you eat."

"I've said nothing about you," declared Andy.

There was a groan from the saloon. Once more all eyes flashed across to Jasper Lanning.

"*Bah!*" snorted Buck Heath, and raised his hand.

To crown the horror, the other stepped back. A little puff of alkali dust attested the movement.

"I'll tell you," roared Buck, "you ain't fittin' for a man's hand to touch, you ain't! A hosswhip is more your style."

From the pommel of his saddle he snatched his quirt. It whirled, hummed in the air, and then cracked on the shoulders of Andrew. In the dimness of the saloon door a gun flashed in the hand of Jasper Lanning. It was a swift draw, but he was not in time to shoot, for Andy, with a cry, ducked in under the whip as it raised for the second blow, and grappled with Buck Heath. They swayed, then separated as though they had been torn apart. But the instant of contact had told Andy a hundred things. He was much smaller than the other, but he knew that he was far and away stronger after that grapple. It cleared his brain, and his nerves ceased jumping.

"Keep off," he said. "I've no wish to harm you."

"You houn' dog!" yelled Buck, and leaped in with a driving fist.

It bounced off the shoulder of Andrew. At the same time he saw those banked heads at the windows of the saloon, and knew it was a trap for him. All the scorn and the grief that had been piling up in him, all the cold hurt went into the effort as he stepped in and snapped his fist into the face of Buck Heath. He rose with the blow. All his energy, from wrist to instep, was in that lifting drive. Then there was a jarring impact that made his arm numb to the shoulder. Buck Heath looked blankly at him, wavered, and pitched loosely forward on his face. And his head bounced back as it struck the ground. It was a horrible thing to see, but it brought one wild yell of joy from the saloon—the voice of Jasper Lanning.

Andrew had dropped to his knees and turned the body upon its back. The stone had been half buried in the dust, but it had cut a deep, ragged gash on the forehead of Buck. His eyes were open, glazed, his mouth sagged, and, as the first panic seized Andy, he fumbled at the heart of the senseless man and felt no beat.

"Dead!" exclaimed Andy, starting to his feet. Men were running toward him from the saloon, and their eagerness made him see a picture he had once seen before. A man standing in the middle of a courtroom—the place crowded—the judge speaking from behind the desk—". . . to be hanged by the neck until. . . ."

A revolver came into the hand of Andrew. And when he found his voice it was as thin and high as the voice of a girl, for there was a snapping tension in it. "Stop!" he called. The scattering line stopped like horses thrown back on their haunches by jerked bridle reins. "And don't make no move," continued Andy, gathering the reins of Buck's horse behind him. A blanket of silence had dropped on the street. "The first gent that shows metal," said Andy, "I'll drill him. Keep steady." He turned and flashed into the saddle. Once more his gun covered them. He found his mind working swiftly, calmly. His knees pressed the long holster of an old-fashioned rifle. He knew that make of gun from toe to foresight; he could assemble it in the dark.

"You, Perkins! Get your hands away from your hip. Higher, I say!"

He was obeyed. His voice was still thin, but it kept that line of hands high above their heads. When he moved his gun, the whole line winced; it was as if his will were communicated to them on electric currents. He sent his horse into a walk, into a trot, then dropped along the saddle, and was plunging at full speed down the street, leaving a trail of sharp alkali dust behind him and a long, tingling yell.

Chapter Four

Only one man in the crowd was old enough to recognize that yell, and the one man was Jasper Lanning. A great, singing happiness filled his heart and his throat. But the shouting of the men, as they tumbled into their saddles, cleared his brain. He called to Deputy Bill Dozier, who was kneeling beside the prostrate form of Buck Heath: "Call 'em off, Bill. Call 'em off, or, by the Lord, I'll take a hand in this! He done it in self-defense. He didn't even pull a gun on Buck. Bill, call 'em off!"

And Bill did it most effectually. He straightened, and then got up. "Some of you fools get some sense, will you?" he called. "Buck ain't dead . . . he's just knocked out!"

It brought them back, a shamefaced crew, laughing at each other.

"Where's a doctor?" demanded Bill Dozier.

Someone who had an inkling of how wounds should be cared for was instantly at work over Buck. "He's not dead," pronounced this authority, "but he's danged close to it. Fractured skull, that's what he's got. And a fractured jaw, too, looks to me."

Jasper Lanning was in the midst of a joyous monologue. "You seen it, boys? One punch done it. That's what the Lannings are . . . the one-punch kind. And you seen him get to his gun? Handy. Lord, but it done me good to see him mosey that piece of iron offen his hip. And you looked sick, Gus, when he had you covered. What was it you said about my boy and nerve today? Maybe you've forgot. Well, I'll promise you I won't never tell him. Neat, wasn't it? Clean getaway. See him take that saddle? Where was you with your gat, Joe? Nowhere! Looked to me like. . . ."

The voice of Bill Dozier broke in: "I want a posse. Who'll ride with Bill Dozier tonight?"

It sobered Jasper Lanning. "What d'you mean by that?" he asked. "Didn't the boy fight clean?"

"Maybe," admitted Dozier. "But Buck may kick out. And if he dies, there's got to be a judge talk to your boy. Come on. I want volunteers."

"Dozier, what's all this fool talk?"

"Don't bother me, Lanning. I got a duty to perform, ain't I? Think I'm going to let 'em say later on that anybody done this, and then got away from Bill Dozier? Not me!"

"Bill," said Jasper, "I read in your mind. You're lookin' for action, and you want to get it out of Andy."

"I want nothin' but to get him back."

"Think he'll let you come close enough to talk? He'll think you want him for murder, that's what. Keep off of this boy, Bill. Let him hear the news . . . then he'll come back well enough."

"You waste my time," said Bill, "and all the while a man that the law wants is puttin' ground between him and Martindale. Now, boys, you hear me talk. Who's with Bill Dozier to bring back this milk-fed kid?"

It brought a snarl from Jasper Lanning. "Why don't you go after him by yourself, Dozier? I had your job once and I didn't ask no helpers on it."

But Bill Dozier apparently had no liking for a lonely ride. He made his demand once more, and the volunteers came out. There is always a fascination about a pursuit, and it acted now to make every one of the crowd come close about the deputy. He chose from them wisely, for he knew them all. He picked them for the sake of their steady hands, their cool heads, and also for their horses. A good many offered themselves out of mere shame, but Bill Dozier knew them, and not one was included. In five minutes he had selected five sturdy men, and every one of the five was a man whose name was known.

They went down the street of Martindale without shouting and at a steady lope that their horses could keep up indefinitely. Old Jasper followed them to the end of the village and kept on watching through the dusk until the six horsemen loomed on the hill beyond against the skyline. They were still cantering, and they rode close together like a tireless pack of wolves. After this old Jasper went back to his house, and, when the door closed behind him, a lonely echo went through the place.

"Bah!" said Jasper. "I'm getting soft."

In the meantime, the posse went on, regardless of direction. There were only two possible paths for a horseman out of Martindale—east and west the mountains blocked the way—and young Lanning had started north. Straight ahead of them the mountains shot up on either side of Grant's Pass, and toward this natural landmark Bill Dozier led the way. Not that he expected to have to travel as far as this. He felt fairly certain that the fugitive would ride out his horse at full speed, and then he would camp for the night and make a fire.

Andrew Lanning was town-bred and soft of skin from the work at the forge. When the biting night air got through his clothes, he would need warmth from a fire.

Bill Dozier led on his men for three hours at a steady pace until they came to Sullivan's ranch house in the valley. The place was dark, but the deputy threw a loose circle of his men around the house, and then knocked at the front door. Old man Sullivan answered in his bare feet. Did he know of the passing of young Lanning? Not only that, but he had sold Andrew a horse. It seemed that Andrew was making a hurried trip, that

Buck Heath had loaned him his horse for the first leg of it, and that Buck would call later for the animal. It had sounded strange, but Sullivan was not there to ask questions. He had led Andrew to the corral and told him to make his choice.

"There was an old pinto in there," said Sullivan. "All leather in that hoss. You know him, Joe. Well, the boy runs his eye over the bunch, and then picks the pinto right off. I said he wasn't for sale, but he wouldn't take anything else. I figured a stiff price, and then added a hundred to it. Lanning didn't wink. He took the horse, but he didn't pay cash. Told me I'd have to trust him."

Bill Dozier bade Sullivan farewell, gathered his five before the house, and made them a speech. Bill had a long, lean face, a misty eye, and a pair of drooping, sad mustaches. As Jasper Lanning once said: "Bill Dozier always looked like he was just away from a funeral or just goin' to one." This night the dull eye of Bill was alight.

"Gents," he said, "maybe you all is disappointed. I heard some talk comin' up here that maybe the boy had laid over for the night in Sullivan's house. While he may be a fool, he sure ain't a plumb fool. But, speakin' personal, this trail looks more and more interestin' to me. Here he's left Buck's hoss, so he ain't exactly a hoss thief . . . yet. And he's promised to pay for the pinto, so that don't make him a crook. But when the pinto gives out, Andy'll be in country where he mostly ain't known. He can't take things on trust, and he'll mostly take 'em, anyway. Boys, looks to me like we was after the real article. Anybody weakenin'?"

It was suggested that the boy would be overtaken before the pinto gave out; it was even suggested that this waiting for Andrew Lanning to commit a crime was perilously like forcing him to become a criminal. To all of this the deputy listened sadly, combing his mustaches. The hunger for the manhunt is like the hunger for food, and Bill Dozier had been starved for many a day. When he stood before the saloon, with his arms held above his head like the rest of the crowd, he had sensed many possibilities in young Lanning, and he was more and more determined as the trail wore on to develop the chances to the uttermost.

"Partner," said Bill to the last speaker, "ain't we makin' all the speed we can? Ain't it what I want to come up to the fool kid and grab him before he makes a hoss thief or somethin' out of himself? You gents feed your hosses the spur and leave the thinkin' to me. I got a pile of hunches."

There was no questioning of such a known man as Bill Dozier. The five went rattling up the valley at a smart pace. Yet Andy's change of horses at Sullivan's place changed the entire problem. He had ridden his first mount to a stagger at full speed, and it was to be expected that, having built up a comfortable lead, he would settle his second horse to a steady pace and maintain it.

All night the five went on, with Bill Dozier's long-striding chestnut setting the pace. He made no effort toward a spurt now. Andrew Lanning led them by a full hour's riding on a comparatively fresh horse, and, unless he were foolish enough to indulge in another wild spurt, they could not wear him down in this first stage of the journey. There was only the chance that he would build a fire recklessly near to the trail, but still they came to no sign of light, and then the dawn broke and Bill Dozier found unmistakable signs of a trotting horse that went straight up the valley. There were no other fresh tracks pointing in the same direction, and this must be Andy's horse. And the fact that he was trotting told many things. He was certainly saving his mount for a long grind. Bill Dozier looked about at his men in the gray morning. They were a hard-faced lot; he had not picked them for tenderness. They were weary now, but the fugitive must be still wearier, for he had fear to burden him.

And now they came to a surprising break in the trail. It twisted from the floor of the valley up a steep slope, crossed the low crest of the hills, dipped into a ravine and out again, and finally came out above a broad and open valley.

"What does he mean," said Bill Dozier aloud, "by breakin' for Jack Merchant's house?"

CHAPTER FIVE

The yell with which Andrew Lanning had shot out of Martindale, and which only Jasper Lanning had recognized, was no more startling to the men of the village than it was to Andrew himself. Mingled in an ecstasy of emotion, there was fear, hate, anger, grief, and the joy of freedom in that cry, but it froze the marrow of Andy's bones to hear it.

Fear, most of all, was driving him out of the village. Just as he rushed around the bend of the street, he looked back to the crowd of men tumbling upon their horses; every hand there would be against him. He knew them. He ran over their names and faces. Thirty seconds before he would rather have walked on the edge of a cliff than rouse the anger of a single one among these men, and now, by one blow, he had started them all after him.

Once, as he topped the rise, the folly of attempting to escape from their long-proved cunning made him draw in on the rein a little, but the horse only snorted and shook his head and burst into a greater effort of speed. After all, the horse was right, Andy decided. For the moment he thought of turning and facing that crowd, but he remembered stories about men who had killed the enemy in fair fight, but who had been tried by a mob jury and strung to the nearest tree.

Any sane man might have told Andrew that those days were some distance in the past, but Andy made no distinction between periods. He knew the most exciting events that had happened around Martindale in the past fifty years, and he saw no difference between one generation and the next. In fact, he was not given to sifting evidence. With Uncle Jasper to manage his affairs he had had little to do with men and their ways, and his small contact with people, in the blacksmith shop, outside of purely business dealings, had all gone to convince him that men near Martindale were a bad lot.

Was not Uncle Jasper himself continually dinning into his ears the terrible possibilities of trouble? Was not Uncle Jasper, even in his old age, when no one but a greaser would dream of lifting a hand against him, religiously exacting in his hour or more of gun exercise each day? Did not Uncle Jasper force Andy to go through the same maneuvers for twice as long between sunset and sunrise? And why all these precautions and endless preparations if Martindale men were not killers?

It might have occurred to Andy that no one had been killed in recent months, but it did not occur. He was thinking back to the stories of Jasper, when Martindale, through a period of one bloody six months, had averaged over two killings a day. That was in a period when a gold-rush population clogged the streets and made the saloons bulge with people. But still Andy was unable to distinguish between past and present. It might seem strange that he could have lived so long among these people without knowing them better, but Andy had taken from his mother a little strain of shyness. He never opened his mind to other people, and they really never opened themselves to Andy Lanning. The men of Martindale wore guns, and the conclusion had always been apparent to Andy: they wore guns because, in a pinch, they were ready to kill men.

And Andy Lanning, with a sob in his throat and his eyes drawn to glinting points, sent his horse rushing down the valley.

The fear of wild beasts is terrible enough, and there are few horrors as great as the terror that the criminal feels when he hears the bloodhounds crying down his trail, but of all fears there is none like the fear of man for man. Because it is intelligence following intelligence. If the pursued conceives the most adroit plan with his hard-working imagination, he can never be sure that one of his enemies may not reach a similar conclusion.

To Andy Lanning, as fear whipped him north out of Martindale, there seemed no pleasure or safety in the world except in the speed of his horse and the whir of the air against his face. When that speed faltered he went to the quirt. He spurred mercilessly. Yet he had ridden his horse out to a stagger before he reached old Sullivan's place. Only when the forehoofs of the mustang began to pound did he realize his folly in exhausting his horse when the race was hardly begun. He went into the ranch house to get a new mount.

He had seen old Sullivan many times before, but he had never seen him with such eyes. The pointed face of the old man held a wealth of cunning and knowledge. When he opened the door, he stood for a long moment simply looking at Andy and saying nothing, and for the space of one or two sickening heartbeats it seemed to Andy that the news must have already reached the ranch house. Knowing that this was impossible, he steadied himself with a great effort. It was simply the habitual silence of Sullivan, and not a suspicion. After a moment they were out in the corral looking over the horses with the aid of a lantern.

There was nothing dangerous in that adventure, but when Andy turned his back on the house and started again up the valley, his nerves were singing. He rehearsed the cock-and-bull story he had stammered out to Sullivan. What if the shrewd old fellow had read everything between the lines?

The muscles of Andy's back quivered in hysterical expectation of the bullet that might strike among them. And then darkness settled around him.

When he was calmer, he would rebuild the scene with Sullivan with more truth. He realized that he had played his part well—astonishingly well. His voice had not quivered. His eye had met that of the old rancher every moment. His hand had been as steady as iron.

Something that Uncle Jasper had said recurred to him, something about iron dust. He felt now that there was indeed a strong, hard metal in him; fear had put it there—or was it fear itself? Was it not fear that had brought the gun into his hand so easily when the crowd rushed him from the door of the saloon? Was it not fear that had made his nerves so rock-like as he faced that crowd and made his getaway?

He was on one side now, and the world was on the other. He turned in the saddle and probed the thick blackness with his eyes, then he sent the pinto on at an easy, ground-devouring lope. Sometimes, as the ravine narrowed, the close walls made the creaking of the saddle leather loud in his ears, and the puffing of the pinto, who hated work. Sometimes the hoofs scuffed noisily through gravel, but usually the soft sand muffled the noise of hoofs, and there was a silence as dense as the night around Andy Lanning.

Thinking back, he felt that it was all absurd and dream-like. He had never hurt a man before in his life. Martindale knew it. Why could he not go back, face them, give up his gun, wait for the law to speak?

But when he thought of this, he thought a moment later of a crowd rushing their horses through the night, leaning over their saddles to break the wind more easily, and all ready to kill on this man trail.

All at once a great hate welled up in him, and he gritted his teeth. It was out of this anger, oddly enough, that the memory of the girl came back to him. She was like the falling of this starlight, pure, aloof, and strange and gentle. It seemed to

Andrew Lanning that the instant of seeing her outweighed the rest of his life, but he would never see her again. He began to think with the yearning of a boy—foolish thoughts. If he could make a bargain with those who followed him. If he could make them let him have time to see her for a moment, he would go on and he would attempt no trick to get away. But how could he see her, even if Bill Dozier and his men allowed it? If he saw her, what would he say to her? It would not be necessary to speak. One glance would be enough. He felt that he could carry away a treasure to last a lifetime in another glance.

But, sooner or later, Bill Dozier would reach him. Why not sooner? Why not take the chance, ride to John Merchant's ranch, break a way to the room where the girl slept, smash open the door, look at her once, and then fight his way out? Another time such a thing would have made him shudder. But what place has modesty when a man flees for his life?

He swung out of the ravine and headed across the hills. From the crest the valley was broad and dark below him, and on the opposite side the hills were blacker still. He let the pinto go down the steep slope at a walk, for there is nothing like a fast pace downhill to tear the heart out of a horse. Besides, it came to him after he started, were not the men of Bill Dozier apt to miss this swinging trail?

In the floor of the valley he sent the pinto again into the stretching canter, found the road, and went on with a thin cloud of the alkali dust about him until the house rose suddenly out of the ground, a black mass whose gables seemed to look at him like so many heads above the treetops.

Chapter Six

The house would have been more in place on the main street of a town than here in the mountain desert, but when the first John Merchant had made his stake and could build his home as it pleased him to build, his imagination harked back to a mid-Victorian model, built of wood, with high, pointed roofs, many carved balconies and windows, and several towers. These houses habitually seem in need of new paint, and, looking on them, one pities the men and women who have lived and died there. Such was the house that the first John Merchant built, a grotesque castle of wood. And here the second John Merchant lived with his son Charles, whose taste had quite outgrown the house.

But to the uneducated eye of Andrew Lanning the Merchant house was a great and dignified building, something of which the whole countryside was proud. They would point it out to strangers: "There's the Merchant house. Can you raise that in your home town?"

The way to the house led for a short distance through a grove of trees, then, rounding an elbow turn, revealed the full view of the house. Andrew reined the pinto under the trees to look up at that tall, black mass. It was doubly dark against the sky, for now the first streaks of gray light were pale along the eastern horizon, and the house seemed to tower up into the center of the heavens. Andy sighed at the thought of stealing through the great halls within. Even if he could find an open window, or if the door were unlatched, how could he find the girl?

Another thing troubled him. He kept canting his ear with eternal expectation of hearing the chorus of many hoofs swinging toward him out of the darkness. After all, it was not a simple thing to put Bill Dozier off the trail. When a horse neighed in one of the corrals, Andy started violently and laid his fingertips on his revolver butt.

That false alarm determined him to make his attempt without further waste of time. He swung from the stirrups and went lightly up the front steps. A board creaked slightly beneath him, and Andy paused with one foot raised. He listened, but there was no stir of alarm in the house. Thereafter his footfall was a feathery thing that carried him like a shadow to the door. It yielded at once under his hand, and, stepping through, he found himself lost in utter blackness.

He closed the door, taking care that the spring did not make the lock click, and then stood perfectly motionless, listening, probing the dark.

After a time the shadows gave way before his eyes, and he could make out that he was in a hall with lofty ceiling. Opposite him there was a faint glimmer; that was a big mirror. Something wound down from above at a little distance, and he made out that this was the stairway. Obviously the bedrooms would be in the second story.

Andy began the ascent.

He had occasion to bless the thick carpet before he was at the head of the stairs; he could have run up if he had wished, and never have made a sound. At the edge of the second hall he paused again. The sense of people surrounded him. That indescribable odor of a house was thick in his nostrils; the scent of cooking, which will not out the taint of tobacco smoke. Then directly behind him a man cleared his throat. As though a great hand had seized his shoulder and wrenched him down, Andy whirled and dropped to his knees, the revolver in his hands pointing uneasily here and there like the head of a snake seeking its enemy.

But there was nothing in the hall. The voice became a murmur, and then Andy knew that it had been some man speaking in his sleep.

At least that room was not the room of the girl. Or was she, perhaps, married? Weak and sick, Andy rested his hand against the wall and waited for his brain to clear. "She won't be married," he whispered to himself in the darkness.

But of all those doors up and down the hall, which would be hers? There was no reasoning that could help him in the midst of that puzzle. He walked to what he judged to be the middle of the hall, turned to his right, and opened the first door. A hinge creaked, but it was no louder than the rustle of silk against silk.

There were two windows in that room, and each was gray with the dawn, but in the room itself the blackness was unrelieved. There was the one dim stretch of white, which was the covering of the bed; the furniture, the chairs, and the table were half merged with the shadows around them, and they were as vague as reflections in muddy water. Andy slipped across the floor, evaded a chair by instinct rather than by sight, and leaned over the bed. It was a man, as he could tell by the heavy breathing, yet he leaned closer in a vain effort to make surer by the use of his eyes.

Then something changed in the face of the man in the bed. It was an indescribable change. It was in effect like the change that comes in the face of one we are talking to when we feel the thought in his mind without noting a single change of muscles, but Andrew knew that the man in the bed had opened his eyes. Before he could straighten or stir hands were thrown up. One struck at his face, and the fingers were stiff; one arm was cast over his shoulders, and Andy heard the intake of breath that precedes a shriek. Not a long interval—no more, say, than the space required for the lash of a snapping blacksnake to flick back on itself—but in that interim the hands of Andy were buried in the throat of his victim.

His fingers, accustomed to the sway and quiver of eight-pound hammers and fourteen-pound sledges, sank through the flesh and found the windpipe. And the hands of the other grappled at his wrists, smashed into his face. Andy could have laughed at the effort. He jammed the shin of his right leg just above the knees of the other, and at once the writhing body was quiet. With all of his blood turned to ice, Andy found what he had discovered when he faced the crowd in Martindale, that his nerves did not jump and that his heart, instead of trembling, merely beat with greater pulses. Fear filled him as wine fills a cup, but it cleared his brain; it sent a tremendous nervous power thrilling in his wrists and elbows. All the while he was watching mercilessly for the cessation of the struggles. And when the wrenching at his forearms ceased, he instantly relaxed his grip.

For a time there was a harsh sound filling the room, the rough intake of the man's breath; he was for the time being paralyzed and incapable of any effort except the effort to fill his lungs. By the glint of the metalwork about the bits Andy made out two bridles hanging on the wall near the bed. Taking them down, he worked swiftly. As soon as the fellow on the bed would have his breath he would scream. Yet the time sufficed Andy; he had his knife out, flicked the blade open, and cut off the long reins of the bridles. Then he went back to the bed and shoved the cold muzzle of his revolver into the throat of the other.

There was a tremor through the whole body of the man, and Andy knew that at that moment the senses of his victim had cleared.

He leaned close to the ear of the man and whispered: "Don't make no loud talk, partner. Keep cool and steady. I don't aim to hurt you . . . unless you play the fool."

Instantly the man answered in a similar whisper: "Get that coat of mine out of the closet. There . . . the door is open. You'll find my wallet in the inside pocket and about all you can want will be in it."

"That's the way," reassured Andy. "Keep your head and use sense. But it isn't the coin I want. You've got a red-headed girl in this house. Where's her room?"

His hand that held the revolver was resting on the breast of the man, and he felt the heart of the other leap. Then there was a current of curses, a swift hissing of invective. And suddenly it came over Andy that since he had killed one man, as he thought, the penalty would be no greater if he killed ten. All at once the life of this prostrate fellow on the bed was nothing to him.

When he cut into that profanity, he meant what he said. "Partner, I've got a pull on this trigger. Another ounce will send you right up against eternity. Now cut out that line of chatter and hear me talk. I don't mean the girl any harm, but I've got to see her."

"You . . . you cur. . . ."

"Easy," said Andy. "That took you a long step on your way. There's a slug in this gun just trembling to get at you. And I tell you honest, friend, I'd as soon drill you as turn around. Now tell me where that girl's room is?"

"Anne Withero?" Only his breathing was heard for a moment. Then: "Two doors down, on this side of the hall. If you lay a hand on her, I'll live to. . . ."

"Partner, so help me heaven, I wouldn't touch a lock of her hair. Now lie easy while I make sure of you." And he promptly trussed the other in the bridle reins. Out of a pillow case folded hard he made a gag and tied it into the mouth of the man. Then he ran his hands over the straps; they were drawn taut.

"If you make any noise," he warned the other, "I'll come back to find out why. S'long."

CHAPTER SEVEN

Every moment was bringing on the dawn more swiftly, and the eyes of Andy were growing more accustomed to the gloom in the house. He found the door of the girl's room at once. When he entered, he had only to pause a moment before he had all the details clearly in mind. Other senses than that of sight informed him in her room. There was in the gray gloom a touch of fragrance such as blows out of gardens across a road, yet here the air was perfectly quiet and chill. The dawn advanced. A lesser place of darkness shone in the gloom across the back of a chair. He touched it—something silken and as light as the air. He gathered it into his hand, and it was reduced to a small thing against his palm.

But all that he could make out was a faint touch of color against the pillow—and that would be her hair. Then with astonishing clearness he saw her hand resting against her breast. Andy stood for a moment with his eyes closed, a great tenderness falling around him. The hush kept deepening, and the sense of the girl drew out to him as if a light were brightening about her. It was a holy moment to Andy. There was a feeling that a third presence was hovering about him, seeing and understanding, and that presence was God, he knew.

He stepped back to the table against the wall, took the chimney from the lamp, and flicked a match along his trousers, for in that way a match would make the least noise. Yet to the hair-trigger nerves of Andy the spurt and flare of the match was like the explosion of a gun. He lighted the lamp, turned down the wick, and replaced the chimney. Then he turned as though someone had shouted behind him. He whirled, as he had whirled in the hall, crouching, and he found himself looking straight into the eyes of the girl as she sat up in bed.

Truly he did not see her face at first, but only the fear in it, parting her lips and widening her eyes. The glow of the lamp caught on her hair and turned it into a red-gold river of light that splashed on white shoulders, and then disappeared behind her. A moment before the room had been nothing—a part of the grayness of the dawn—but the lighting of the lamp had shut out the rest of the world, and all the mind, all the soul of Andy was cupped and poured against that tide of bronze light and against the face of the girl. She did not speak; her only movement was to drag up the coverlet of the bed and hold it against the base of her throat.

Andy drew off his hat and stood, crushing it against his breast. His hair, wild from the ride, became wilder as a morning wind drove through the window and made the flame jump in the throat of the lamp. Altogether he was a savage figure, and he saw the fear of him go into the face of the girl as plainly as though he stood in front of a mirror. And it hurt Andy like a bullet tearing through him.

He stepped a little closer; she winced against the back of the bed.

Then Andy came stockstill. "Do you know me?" he asked. He watched her as she strove to speak, but if her lips stirred, they made no sound. It tortured him to see her terror, and yet he would not have had her change. This crystal pallor or a flushed joy—in one of the two she was most beautiful. "You saw me in Martindale," he continued. "I am the blacksmith. Do you remember?"

She nodded, still watching him with those haunted eyes.

"I saw you for the split part of a second," said Andy, "and you stopped my heart. I've come to see you for two minutes . . . I swear I mean you no harm. Will you let me have those two minutes for talk?"

Again she nodded. But he could see that the terror was being tempered a little in her face. There was more plain excitement behind her eyes. She was beginning to think, to wonder. It seemed a natural thing for Andy to go forward a pace closer to the bed, but, lest that should alarm her, it seemed also natural for him to drop upon one knee. It brought the muzzle of the revolver jarringly home against the floor.

The girl heard that sound of metal and it shook her, but it requires a very vivid imagination to fear a man upon his knees. And now that he was not so tall she could look directly into his face, and she saw that he was only a boy, not more than two or three years older than herself. For the first time she remembered the sooty figure that had stood in the door of the blacksmith shop. The white face against the tawny smoke of the shop that had attracted her eyes before. It was the same white face now, but subtly changed. A force exuded from him; indeed, he seemed neither young nor old. Here he was upon his knees. And one wildly romantic thought brushed through her mind, to be instantly dismissed.

She heard him speaking in a voice not louder than a whisper, rapid, distinct, and there was a quality of emotion behind it. She had heard that same quality in the voice of great actors—men who knew how to talk from the heart, or to seem to talk from the heart.

"When you came through the town, you waked me up like a whiplash," he was saying. "When you left, I kept thinking about you. Then along came a trouble. I killed a man. A posse started after me. It's on my heels. I rode like the wind, for I knew it was life or death if they caught me, but I had to see you again. Do you understand?"

A ghost of color was going up her throat, staining her cheeks.

"I had to see you," he repeated. "It's my last chance. Tomorrow they may get me. Two hours from now they may have me salted away with lead. But before I kick out, I had to have one more look at you. So I swung out of my road and came straight to this house. I came up the stairs. I went into a room down the hall and made a man tell me where to find you."

There was a flash in the eyes of the girl like the wink of sun on a bit of quartz on a faraway hillside, but it cut into the speech of Andrew Lanning. "He told you where to find me?" she asked in a voice no louder than the swift, low voice of Andy. But what a world of meaning. What a rush and outpour of contempt and scorn.

"He had a gun shoved into the hollow of his throat," said Andy. "He had to tell . . . two doors down the hall. . . ."

"It was Charlie," said the girl softly. She seemed to forget her fear. Her head raised as she looked at Andy.

It made him flush to see her like that. "I came in here," said Andy. "I lighted the lamp to look at you once. I didn't mean to speak to you. But I had to see you before I go. Do you believe me?"

She brooded on him, excited, fearless now. And she answered: "The other man . . . the one you . . . why. . . ."

"The man I killed doesn't matter," said Andy. "Nothing matters except that I've got this minute here with you."

"But where will you go? How will you escape?"

"I'll go to death, I guess," said Andy quietly. "But I'll have a grin for Satan when he lets me in. I've beat 'em, even if they catch me."

"Tell me your name."

"What's my name? Nothing. And don't waste time on things like that."

The coverlet dropped from her breast; her hand was suspended with stiff fingers. There had been a sound as of someone stumbling on the stairway, the unmistakable slip of a heel and the recovery, then no more sound. Andy was on his feet. She saw his face whiten, and then there was a glitter in his eyes, and she knew that the danger was nothing to him. But Anne Withero whipped out of her bed.

"Did you hear?"

"I tied and gagged him," said Andy, "but he's broken loose, and now he's raising the house on the quiet."

For an instant they stood listening, staring at each other.

"They . . . they're coming up the hall," whispered the girl. "Listen."

It was no louder than a whisper from without—the creak of a board. Andrew Lanning slipped to the door and turned the key in the lock. When he rejoined her in the middle of the room, he gave her the key.

"Let 'em in if you want to," he said.

But the girl caught his arm, whispering: "Hide there in the closet . . . among my clothes. Quick. They . . . they won't dare come in here."

"There's men coming who'll dare a lot more than that. But they don't matter. It's as well here as the next place."

"You mean you're not going to try to get away?"

"Maybe that. Don't you see that I'm happy, Anne Withero?"

"You're not afraid?"

"I'm plumb froze with fear, but with happiness, too."

Looking past him, she saw the knob of the door turn slightly, slowly. She caught her breath. "There's still time. You can get out that window onto the top of the roof below, then a drop to the ground. But hurry before they think to guard that way."

"Confound them and the ways they guard. One minute more of you and me and God, Anne."

"You're throwing yourself away."

"Stand there like that. With your head high. You're beautiful, Anne. And this is worth dyin' for."

His voice shook her. It was as if she were sobbing.

"Then go for my sake," she pleaded.

"I'll go for one thing."

"Name it. Name it." She began to wring her hands, and the lamplight caught at her hair and she was covered to the waist with the ripples of her red-gold hair. Fear had whitened her lips, but her eyes were glorious.

"When you know they've blown me to the four winds, will you say this thing to yourself . . . 'He was no good, but he loved me.' Will you say that?"

"I will. I promise you I will." She was dragging him toward the window.

"Anne!" called a voice suddenly from the hall.

Andy threw up the window, and, turning toward the door, he laughed his defiance and his joy.

"Hurry!" she was demanding. A great blow fell on the door of her room, and at once there was shouting in the hall: "Pete, run outside and watch the window!"

"Will you go?" cried the girl desperately.

He turned toward the window. He turned back like a flash and swept her close to him. "Do you fear me?" he whispered.

"No," said the girl.

"Will you remember me?"

"Forever!"

"God bless you," said Andy as he leaped through the window.

She saw him take the slope of the roof with one stride; she heard the thud of his feet on the ground below. Then a yell from without, shrill and high and sharp.

When the door fell with a crash, and three men were flung into the room, Charles Merchant saw her standing in her nightgown by the open window. Her head was flung back against the wall, her eyes closed, and one hand was pressed across her lips.

"He's out the window. Down around the other way. Curse him!" cried Charles Merchant.

The stampede swept out of the room. Charles was beside her.

She knew that vaguely, and that he was speaking, but not until he touched her bare shoulder did she hear the words: "Anne, are you unhurt . . . has . . . for heaven's sake speak, Anne. What's happened?"

She reached up and pushed his hand away. "Charles," she said, "call them back. Don't let them follow him."

"Are you mad, dear?" he asked. "That murdering. . . ." He found a tigress in front of him.

"If they hurt a hair of his head, Charlie, I'm through with you. I'll swear that!"

It stunned Charles Merchant. And then he went stumbling from the room.

His cowpunchers were out from the bunkhouse already; the guests and his father were saddling or in the saddle.

"Come back!" shouted Charles Merchant. "Don't follow him. Come back! No guns. He's done no harm."

Two men came around the corner of the house, dragging a limp figure between them.

"Is this no harm?" they asked. "Look at Pete, and then talk."

They lowered the tall, limp figure of the man in pajamas to the ground; his face was a crimson smear.

"Is he dead?" asked Charles Merchant.

"No move out of him," they answered.

Other people, most of them on horseback, were pouring back to learn the meaning of the strange call from Charles Merchant.

"I can't tell you what I mean," he was saying in explanation.

"But you, Dad, I'll be able to tell you. All I can say is that he mustn't be followed . . . unless Pete here. . . ."

The eyes of Pete opportunely opened. He looked hazily about him. "Is he gone?" asked Pete.

"Yes."

"Thank the Lord."

"Did you see him? What's he like?"

"About seven feet tall. I saw him jump off the roof of the house. I was right under him. Tried to get my gun on him while he was sprawling after his jump, but he came up like a wildcat and went straight at me. Had his fist in my face before I could get my finger on the trigger. And then the earth came up and slapped me in the face."

"There he goes!" cried someone.

The sky was now of a brightness not far from day, and, turning east, in the direction pointed out, Charles Merchant saw a horseman ride over a hilltop, a black form against the coloring horizon. He was moving leisurely, keeping his horse at the cattle pony's lope. Presently he dipped away out of sight.

John Merchant dropped his hand on the shoulder of his son. He was a stern man, was John Merchant, and his face was not pleasant as Charles turned and looked up at it. But if John Merchant was stern, the face of his son was that of a soul in torment.

"What is it?" asked the father.

"Heaven knows. Not I."

"Here are more people. What's this? A night of surprise parties?"

Six riders came through the trees, rushing their horses, and John Merchant saw Bill Dozier's well-known, lanky form in the lead. He brought his horse from a dead run to a halt in the space of a single jump and slide. The next moment he was demanding fresh mounts.

"Can you give 'em to me, Merchant? But what's all this?"

"You make your little talk," said Merchant, "and then I'll make mine."

"I'm after Andy Lanning. He's left a gent more dead than alive back in Martindale, and I want him. Can you give me fresh horses for me and my boys, Merchant?"

"But the man wasn't dead? He wasn't dead?" cried the voice of a girl. The group opened; Bill Dozier found himself facing a bright-haired girl wrapped to the throat in a long coat, with slippers on her feet.

"Not dead and not alive," he answered. "Just betwixt and between."

"Thank God," whispered the girl. "Thank God."

There was only one man in the group who should not have heard that whispered phrase, and that man was Charles Merchant. He was standing at her side.

CHAPTER EIGHT

It took less than five minutes for the deputy sheriff to mount his men; he himself had the pick of the corral, a dusty roan, and, as he drew the cinch taut, he turned to find Charles Merchant at his side.

"Bill," said the young fellow, "what sort of a man is this Lanning?"

"He's been a covered card, partner," said Bill Dozier. Not since Charles Merchant went away to school had he been able to remember the first name of Dozier, and Bill Dozier's lips were twitching behind his faded mustache. "He's been a covered card that seemed pretty good. Now he's in the game, and he looks like the rest of the Lannings . . . a good lump of daring and defiance. Why d'you ask?"

"Are you keen to get him, Bill?" continued Charlie Merchant eagerly.

"I could stand it. Again, why?"

"You'd like a little gun play with that fellow?"

"I wouldn't complain none."

"*Ah?* One more thing . . . could you use a bit of ready cash?"

"I ain't pressed," said Bill Dozier, working away behind the eyes of the younger man with his own ferret glance. "On the other hand, I ain't of a savin' nature." Then he added: "Get it out, Charlie. I think I follow your drift. And you can go as far as you like." He put out his jaw in an ugly way as he said it.

"It would be worth a lot to me to have this cur done for, Bill.

51

You understand?"

"My time's short. Talk terms, Charlie."

"A thousand."

"The price of a fair hoss."

"Two thousand, old man."

"Hoss and trimmin's."

"Three thousand."

"Charlie, you seem to forget that we're talkin' about a man and a gun."

"Bill, it's worth five thousand to me."

"That's turkey. Let me have your hand."

They shook hands.

"And if you kill the horses," said Charles Merchant, "you won't hurt my feelings. But get him."

"I've got nothing much on him," said Bill Dozier, "but some fools resist arrest." He smiled in a manner that made the other shudder. And a moment later the deputy led his men out on the trail.

They were a weary lot by this time, but they had beneath the belt several shots of the Merchant whiskey that Charles had distributed. And they had that still greater stimulus—fresh horses running, smooth and strong, beneath them. Another thing had changed. They saw their leader, Bill Dozier, working at his revolver and his rifle as he rode, looking to the charges, trying the pressure of the triggers, getting the balance of the weapons with a peculiar anxiety, and they knew, without a word being spoken, that there was small chance of that trail ending at anything short of a red mark in the dust.

It made some of them shrug their shoulders, but here again it was proved that Bill Dozier knew the men of Martindale, and had picked his posse well. They were the common, hard-working variety of cowpuncher, and presently the word went among them from the man riding nearest to Bill that if young Lanning were taken, it would be worth $100 to each of them. Two months' pay for two days' work. That was fair enough. They also began to look to their guns. It was not that a single one of them could have been bought for a man-killing at that or any other price, perhaps, but this was simply a bonus to carry them along toward what they considered an honest duty.

Nevertheless, it was a different crew that rode over the hills away from the Merchant place. There was even something different in their riding. They had begun for the sake of the excitement. Now they were working carefully, riding with less abandon, jockeying their horses, for each man was laboring to be in on the kill.

They had against them a good horse and a stanch horseman. Never had the pinto dodged his share of honest running, and this day was no exception. He gave himself wholeheartedly to his task, and he stretched the legs of the ponies behind him. Yet he had a great handicap. He was tough, but the ranch horses of John Merchant were of the Morgan breed, vicious, a good many of them, but solid and wiry and fast enough for any purpose— such as clinging to a long trail over hill and valley. Above all, they came out from a night of rest. Their lungs were clean of dust. Their legs were full of running. And the pinto, for all his courage, could not meet that handicap and beat it.

That truth slowly sank in upon the mind of the fugitive as he put the game little cattle pony into his best stride. He tried the pinto in the level going. He tried him in the rough. And in both conditions the posse gained slowly and steadily, until it became apparent to Andrew Lanning that the deputy held him in the hollow of his hand, and in half an hour of stiff galloping could run his quarry into the ground, whenever he chose.

Andy turned in the saddle and grinned back at the followers. He could distinguish Bill Dozier most distinctly. The broad brim of Bill's hat was blown up stiffly. And the sun glinted now and again on those melancholy mustaches of his. Andy was puzzled. Bill had horses that could outrun the fugitive, and why did he not use them?

Almost at once Andy received his answer.

The deputy sheriff sent his horse into a hard run, and then brought him suddenly to a standstill. Looking back, Andy saw a rifle pitch to the shoulder of the deputy. It was a flashing line of light that focused suddenly in a single, glinting dot. That instant something hummed evilly beside the ear of Andy. A moment later the report came barking and echoing in his ear with the little metallic ring in it which tells of the shiver of a gun barrel.

That was the beginning of a running fusillade. Technically these were shots fired to warn the fugitive that he was wanted by the law, and to tell him that, if he did not halt, he would be shot at to be killed. But the deputy did not waste warnings. He began to shoot to kill. And so did the rest of the posse. They saw the deputy's plan at once, and they grinned at it. If they rode down in a mob, the boy would no doubt surrender. But if they goaded him in this manner from a distance, he would probably attempt to return the fire. And if he fired one shot in reply, unwritten law and strong public opinion would be on the side of Bill Dozier in killing this criminal without quarter. In a word, the whiskey and the little promise of money were each taking effect on the posse.

They spurted ahead in pairs, halted, and delivered their fire, then the next pair spurted ahead and fired. Every moment or so two bullets winged through the air near and nearer Andy. It was really a wonder that he was not cleanly drilled by a bullet long before that fusillade had continued for ten minutes. But it is no easy thing to hit a man on a galloping horse when one sits on the back of another horse, and that horse heaving from a hard run. Moreover, Andy watched, and, when the pairs halted, he made the pinto weave.

At the first bullet he felt his heart come into his throat. At the second he merely raised his head. At the next he smiled, and thereafter he greeted each volley with a yell and with a wave of his hat. It was like dancing, but greater fun. The cold, still terror was in his heart every moment, but yet he felt like laughing, and, when the posse heard him, their own hearts went cold. It disturbed their aim. They began to snarl at each other, and they also pressed their horses close and closer before they even attempted to fire.

And the result was that Andy, waving his hat, felt it twitched sharply in his hand, and then he saw a neat little hole clipped out of the very edge of the brim. It was a pretty trick to see, until Andy remembered that the thing that had nicked that hole would also cut its way through him, body and bone. He leaned over the saddle and spurred the pinto into his racing gait.

"I nicked him!" yelled the deputy. "Come on, boys! Close in!"

But within five minutes of racing, Andy drew the pinto to a sudden halt and raised his rifle. The posse laughed. They had been shooting for some time, and always for a distance even less than Andy's, yet not one of their bullets had gone home. So they waved their hats recklessly and continued to ride to be in at the death. And everyone knew that the end of the trail was not far off when the fugitive had once begun to turn at bay.

Andy knew it as well as the rest, and his hand shook like a nervous girl's, while the rifle barrel tilted up and up, the blue barrel shimmering wickedly. In a frenzy of eagerness he tried to line up the sights. It was vain. The circle through which he squinted wobbled crazily. He saw two of the pursuers spurt ahead, take their posts, raise their rifles for a fire that would at least disturb his. For the first time they had a stationary target.

And then, by chance, the circle of Andy's sight embraced the body of a horseman. Instantly the left arm, stretching out to support his rifle, became a rock; the forefinger of his right hand was as steady as the trigger it pressed. It was like shooting at a target. He found himself breathing easily.

It was very strange. Find a man with his sights? He could follow his target as though a magnetic power attracted his rifle. The weapon seemed to have volition of its own. It drifted along with the canter of Bill Dozier. With incredible precision the little finger of iron inside the circle dwelt in turn on the hat of Bill Dozier, on his sandy mustaches, on his fluttering shirt. And Andy knew that he had the life of a man under the command of his fore finger.

And why not? He had killed one. Why not a hundred?

The punishment would be no greater. And to tempt him there was this new mystery, this knowledge that he could not miss. It had been vaguely present in his mind when he faced the crowd at Martindale, he remembered now. And the same merciless coldness had been in his hand when he pressed his gun into the throat of Charles Merchant.

He turned his eyes and looked down the guns of the two men who had halted. Then, hardly looking at his target, he snapped his rifle back to his shoulder and fired. He saw Bill Dozier throw up his hands, saw his head rock stupidly back and forth, and then the long figure toppled to one side. One of the posse rushed alongside to catch his leader, but he missed, and Bill, slumping to the ground, was trampled underfoot.

Chapter Nine

At the same time the rifles of the two men of the posse rang, but they must have seen the fall of their leader, for the shots went wild, and Andy Lanning took off his hat and waved to them. But he did not flee again. He sat in his saddle with the long rifle balanced across the pommel while two thoughts went through his mind. One was to stay there and watch. The other was to slip the rifle back into the holster and with drawn revolver charge the five remaining members of the posse. These were now gathering hastily about Bill Dozier. But Andy knew their concern was vain. He knew where that bullet had driven home, and Bill Dozier would never ride again.

One by one he picked up those five figures with his eyes, fighting temptation. He knew that he could not miss if he fired again. In five shots he knew that he could drop as many men, and within him there was a perfect consciousness that they would not hit him when they returned the fire.

He was not filled with exulting courage. He was cold with fear. But it was the sort of fear that makes a man want to fling himself from a great height. But, sitting there calmly in the saddle, he saw a strange thing—the five men raising their dead leader and turning back toward the direction from which they had come. Not once did they look toward the form of Andy Lanning. They knew what he could not know, that the gate of the law had been open to this man as a retreat, but the bullet that struck down Bill Dozier had closed the gate and thrust him out from mercy. He was an outlaw, a leper now. Anyone who shared his society from this moment on would fall under the heavy hand of the law.

But as for running him into the ground, they had lost their appetite for such fighting. They had kept up a long running fight and gained nothing, but a single shot from the fugitive had produced this result. They turned now in silence and went back, very much as dogs turn and tuck their tails between their legs when the wolf, which they have chased away from the precincts of the ranch house, feels himself once more safe from the hand of man and whirls with a flash of teeth. The sun gleamed on the barrel of Andy Lanning's rifle, and these men rode back in silence, feeling that they had witnessed one of those prodigies that were becoming fewer and fewer and farther and farther between around Martindale—the birth of a desperado.

Andrew watched them skulking off with the body of Bill Dozier held upright by a man on either side of the horse. He watched them draw off across the hills, still with that nervous, almost irresistible impulse to raise one wild, long cry and spur after them, shooting, swift and straight, over the head of the pinto. But he did not move, and now they dropped out of sight. And then, looking about him, Andrew Lanning felt how vast were those hills, how wide they stretched, and how small he stood among them. He was alone. He was utterly alone. He almost wished that Bill Dozier were back at the head of the posse hunting for his life. At least, that had been a sort of savage company. But now there was nothing but the hills and a sky growing pale with heat and the patches of olive-gray sagebrush in the distance. The wind picked up a cloud of dust, molded it into the strangely life-like figure of a horseman, and rushed that form across the valley at his left; it melted into thin air, as many a man had melted to nothingness in the mountain desert.

A great melancholy dropped upon Andy. He felt a childish

weakness; dropping his elbows upon the pommel of the saddle, he buried his face in his hands. In that moment he needed desperately something to which he could appeal for comfort. In that moment a child of ten coming upon him could have stuck up Andy with a wooden imitation of a gun and driven him without resistance back to Martindale.

The weakness passed slowly.

He dismounted and looked to the pinto, for the pinto had worked hard, and now he stood with his forelegs somewhat apart and braced, and his head hung low. Every muscle of his body was relaxed, and, like a good cattle pony, not knowing what strange and violent exertion might be demanded of him the next moment, he made the most of this instant of rest. And now the cinches were loosened; the sweat was rubbed carefully from him. Since he stood sagging to the right side and pointing the toe of his off hind hoof, Andy anxiously lifted that hoof to make sure that his horse had not picked up a stone. The pinto rewarded him by coming to life and raising his head just long enough to gauge and deliver a kick at Andy's head. It missed its mark by the proverbial breadth of a hair, and the pinto dropped his head again with a grunt of disappointment.

It made his rider grin with relief, that vicious little demonstration. When the cinches were drawn up again, a moment later, the pinto distended his lungs to make a slack after the girths were fastened, but Andy put his knee into the refractory ribs and crushed them to the breaking point. So the pinto with a sigh expelled his breath and allowed the cinching to be properly finished. The tender care had for a moment given him a thought that this man was no master, but the knee in the ribs removed all doubts. And from that moment the pinto was ready to die for Andy.

The rider, after this little exhibition of temper, stepped back and looked his horse over more carefully. The pinto had many good points. He had ample girth of chest at the cinches, where lung capacity is best measured. He had rather short forelegs, which promised weight-carrying power and some endurance, and he had a fine pair of sloping shoulders. But his belly was a trifle fine drawn, and, although he might stand a drive of a day or two admirably, it was very doubtful if he could endure a long siege of such life as Andy was apt to live. Also, the croup of the pinto sloped down too much, and he had a short neck. Andy knew perfectly well that no horse with a short neck can run fast for any distance. He had chosen the pinto for endurance, and endurance he undoubtedly had, but there was no question that he must have a horse superior in every respect—a horse capable of running his distance and also able to spurt like a trained racer for short distances. For many a time in his life he would need a horse that could put him out of short-shooting distance, and do it quickly. And many a time he would face a long grind across mountain and desert, and both together.

There were no illusions in the mind of Andrew Lanning about what lay before him. Uncle Jasper had told him too many tales of his own experiences on the trail in enemy country.

"There's three things," the old man had often said, "that a man needs when he's in trouble . . . a gun that's smooth as silk, a horse full of running, and a friend."

For the gun Andy had his Colt in the holster, and he knew it like his own mind. There were newer models and trickier weapons, but none that worked so smoothly under the touch of Andy. Thinking of this, he produced it from the holster with a flick of his fingers. The sight had been filed away. When he was a boy in short trousers he had learned from Uncle Jasper the two main articles of a gunfighter's creed—that a revolver must be fired by pointing, not sighting, and that there must be nothing about it liable to hang in the holster to delay the draw. The great idea was to get the gun on your man with lightning speed, and then fire from the hip with merely a sense of direction to guide the bullet. Just as one raises his hand and points the finger. As a rule, one will point with astonishing closeness to the object, but he needs a wrist of iron, and many a long year of practice, to do that accurate pointing when there is a .45 gun in the hand. Uncle Jasper had given him that training, and he blessed the old man for it now.

He had a gun, therefore, and one necessity was his. Sorely he needed a horse of quality as few men needed one. And he needed still more a friend, a haven in time of crisis, an adviser in difficulties. And although Andy knew that it was death to go among men, he knew also that it was death to do without these two things.

He believed that there was one chance left to him, and that was to outdistance the news of the two killings by riding straight north. There he would stop at the first town, in some manner fill his pockets with money, and in some way find horse and friend.

Andrew Lanning was both simple and credulous, but it must be remembered that he had led a sheltered life, comparatively speaking; he had been brought up between a blacksmith shop on the one hand and Uncle Jasper on the other, and the gaps in his knowledge of men were many and huge. The prime necessity now was speed to the northward. So Andy flung himself into the saddle and drove his horse north at the jogging, rocking lope of the cattle pony.

He was in a shallow basin that luckily pointed in the right direction for him. The hills sloped down to it from either side in long fingers, with narrow gullies between, but as Andy passed the first of these pointing fingers a new thought came to him.

It might be—why not?—that the posse had made only a pretense of withdrawing at once with the body of the dead man. No doubt Bill Dozier had taken five hand-picked fellows from the crowd, and it seemed strange, indeed, if they would give up the battle when the odds were still five to one in their favor. Perhaps, then, they had only waited until they were out of sight and had then circled swiftly around, leaving one man with the body. They might be waiting now at the mouth of any of these gullies.

No sooner had the thought come to Andy than he whitened. The pinto had been worked hard that morning and all the night before, but now Andy sent the spurs home without mercy as he shot up the basin at full speed. Each spur of hills pointed at him accusingly. Each shadowy cañon yawned like a door of danger as he passed, and he went with his revolver drawn, ready for a snap shot, and a drop behind the far side of his horse.

For half an hour he rode in this fashion with his heart beating at his teeth. And each cañon as he passed was empty, and each had some shrub, like a crouching man, to startle him and upraise the revolver. At length, with the pinto wheezing from this new effort, he drew back to an easier gait. But still he had a companion ceaselessly following like the shadow of the horse he rode. It was fear, and it would never leave him.

CHAPTER TEN

In her room, Anne Withero was reading. She had always disliked that room, for her tastes were by no means idle standards but tyrants, and the flowered wallpaper of that old-fashioned place and the vivid red of the carpet were a torture to her eyes. The room had not changed overnight, yet now she preferred it to any other place in the house. And there was only one possible explanation. Once, twice, and again she got up from her chair to examine the sill of her window. On it there was a dotted scratch in the paint, such a scar as the sharp rowel of a spur might make. And on the slant roof of the verandah below her there was a broken shingle on which she could make out—or perhaps this was imagination—the print of a heel. At any rate, the window sill fascinated her.

After that forced and early rising the rest of the house had remained awake, but Anne Withero was gifted with an exceptionally strong set of nerves. She had gone back to bed and fallen promptly into a pleasant sleep. And when she wakened all that had happened in the night was filmed over and had become dream-like.

No one disturbed her rest, but, when she went down to a late breakfast, she found Charles Merchant lingering in the room. He had questioned her closely, and after a moment of thought she told him exactly what had happened, because she was perfectly aware that he would not believe a word of it. And she was right. He had sat opposite her, drumming his fingers without noise on the table, with a smile now and then that might be plain amusement, but that was tinged, she thought, with insolence.

Yet he seemed oddly undisturbed. She had expected some jealous outburst, some keen questioning of the motives that had made her beg them not to pursue this man. But Charles Merchant was only interested in what the fellow had said and done when he talked with her. "He was just like a man out of a book," said the girl in conclusion, "and I'll wager that he's been raised on romances. He had the face for it, you know . . . and the wild look."

"A blacksmith . . . in Martindale . . . raised on romances?" Charles had said as he fingered his throat, which was patched with black and blue.

"A blacksmith . . . in Martindale," she had repeated slowly. And it brought a new view of the affair home to her. It had all seemed quite clear before. This romantic fellow caught a glimpse of her, thought he was in love with a face, got into a scrape, and like a wild boy risked his life to see that face again while he was being pursued. Besides, now that they knew from Bill Dozier that the victim in Martindale had been only injured, and not actually killed, the whole matter became rather a farce. It would be an amusing tale. But now, as Charles Merchant repeated the words—"blacksmith," "Martindale"—the new idea shocked her, the new idea of Andrew Lanning, for Charles had told her the name.

The new thought stayed with her when she went back to her room after breakfast ostensibly to read, but really to think, for Anne Withero was still young enough to love to turn adventures over her tongue like a wine-taster.

Remembering Andrew Lanning, she got past the white face and the brilliant black eyes; she felt, looking back, that he had shown a restraint that was something more than boyish. When he had taken her in his arms just before he fled, he had not kissed her, although for that matter she had been perfectly ready to let him do it.

That moment kept recurring to her—the beating on the door, the voices in the hall, the shouts, and the arms of Andrew Lanning around her, and his tense, desperate face close to hers. It became less dream-like that moment. It became a living thing that grew more and more vivid. She began to understand that if she lived to be a hundred, she would never find that memory dimmer. Men had made love to her, had poured out their hearts before her, but only once she had seen the soul of a man. And very naturally she kept thinking: *What did he see in return?* No, he had not seen the truth, but he had taken away a picture to worship. It was not strange that she did not hold this against young Lanning.

When her eyes were misty with this thought, and a half-sad, half-happy smile was touching the corners of her mouth, Charles Merchant knocked at her door. Truly it was a most inopportune moment, but, since she had promised to become his wife, Charles made a common masculine mistake—he considered that she was already a possession and that even her thoughts belonged to him. She gave herself one moment in which to clear the wistfulness from her face, one moment to banish the queer pain of knowing that she would never see this wild Andrew again, and then she told Charles to come in.

In fact, he was already opening the door, and she resented this fiercely. Besides, there was a ragged crack across the door where they had battered it down early that day. Then Charles stood before her. He was calm of face, but she guessed an excitement beneath the surface.

"I've got something to show you," he said.

A great thought made her sit up in the chair, but she was afraid just then to stand up. "I know. The posse has reached that silly boy and brought him back. But I don't want to see him again. Handcuffed, and all that."

"The posse is here, at least," said Charles noncommittally.

She was finding something new in him. The fact that he could think and hide his thoughts from her was indeed very new, for, when she first met him, he had seemed all surface, all clean young manhood without a stain, frank, careless, gay. Also, he danced wonderfully, and could wear his clothes. Everything between them had grown out of that, and an impulse.

"Do you want me to see the six brave men again?" she asked, smiling, but really she was prying at his mind to get a clue of the truth. "Well, I'll come down."

And she went down the stairs with Charles Merchant beside her; he kept looking straight ahead, biting his lips, and this made her wonder. She began to hum a gay little tune, and the first bar made the man start. So she kept on. She was bubbling with apparent good nature when Charles, all gravity, opened the door of the living room.

The shades were drawn. The quiet in that room was a deadly, living thing. And then she saw, on the sofa at one side of the place, a human form under a sheet.

"Charles," whispered the girl. She put out her hand and touched his shoulder, but she could not take her eyes off that ghastly dead thing. "They . . . they . . . he's dead . . . Andrew Lanning. Why did you bring me here?"

"Take the cloth from his face," commanded Charles Merchant, and there was something so hard in his voice that she obeyed.

She did not want to see the horror beneath, but she followed his order in a daze. The sheet came away under her touch, and she was looking into the sallow face of Bill Dozier. She had remembered him because of the sad mustaches, that morning, and his big voice.

"That's what your romantic boy out of a book has done," said Charles Merchant. "Look at his work."

But she dropped the sheet and whirled on him. "And they left him . . . ," she said.

"Anne," he said, "are you thinking about the safety of that murderer . . . now? He's safe, but they'll get him later on . . . he's as good as dead, if that's what you want to know."

"God help him," said the girl. And going back a pace, she stood in the thick shadow, leaning against the wall, with one hand across her lips.

It reminded Charles of the picture he had seen when he broke into her room after Andrew Lanning had escaped. And she looked now, as then, more white, more beautiful, more wholly to be desired than he had ever known her before. Yet he could neither move nor speak. He saw her go out of the room with staring eyes. Then, without stopping to replace the sheet, he followed.

He had hoped to wipe the last thought of that vagabond blacksmith out of her mind with the shock of this horror. Instead, he knew now that he had done quite another thing. And in addition he had probably made her despise him for taking her to confront such a sight.

All in all, Charles Merchant was exceedingly thoughtful as he closed the door and stepped into the hall. He ran up the stairs to her room. The door was closed. There was no answer to his knock, and by trying the knob he found that she had locked herself in. And the next moment he could hear her sobbing. He stood for a moment more, listening, and wishing Andrew Lanning dead with all his heart.

Then he went down to the garage, climbed into his car, and burned up the road between his place and that of Hal Dozier. There was very little similarity between the two brothers. Bill had been tall and lean; Hal was compact and solid, and he had the fighting agility of a starved coyote. He had a smooth-shaven face as well, and a clean eye, which was known wherever men gathered in the mountain desert. There was no news to give him. A telephone message had already told him of the death of Bill Dozier.

"But," said Charles Merchant, "there's one thing I can do. I can set you free to run down this Lanning."

"How?"

"You're needed on your ranch, Hal, but I want you to let me stand the expenses of this trip. Take your time, make sure of him, and run him into the ground."

"My friend," said Hal Dozier, "you turn a pleasure into a real party."

And Charles Merchant left, knowing that he had signed the death warrant of young Lanning. In all the history of the mountain desert there was a tale of only one man who had escaped, once Hal Dozier took his trail, and that man had blown out his own brains.

CHAPTER ELEVEN

Far away in the western sky Andy Lanning saw a black dot that moved in wide circles and came up across the heavens slowly, and he knew it was a buzzard that scented carrion and was coming up the wind toward that scent. He had seen them many a time before on their gruesome trails, and the picture that he carried was not a pleasant one.

But now the picture that drifted through his mind was still more horrible. It was a human body lying face downward in the sand with the wind ruffling in the hair and the hat rolled a few paces off and the gun close to the outstretched hand. That was the way they would leave him when they found him. And he knew from Uncle Jasper that no matter how far the trail led, or how many years it was ridden, the end of the outlaw was always the same—death and the body left to the buzzards. Or else, in some barroom, a footfall from behind and a bullet through the back.

The flesh of Andy crawled. Hunger was a sharp pain in his vitals. He smoked a cigarette and forgot it. His eyes dimmed from long wakefulness and from squinting across the sand, but one rub of his hand restored the freshness of his sight. It was not possible for him to relax in vigilance for a moment, lest danger come upon him when he least expected it. Perhaps, in some open space like this. He could feel the muscles of his face drawing with the test, but he went on until the sun was low in the west and all the sky was rimmed with color.

The mountain desert changed now. The hills were hung with blue on the eastern sides. The coolness seemed to come out of the ground, and the wind changed its direction. But for Andy these were not pleasant things. Night had become an enemy. And the first moments of his long torment were beginning— men, who made up his danger, were also a necessity, and he felt that any danger were better than this solitude and the dark.

The sun was down, and dusk had come over the hills in a rush, when he saw a house half lost in the shadows. It was a narrow-fronted, two-storied, unpainted, lonely place, without sign of a porch. It was obviously not made to be lived in and enjoyed. It was only a shelter into which people crept for the night, or where they ate their meals. And here certainly, where there was no vestige of a town near, and where there was no telephone, the news of the deaths of Bill Dozier and Buck Heath could not have come. Andy accepted the house as a blessing and went straight toward it.

But the days of carelessness were over for Andy, and he would never again approach a house without searching it like a human face. He studied this shack as he came closer. It was an evil-appearing building, with no sign of smoke from the stovepipe until he was almost on the house, and then he saw a meager wisp of vapor, showing that the fire had almost burned down. And if there were people in the building, they did not choose to show a light. The windows were black inside, and on the outside they glimmered with the light reflected from the sky.

Andy went around to the rear of the house, where there was a low shed beside the corral, half tumbled down because the owner had fed from it carelessly, but in the corral were five or six fine horses—wild fellows with bright eyes and long forelocks. They had the long necks of speed, and lithe, strong bodies. Andy looked upon them wistfully. Not one of them but was worth the price of three of the pinto, but as for money there was not $5 in the pocket of Andy.

Stripping the saddle from the pinto, he put it under the shed and left the mustang to feed and find water in the small pasture. Then he went with the bridle, that immemorial sign of one who seeks hospitality in the West, toward the house. He was met halfway by a tall, strong man of middle age or more. There was no hat on his head, which was covered with a shock of brown hair much younger than the face beneath it. He beheld Andy without enthusiasm.

"You figure on layin' over here for the night, stranger?" he asked.

"That's it," said Andy.

"I'll tell you how it is," said the big man in the tone of one who is willing to argue a point. "We ain't got a very big house . . . you see it . . . and it's pretty well filled right now. If you was to slope over the hills there, you'd find Gainorville inside of ten miles."

Andy explained that he was at the end of a hard ride. He pointed to the pinto, which, in spite of a roll in the pasture, still bore the distinct outlines of the saddle, black with sweat, and all the rest of him dusted with salt, where the perspiration had come out and repeatedly dried in layers. "Ten more miles would kill the pinto," he said simply. "But if you don't mind, I'll have a bit of chow, and then turn in out there in the shed. That won't crowd you in your sleeping quarters, and it'll be fine for me."

The big man opened his mouth to say something more. Andy, watching him with active eyes, saw three distinct shades of expression cross the face of the other, then his host turned on his heel.

"I guess we can fix you up," he said. "Come on along."

At another time Andy would have lost a hand rather than accept such churlish hospitality, but he was in no position to choose. The pain of hunger was like a voice speaking in him.

It was a four-room house. The rooms on the ground floor were the kitchen, where Andy cooked his own supper of bacon and coffee and flapjacks, and the combination living room/dining room, and, from the bunk covered with blankets on one side, the bedroom. Upstairs there must have been two more rooms of the same size.

Seated about a little kitchen table in the front room, Andy found three men playing an interrupted game of blackjack, which was resumed when the big fellow took his place before his hand. The three gave Andy a look and a grunt, but otherwise they paid no attention to him. And if they had consulted him, he could have asked for no greater favor. Yet he had an odd hunger about seeing them. They were the last men in many a month perhaps whom he could look at or who he could permit to see him without a fear. He brought his supper into the living room and put his cup of coffee on the floor beside him. While he ate, he watched them together and in detail.

They were, all in all, the least prepossessing group he had ever seen. The man who had brought him in was far from well-favored, but he was handsome compared with the others. Opposite him sat a tall fellow very erect and stiff in his chair. A candle had recently been lighted, and it stood on the table near this man. It showed a wan face of excessive leanness, and lank hair that seemed damp straggling across his forehead. His eyes were deep under bony brows, and they alone of the features showed any expression as the game progressed, turning now and again to the other faces with glances that burned; he was losing steadily. A red-headed man was on his left, with his back to Andy, but now and again he turned, and Andy saw a heavy jowl and a skin blotched with great, rusty freckles. His shoulders overflowed the back of his chair, which creaked whenever he moved, and Andy knew the man was a veritable Hercules—when he dropped his arm the tips of his fingers brushed close to the floor.

The man who faced the redhead was as light as his companion was ponderous. He had frail hands and wrists, almost girlish; he was dressed also in a sort of feminine neatness and display; his voice was gentle, his eyes large and soft, and his profile was exceedingly handsome. But in the full view Andy saw nothing except a grisly, purple scar that twisted down beneath the right eye of the man. It drew down the lower lid of that eye, and it pulled the mouth of the man a bit awry, so that he seemed to be smiling in a smug, half-apologetic manner. In spite of his youth and his gentle manner he was unquestionably the dominant spirit here. Once or twice the others lifted their voices in argument, and a single word from him cut them short. And when he raised his head, now and again, to look at Andy, it gave the latter a feeling that his secret was read and all his past known.

These strange fellows had not asked his name, and neither had they introduced themselves, but from their table talk he gathered that the redhead was named Jeff, the funereal man with the bony face was Larry, the brown-haired one was Joe, and he of the scar and the smile was Henry. It occurred to Andy as odd that such rough boon companions had not shortened that name for convenience.

They played with the most intense concentration. As the night deepened and the windows became black slabs Joe brought another candle and reinforced this light by hanging a lantern from a nail on the wall. This illuminated the entire room, but in a partial and dismal manner. The game went on. They were playing for high stakes; Andrew Lanning had never seen so much cash assembled at one time. They had stacks of unmistakable yellow gold before them—actually stacks. He counted fifty $10 gold pieces before Jeff; Henry lost steadily, but replaced his losses from an apparently inexhaustible purse; Joe had about the same amount as Jeff, but the winner was

Larry. That skull-faced gentleman was fairly barricaded behind heaps of money. Andy estimated swiftly that there must be well over $2,000 in those stacks.

He finished his supper, and, having taken the tin cup and plate out into the next room and cleaned them, he had no sooner come back to the door, on the verge of bidding them good night, than Henry invited him to sit down and take a hand.

CHAPTER TWELVE

He had never studied any men as he had watched these men at cards. Andrew Lanning had spent most of his life quite indifferent to the people around him, but now it was necessary to make quick judgments and sure. He had to read unreadable faces. He had to guess motives. He had to sense the coming of danger before it showed its face. And, watching them with such intentness, he understood that at least three of them were cheating at every opportunity. Henry, alone, was playing a square game; as for the heavy winner, Larry, Andrew had reason to believe that he was adroitly palming an ace now and again—luck ran too consistently his way. For his own part, he was no card expert, and he smiled as Henry made his offer.

"I've got eleven dollars and fifty cents in my pocket," he said frankly. "I won't sit in at that game."

"Then the game is three-handed," said Henry as he got up from his chair. "I've fed you boys enough," he continued in his soft voice. "I know a three-handed game is no good, but I'm through. Unless you'll try a round or two with 'em, stranger? They've made enough money. Maybe they'll play for silver for the fun of it, eh, boys?"

There was no enthusiastic assent. The three looked gravely at a victim with $11.50, the chair of big Jeff creaking noisily as he turned. "Sit in," said Jeff. He made a brief gesture, like one wiping an obstacle out of the way.

"All right." Andy nodded, for the thing began to excite him.

He turned to Henry. "Suppose you deal for us?"

The scar on Henry's face changed color, and his habitual smile broadened. "Well!" exclaimed Larry. "Maybe the gent don't like the way we been runnin' this game in other ways. Maybe he's got a few more suggestions to make, sittin' in? I like to be obligin'." He grinned, and the effect was ghastly.

"Thanks," said Andy. "That lets me out as far as suggestions go." He paused with his hand on the back of the chair, and something told him that Larry would as soon run a knife into him as take a drink of water. The eyes burned up at him out of the shadow of the brows, but Andy, although his heart leaped, made himself meet the stare. Suddenly it wavered, and only then would Andy sit down.

Henry had drawn up another chair. "That idea looks good to me," he said. "I think I shall deal." And forthwith, as one who may not be resisted, he swept up the cards and began to shuffle.

The others at once lost interest. Each of them nonchalantly produced silver, and they began to play negligently, careless of their stakes.

But to Andy, who had only played for money half a dozen times before, this was desperately earnest. He kept to a conservative game, and slowly but surely he saw his silver being converted into gold. Only Larry noticed his gains—the others were indifferent to it, but the skull-faced man tightened his lips as he saw. Suddenly he began betting in gold, $10 for each card he drew. The others were out of that hand. Andy, breathless, for he had an ace down, saw a three and a two fall—took the long chance, and, with the luck behind him, watched a five spot flutter down to join his draw. Yet Larry, taking the same draw, was not busted. He had a pair of deuces and a four. There he stuck, and it stood to reason that he could not win. Yet he bet recklessly, raising Andy twice, until the latter had no more money on the table to call a higher bet. The showdown revealed an ace under cover for Larry, also. Now he leaned across the table, smiling at Andrew.

"I like the hand you show," said Larry, "but I don't like your face behind it, my friend." His smile went out—his hand jerked back—and then the lean, small hand of Henry shot out and fastened on the tall man's wrist.

"You skunk," said Henry. "D'you want to get the kid for that beggarly mess? *Bah!*"

Andy, colorless, his blood cold, brushed aside the arm of the intercessor. "Partner," he said, leaning a little forward in turn, and thereby making his holster swing clear of the seat of his chair, "partner, I don't mind your words, but I don't like the way you say 'em."

When he began to speak, his voice was shaken; before he had finished, his tones rang and he felt once more that overwhelming desire that was like the impulse to fling himself from a height. He had felt it before, when he watched the posse retreat with the body of Bill Dozier. He felt it now—a vast hunger, an almost blinding eagerness to see Larry make an incriminating move with his bony, hovering, right hand. The bright eyes burned at him for a moment longer out of the shadow. Then, again, they wavered, and turned away.

Andy knew that the fellow had no more stomach for a fight. Shame might have made him go through with the thing he started, however, had not Henry cut in again and given Larry a chance to withdraw gracefully.

"The kid's called your bluff, Larry," he said. "And the rest of us don't need to see you pull any target practice. Shake hands with the kid, will you, and tell him you were joking."

Larry settled back in his chair with a grunt, and Henry, without a word, tipped back in his chair and kicked the table. Andy, beside him, saw the move start, and he had just time to scoop his own winnings, including that last rich bet, off the table top and into his pocket. As for the rest of the coin, it slid with a noisy jangle to the floor and it turned the other three men into scrambling madmen. They scratched and clawed at the money, cursing volubly, and Andy, stepping back out of the fracas, saw the scar-faced man watching with a smile of contempt. There was a snarl. Jeff had Joe by the throat, and Joe was reaching for his gun. Henry moved forward to interfere once more, but this time he was not needed. A clear whistling sounded outside the house, and a moment later the door was kicked open. A man came in with his saddle on his hip.

His appearance converted the threatening fight into a scene of jovial good nature. The money was swept up at random, as though none of them had the slightest care what became of it. Coin appeared to be made cheap by the appearance of this fifth man.

"Havin' one of your little parties, eh?" said the stranger. "What started it?"

"He did, Scottie," answered Larry, and, stretching out an arm of enormous length, he pointed at Andrew.

Again it required the intervention of Henry to explain matters, and Scottie, with his hands on his hips, turned and surveyed Andrew with considering eyes. He was much different from the rest. Whereas they had one and all a peculiarly unhealthy effect upon Andy, this newcomer was a cheery fellow, with an eye as clear as crystal, and color in his tanned cheeks. He had one of those long faces that invariably imply shrewdness, and he canted his head to one side while he watched Andy.

"You're him that put the pinto in the corral, I guess?" he said.

Andy nodded.

There was no further mention of the troubles of that card game. Jeff and Joe and Larry were instantly busied about the kitchen and in arranging the table, while Scottie, after the manner of a guest, bustled about and accomplished little.

But the eye of Andrew, then and thereafter, whenever he was near the five, kept steadily upon the scar-faced man. Henry had tilted his chair back against the wall. The night had come on chill, with a rising wind that hummed through the cracks of the ill-built wall and tossed the flame in the throat of the chimney. Henry draped a coat like a cloak around his shoulders and buried his chin in his hands, separated from the others by a vast gulf. Presently Scottie was sitting at the table. The others were gathered around him in expectant attitudes. One or two unavoidable side glances flashed across at Andy, and he knew that he was not wanted, but he was too much fascinated by this strange society to leave.

Red-headed Jeff, his burly face twisting with anxiety, asked: "And did you see her, man?"

"Sure did I," Scottie answered. "She's doin' fine. Nothin' to be asked better. She had some messages to send you, lad." He smiled at Jeff, who sighed. Then he turned to Larry; "I sent the money," he said, and the skull-faced man nodded. To Joe: "The kid weighs eighty-seven pounds. Looks more a ringer for you every day."

To each of them one important message, except for Henry.

"What else is new?" they exclaimed in one voice.

"Oh, about a million things. Let me get some of this ham into my face, and then I'll talk. I've got a batch of newspapers yonder. There's a gold rush on up to Tolliver's Creek."

Andy blinked, for that news was at least four weeks old. But now came a tide of other news, and almost all of it was stale stuff to him. But the men drank it in—all except Henry, silent in his corner. He was relaxed, as if he slept. "But the most news is about the killing of Bill Dozier."

CHAPTER THIRTEEN

"Bill!" grunted red-headed Jeff. "Well, I'll be hung. There's one good deed done. He was overdue, anyways."

Andy, waiting breathlessly, watched lest the eye of the narrator should swing toward him for the least part of a second. But Scottie seemed utterly oblivious of the fact that he sat in the same room with the murderer.

"Well, he got it," said Scottie. "And he didn't get it from behind. Seems there was a young gent in Martindale . . . all you boys know old Jasper Lanning?" There was an answering chorus. "Well, he's got a nephew, Andrew Lanning. This kid was sort of a bashful kind, they say. But yesterday he up and bashed a fellow in the jaw, and the man went down. Whacked his head on a rock, and young Lanning thought his man was dead. So he holds off the crowd with a gun, hops a horse, and beats it."

"Pretty, pretty," murmured Larry. "But what's that got to do with that hyena Bill Dozier?"

"I don't get it all hitched up straight. Most of the news come from Martindale to town by telephone. Seems this young Lanning was follered by Bill Dozier. He was always a hound for a job like that, eh?"

There was a growl of assent.

"He hand-picked five rough ones and went after Lanning. Chased him all night. Landed at John Merchant's place. The kid had dropped in there to call on a girl. Can you beat that for cold nerve, him figuring that he'd killed a man, and Bill Dozier and five more on his trail to bring him back to wait and see whether the buck he dropped, lived or died . . . and then to slide over and call on a lady? No, you can't raise that."

But the tidings were gradually breaking in upon the mind of Andrew Lanning. Buck Heath had not been dead; the pursuit was simply to bring him back on some charge of assault; now . . . Bill Dozier. . . . The head of Andrew swam.

"Seems he didn't know her, either. Just paid a call around about dawn and then rode on. Oh, that's the frosty nerve for you. Bill comes along a little later on the trail, gets new horses from Merchant, and runs down Lanning early this morning. Runs him down, and then Lanning turns in the saddle and drills Bill through the head at five hundred yards."

Henry came to life. "How far?" he said.

"That's what they got over the telephone," said Scottie apologetically.

"Then the news got to Hal Dozier from Merchant's house. Hal hops on the wire and gets in touch with the governor, and in about ten seconds they make this Lanning kid an outlaw and stick a price on his head . . . five thousand, I think, and they say Merchant is behind it. The telephone was buzzing with it when I left town, and most of the boys were oiling up their gats and getting ready to make a play. Pretty easy money, eh, for putting the rollers under a kid?"

Andrew Lanning muttered aloud: "An outlaw."

"Not the first time Bill Dozier has done it," said Henry calmly. "That's an old maneuver of his . . . to hound a man from a little crime to a big one."

The throat of Andrew was dry. "Did you get a description of young Lanning?" he asked.

"Sure." Scottie nodded. "Twenty-three years old, about five feet ten, black hair and black eyes, good-looking, big shoulders, quiet spoken."

Andrew made a gesture and looked carelessly out the back window, but, from the corner of his eyes, he was noting the five men. Not a line of their expressions escaped him. He was seeing, literally, with eyes in the back of his head, and if, by the interchange of one knowing glance, or by a significant silence, even, these fellows had indicated that they remotely guessed his identity, he would have been on his feet like a tiger, gun in hand, and backing for the door. $5,000! What would not one of these men do for that sum? And yet, money seemed plentiful among them. But $5,000! A man could buy twenty fine horses for that price; he could buy a store and set up in business for that price. A struggling family could lift its mortgage and breathe freely for a smaller sum than that. And of his few friends, what one was there who would shelter him or aid him? What human being in the world would prefer him to $5,000?

All of this ran through the brain of Andy in the second in which he turned his head toward the window. He had been keyed to the breaking point before, but his alertness was now trebled, and, like a sensitive barometer, he felt the danger of Larry, the brute strength of Jeff, the cunning of Henry, the grave poise of Joe, to say nothing of Scottie—an unknown force.

But Scottie was running on in his talk; he was telling of how he met the storekeeper in town; he was naming everything he saw. These fellows seemed to hunger for the minutest news of men. They poured forth a chorus of questions about a new house that was being built; they broke into admiring laughter when Scottie told of his victorious tilt of jesting with the storekeeper's daughter; even Henry came out of his patient gloom long enough to smile at this, and the rest were like children. Larry was laughing so heartily that his eyes began to twinkle. He even invited Andrew in on the mirth.

At this point Andy stood up and stretched elaborately—but in stretching he put his arms behind him, and stretched them down rather than up, so that his hands were never far from his hips.

"I'll be turning in," said Andy, and, stepping back to the door so that his face would be toward them until the last instant of his exit, he waved good night.

There was a brief shifting of eyes toward him, and a grunt from Jeff, that was all. Then the eye of everyone reverted to Scottie. But the latter broke off his narrative.

"Ain't you sleepin' in?" he asked. "We could fix you a bunk upstairs, I guess?"

Once more the glance of Andrew flashed from face to face, and yet he did not allow his eyes actually to stir from Scottie. He was waiting for some significant change of expression, but that change did not come. They glanced at him again, but impatiently. And then he saw the first suspicious thing. Scottie was looking straight at Henry in the corner, as though waiting for a direction, and, from the corner of his eye, Andrew was aware that Henry had nodded ever so slightly.

"Here's something you might be interested to know," said Scottie. "This young Lanning was riding a pinto horse." He added, while Andrew stood rooted to the spot: "You seemed sort of interested in the description. I allowed maybe you'd try your hand at findin' him."

Andy understood perfectly that he was known, and, with his left hand frozen against the knob of the door, he flattened his shoulders against the wall and stood ready for the draw. In the crisis, at the first hostile move, he decided that he would dive straight for the table, low. It would tumble the room into darkness as the candles fell—a semidarkness, for there would be a sputtering lantern still.

Then he would fight for his life. And looking at the others, he saw that they were changed, indeed. They were all facing him, and their faces were alive with interest, yet they made no hostile move. No doubt they awaited the signal of Henry; there was the greatest danger, and now Henry stood up.

His first word was a throwing down of disguises. "Mister Lanning," he said, "I think this is a time for introductions."

That cold exultation, that wild impulse to throw himself into the arms of danger, was sweeping over Andrew. Not a nerve in his body quivered, but every one of them seemed to be tightened to the breaking point. He was ready to move like lightning—like intelligent lightning, choosing its targets. He made no gesture toward his gun, though his fingers were curling, but he said; "Friends, I've got you all in my eye. I'm going to open this door and go out. No harm to any of you. But if you try to stop me, it means trouble."

Just a split second of suspense. If a foot stirred, or a hand raised, the curling hand of Andrew's would jerk up and bring out a revolver, and every man in the room knew it.

Then the voice of Henry: "You'd plan on fighting us all?"

"Take my bridle off the wall," said Andrew, looking straight before him at no face, and thereby enabled to see everything, just as a boxer looks in the eye of his opponent and thereby sees every move of his gloves. "Take my bridle off the wall, you, Jeff, and throw it at my feet."

The bridle rattled at his feet.

"This has gone far enough," said Henry. "Lanning, you've got the wrong idea. I'm going ahead with the introductions. The red-headed fellow we call Jeff is better known to the public as Jeff Rankin. Does that mean anything to you?" Jeff Rankin acknowledged the introduction with a broad grin, the corners of his mouth being lost in the heavy fold of his jowls. "I see it doesn't," went on Henry. "Very well. Joe's name is Joe Clune. Yonder sits Scottie Macdougal. There is Larry la Roche. And I am Henry Allister."

The edge of Andrew's alertness was suddenly dulled. The last name swept into his brain a wave of meaning, for of all words on the mountain desert there was none more familiar, more hauntingly well-known than Henry Allister. Scar-Faced Allister, they called him. He had not yet reached middle age, and yet, for nearly twenty years, his had been a name to conjure with, a thing to frighten strong men by the bare mention. Of those deadly men who figured in the tales of Uncle Jasper, Henry Allister was the last and the most grim. A thousand stories clustered about him: of how he killed Watkins; of how Langley, the famous federal marshal, trailed him for five years and was finally killed in the duel that left Allister with that scar; of how he broke jail at Garrisonville and again at St. Luke City. In the imagination of Andrew he had loomed like a giant, some seven-foot prodigy, whiskered, savage of eye, terrible of voice. And, turning toward him, Andrew saw him in profile with the scar obscured—and his face was of almost feminine refinement.

$5,000?

A dozen rich men in the mountain desert would each pay more than that for the apprehension of Allister, dead or alive. And bitterly it came over Andrew that this genius of crime, this heartless murderer as story depicted him, was no danger to him but almost a friend. And the other four ruffians of Allister's band were smiling cordially at him, enjoying his astonishment. The day before his hair would have turned white in such a place among such men; tonight they were his friends.

"Gentlemen," said Andrew, "I'm glad to meet you."

A chorus boomed back at him; he made out the different voices; even the savage Larry la Roche was smiling. "Well, kid, this is one on you." "Sit down and tell us about it." "So you bumped off Bill Dozier . . . the skunk?" "Hang up your hat and make yourself to home." "You can share my bunk."

Tears came to Andrew's eyes.

CHAPTER FOURTEEN

After that things happened to Andrew in a swirl. They were shaking hands with him. They were congratulating him on the killing of Bill Dozier. They were patting him on the back. Larry la Roche, who had been so hostile, now stood up to the full of his ungainly height and proposed his health. And the other men drank it standing. Andy received a tin cup half full of whiskey, and he drank the burning stuff in acknowledgment. The unaccustomed drink went to his head, his muscles began to relax, his eyes swam. Voices began to boom at him out of a haze. "Why, he's only a young kid. One shot put him under the weather."

"Shut up, Larry. He'll learn fast enough."

"Ah, yes," said Larry to himself, "he'll learn fast enough."

Presently he was lifted and carried by strong arms up a creaking stairs. He looked up, and he saw the red hair of the mighty Jeff, who carried him as if he had been a child, and deposited him among some blankets, with as much care as if he had been a child.

"I didn't know," Larry la Roche was saying. "How could I tell he didn't know how to handle his booze? How could I tell a man-killer like him couldn't stand no more than a girl?"

"Shut up and get out," said another voice.

Heavy footsteps retreated, then Andrew heard them once more grumbling and booming below him.

After that his head cleared rapidly. Two windows were open

in this higher room, and a sharp current of the night wind blew across him, clearing his mind as rapidly as wind blows away a fog. The alcohol had only stupefied him for the moment. It was not enough to make him sleep, and, instead, it reacted presently as a stimulus, making his heart flutter, while a peculiar sense of depression and guilt troubled him. Now he made out that one man had not left him; the dark outline of him was by the bed, waiting.

"Who's there?" asked Andrew.

"Allister. Take it easy."

"I'm all right. I'll go down again to the boys."

"That's what I'm here to talk to you about, kid. Are you sure you want to go down?" He added slowly: "Are you sure your head's clear?"

"Yep. Sure thing."

"Then listen to me, Lanning, while I talk. It's important. Stay here till the morning, then ride on."

"Where?"

"Oh, away from Martindale, that's all."

"Out of the desert? Out of the mountains?"

"Of course. They'll hunt for you here." Allister paused, then went on. "And when you get away what'll you do? Go straight?"

"God willing," said Andrew fervently. "It . . . it was only luck, bad luck, that put me where I am."

The outlaw scratched a match and lighted a candle, then he dropped a little of the melted tallow on a box, and by that light he peered earnestly into the face of Andrew. He appeared to need this light to read the expression of Andrew. It also enabled Andrew to see the bare rafters and the cobwebs across the ceiling, and it showed him the face of Allister. Sometimes the play of shadows made that face unreal as a dream, sometimes the face was filled with poetic beauty, sometimes the light gleamed on the scar and the sardonic smile, and then it was a face out of hell.

"You're going to get away from the mountain desert and go straight," said Allister in résumé.

"That's it." He saw that the outlaw was staring with a smile, half grim and half sad, into the shadows and far away.

"Lanning, let me tell you. You'll never get away."

"You don't understand," said Andrew. "Those fellows downstairs wouldn't have known what I was talking about, but I can explain to you. Allister, I don't like fighting. It . . . it makes me sick inside. It isn't easy to say, but I'll whisper it to you . . . Allister, I'm not a brave man."

He waited to see the contempt come on the face of the famous leader, but there was nothing but grave attention.

"Why," he went on in a rush of confidence, "everybody in Martindale knows that I'm not a fighter. My uncle made me work with guns. He's a fighter. He wanted to make a fighter out of me. But I don't want to be one. I feel friendly toward people, Allister. I want them to like me. When they sneer at me, it hurts me like knives. The only reason I ever wanted to do any fighting was just to get the respect of people. Those fellows downstairs think that I'm a sort of bad *hombre*. I'm not. I want to abide by the law. I want to play clean and straight. Why, Allister, when I turned over Buck Heath and saw his face, I nearly fainted, and then. . . ."

"Wait," cut in the other. "That was your first man. You didn't kill him, but you thought you had. You nearly fainted, then. But as I gather it, after you shot Bill Dozier you simply sat on your horse and waited. Did you feel like fainting then?"

"No," explained Andrew hastily. "I wanted to go after them and shoot 'em all. But that was because they'd hounded me and chased me. They could have rushed me and taken me prisoner easily, but they wanted to shoot me from a distance . . .

and it made me mad to see them work it. I . . . I hated them all, and I had a reason for it. Curse them!" He added hurriedly: "But I've no grudge against anybody. All I want is a chance to live quiet and clean."

There was a faint sigh from Allister. "Lanning," he murmured. "I'll tell you a story. Away east from here there was a young chap of a mighty good family, but rather gay habits . . . nothing vicious. He simply spent a little too much money, and his father didn't approve of it. Well, one day his father gave him twenty dollars to take to another man. Mind that . . . just twenty dollars. Our young fellow started out, but in the crowd his pocket was picked. It made him sick when he found that he hadn't that money. He knew that his father would put it down to a lie. His father would think that he'd spent that money on himself, and the idea of another row with the governor made the boy sick inside. Just the way you felt about fighting.

"He told himself he couldn't go home until he had that money back. He couldn't face his father, you see? Well, he was pretty young and pretty foolish. He went into an alley that evening, pulled a cloth over his face with eyeholes in it, and waited until a well-dressed fellow came through. He held up that man by putting a little toy pistol under the man's nose. Then he went through his victim's pockets and took twenty dollars . . . just that, and left over a hundred. And he went away.

"There was a hue and cry, but our young chap was safe at home in one of the most respectable families in the city. Who'd think of looking there?

"But one night at a party . . . a sort of town dance, you see . . . our young chap was talking in one of the anterooms. Pretty soon a big fellow stepped up and drew him to one side. 'Youngster, I recognized your voice,' he said. 'You're the one who stuck me up in the alley and got twenty bucks from me, eh?'

"Of course, our friend could have denied it. But he didn't think of that. He was afraid. He turned white. Then he took out twenty dollars and put it into the other man's hand. 'It was a joke,' he said. 'Forget about it.' 'Sure,' said the other. 'It was a joke.' But ten days later the victim of the hold-up came again. He was in trouble. He wanted a hundred dollars. And the young chap had to get that money . . . otherwise he'd be exposed.

"And a week after that there was another call for money. It came while the youngster was in the garden of the girl he loved, talking to her. This big chap looked over the hedge and called. He had to come. He was afraid. Also, he was cold inside. But his nerves were steady. He was frightened to death, he was white, but his brain was clear. Ever feel like that, Lanning?"

"Go on," said Andrew hoarsely.

"He said to the big man . . . 'Go away from here, or I'll kill you.' Of course the big man laughed. And the hands of the youngster went up of their own accord and fastened in that fellow's throat. There wasn't a sound. But in one minute he had become a murderer. All the time he was frightened to death, but he felt that he had to kill that man.

"Then he ran. He got on a train. He went two thousand miles. He stayed in a small town a month, then the police were on his trail. He broke away. He went on a ship to the other side of the world. The police dropped in on him, and, in one terrible ten seconds, he shot down and killed three men. He doubled straight back on his trail. He landed in the mountain desert. All he wanted was a chance to play clean . . . to settle down and be a good citizen. But the law wouldn't let him. It kept dogging him. It kept haunting him. And wherever it crossed his path, there was a little cross of blood. And, finally, a good many years later, this youngster of ours, grown into a man, sat in an attic of an old shanty and told another youngster what was coming to him."

"You?" murmured Andrew breathlessly.

"I," said Allister calmly. "And this is what you have to hear. All the time I thought that I was trying to run away from trouble, but really I was hungry for the fighting. I wanted the excitement. What I thought was fear was simply a set of nerves that could be tuned up to a thrilling point, but that would never break. I'll tell you why. I had the metal in me from the first. In the blood . . . in my muscles. A queer sort of foreknowledge of things. Lanning, the moment I lay eyes on a man, I know whether I can beat him or not. I even know whether his bullet will strike me. Queer, isn't it? And when I meet the man who is going to kill me in a fair fight, I'll know I'm a dead man before the bullet goes through my heart. Oh, it's nothing altogether peculiar to me. I've talked with other men of the ilk. It's a characteristic . . . it's in my blood . . . it's iron dust inside me, that's all."

Andrew caught a great breath.

"Now I'll tell you why I say all this, Lanning. The minute I laid eyes on you, I knew you were one of my kind. In all my life I've known only one other with that same chilly effect in his eyes . . . that was Marshal Langley . . . only he happened to be on the side of the law. No matter. He had the iron dust in him. He was cut out to be a man-killer. You say you want to get away . . . Lanning, you can't do it. Because you can't get away from yourself. I'm making a long talk to you, but you're worth it. I tell you I read your mind. You plan on riding north and getting out of the mountain desert before the countryside there is raised against you the way it's raised to the south. In the first place I don't think you'll get away. Hal Dozier is on your trail and he'll get to the north and raise the whole district and stop you before you hit the towns. You'll have to go back to the mountain desert. You'll have to do it eventually, why not do it now? Lanning, if I had you at my back, I could laugh at the law the rest of our lives. Stay with me. I can tell a man when I see him. I saw you call Larry la Roche. And I've never wanted a man the way I want you. Not to follow me, but as a partner. Shake and say you will."

The slender hand was stretched out through the shadows, the light from the candle flashed on it. And a power outside his own will made Andrew move his hand to meet it. He stopped the gesture with a violent effort.

The swift voice of the outlaw, with a fiber of earnest persuasion in it, went on: "You see what I risk to get you. Hal Dozier is on your trail. He's the only man in the world I'd think twice about before I met him face to face. But if I join to you, I'll have to meet him sooner or later. Well, Lanning, I'll take that risk. I know he's more devil than man when it comes to gun play, but we'll meet him together. Give me your hand."

There was a riot in the brain of Andrew Lanning. The words of the outlaw had struck something in him that was like metal chiming on metal. Iron dust? That was it! The call of one blood to another, and he realized the truth of what Allister said. If he touched the hand of this man, there would be a bond between them that only death could break. In one blinding rush he sensed the strength and the faith of Allister.

But another voice was at his ear, and he saw the crystal purity of the eyes of Anne Withero, as she had stood for that moment in his arms in her room. It came over him with a chill like cold moonlight, it came over him with a chill like the bouquet of a fine wine.

"Do you fear me?" he had whispered.

"No."

"Will you remember me?"

"Forever!"

And with that ghost of a voice in his ear Andrew Lanning groaned to the man beside him: "Partner, I know you're nine-tenths man, and I thank you out of the bottom of my heart. But there's someone else has a claim to me . . . I don't belong to myself."

There was a breathless moment of pause. Anger contracted the face of Henry Allister, and then he nodded his head gravely.

"It's the girl you went back to see," said Allister.

"Yes."

"Well, then, go ahead and try to win through. Try to get out of the desert and get away among men. I wish you luck. But if you fail, remember what I've said. Now, or ten years from now, what I've said goes for you. Now roll over and sleep. Good bye, Lanning, or rather, *au revoir.*"

Chapter Fifteen

The excitement kept Andrew awake for a little time, but then the hum of the wind, the roll of voices below him, and the weariness of the long ride, rushed on him like a wave and washed him out into an ebb of sleep.

When he wakened, the aches were gone from his limbs, and his mind was a happy blank. Only when he started up from his blankets and rapped his head against the slanting rafters just above him, he was brought to a painful realization of where he was. He turned, scowling, and the first thing he saw was a piece of brown wrapping paper held down by a shoe and covered with a clumsy scrawl.

These blankets are yours and the slicker along with them and heres wishin you luck while youre beatin it back to civlizashun. your friend

Jeff Rankin

Andy glanced swiftly about the room and saw that the other bunks had been removed. He swept up the blankets and went down the stairs to the first floor. It was gutted of everything except the crazy-legged chairs and the boxes that had served as tables. The house reeked of emptiness; broken bottles, a twisted tin plate in which some one had set his heel, were the last signs of the outlaws of Henry Allister's gang. A bundle stood on the table with another piece of the wrapping paper near it. The name of Andrew Lanning was on the outside. He unfolded the sheet and read in a precise, rather feminine writing:

Dear Lanning: We are, in a manner, sneaking off. I've already said good bye, and I don't want to tempt you again. Now you're by yourself and you've got your own way to fight. The boys agree with me. We all want to see you make good. We'll all be sorry if you come back to us. But once you're here, once you've found out that it's no go trying to beat back to good society, we'll be mighty happy to have you with us. In the meantime, we want to do our bit to help Andrew Lanning make up for his bad luck.

For my part, I've put a chamois sack on top of the leather coat with the fur lining. You'll find a little money in that purse. While you slept, I took occasion to run through your pockets, and I see that you aren't very well supplied with cash. Don't be foolish. Take the money I leave you, and, when you're back on your feet, I know that you'll repay it at your own leisure.

And here's best luck to you and the girl,

Henry Allister

Andrew lifted the chamois sack carelessly, and out of its mouth tumbled a stream of gold. One by one he picked up the pieces and replaced them; he hesitated, and then put the sack in his pocket. How could he refuse a gift so delicately made?

A broken kitchen knife had been thrust through a bit of the paper on the box. He read this next.

Your hoss is known. So Im leavin you one in place of the pinto. He goes good and he dont need no spurrin but when you come behind him keep watchin your step. your pal,

Larry la Roche

Blankets and slicker, money, a horse! A flask of whiskey stood on another slip of the paper. And the writing on this was much more legible.

Here's a friend in need. When you come to a pinch, use it. And when you come to a bigger pinch send word to your friend,

Scottie Macdougal

Andrew picked it up, set it down again, and smiled.

On the fur coat there was a fifth tag. Not one of the five, then, had forgotten him.

Its comin on cold, partner. Take this coat and welcome. When the snows get on the mountains if you aint out of the desert put on this coat and think of your partner,

Joe Clune

P.S.—I seen you first, and I have first call on you over the rest of these gents and your can figure that you have first call on me.

J.C.

When he had read all these little letters, when he had gathered his loot before him, Andrew lifted his head and could have burst into song. A tenderness for all men was surging up in him. This much thieves and murderers had done for him; what would the good men of the world do?

He went into the kitchen. They had forgotten nothing. There was a quantity of chuck—flour, bacon, salt, coffee, a frying pan, a cup, a canteen. And this inscription was on it: *To Andy from the boys.*

It brought the tears into his eyes and a lump in his throat. He cast open the back door, and, standing in the little pasture, he saw only one horse remaining. It was a fine young chestnut gelding with a Roman nose and long, mulish ears. His head was not beautiful to see from any angle, but Andrew saw only the long, powerful, sloping shoulders, the long neck, burdened by no spare flesh, the legs fine-drawn as hammered bronze, and appearing fully as strong. Every detail of the body spelled speed, and speed meant safety. From the famous gray stallion of Hal Dozier this gelding could never escape, Andrew knew, but the chestnut could undoubtedly distance any posse that had no greater speed than the pace of its slowest horse. And he saw with pleasure, too, the deep chest and the belly not too finely drawn. That chest meant staying powers, and that stomach meant a horse that would not be "ganted" in a few days of hard work.

What wonder, then, that Andrew began to see the world through a bright mist? What wonder that, when he had finished his breakfast, he sang while he roped the chestnut, built the pack behind the saddle, and filled the saddlebags. When he was in the saddle, the gelding took at once the cattle path with a long and easy canter that did the heart of the young rider good.

He gave the chestnut a mile of that pace. Then he shook him out into a smart gallop, and then he sent him into a headlong racing pace for a quarter of a mile. That done, he reined in the horse to a lope again and, leaning far over, he listened. The breath of the gelding came in deep puffs, but it whistled down as cleanly as if the horse had just cantered across the pasture.

With his head cleared by sleep, his muscles and nerves relaxed, his heart made strong by the gifts of the outlaws, Andrew began to plan his escape with more calm deliberation than before.

If what Scottie had heard was true, and he had been proclaimed an outlaw, it would still be some time before the state could rush the posters from the printing press and distribute them through the countryside—the printed posters announcing the size of the reward, and containing a minute description of Andrew Lanning—height, weight, color of eyes and hair. And in the interval before those posters came out, Andy must break out of the mountain desert and lose himself among the towns beyond the hills. There he could start to work, not as a blacksmith but as a carpenter, and drift steadily east with his new profession of a builder until he was lost in the multitude of some great city. And after that it would be a long road indeed—but after that, there was the back trail to Anne Withero. And no matter how long, she had promised that she would never forget.

The first goal, then, was the big blue cloud on the northern horizon—a good week's journey ahead of him—the Little Canover Mountains. Among the foothills lay the cordon of small towns that it would be his chief difficulty to pass. For, if the printed notices describing him were circulated among them, the countryside would be up in arms prepared to intercept his flight. Otherwise, there would be nothing but telephoned and telegraphed descriptions of him, which, at best, could only come to the ears of a few, and these few would be necessarily put out by the slightest difference between him and the description. Such a vital difference, for instance, as the fact that he now rode a chestnut, while the instructions called for a man on a pinto.

Moreover, it was by no means certain that Hal Dozier, great trailer though he was, would know that the fugitive was making for the northern mountains. With all these things in mind, in spite of the pessimism of Henry Allister, Andrew felt that he had far more than a fighting chance to break out of the mountain desert and into the comparative safety of the crowded country beyond.

He made one mistake in the beginning. He pushed the chestnut too hard the first and second days, because the blue cloud of the Little Canovers did not grow clearer, and, when the atmosphere thickened toward the evening, they entirely disappeared, so that on the third day he was forced to give the gelding his head and go at a jarring trot most of the day. On the fourth and fifth days, however, he had the reward for his caution. The chestnut's ribs were beginning to show painfully, but he kept doggedly at his work with no sign of faltering. The sixth day brought Andrew Lanning in close view of the lower hills. And on the seventh day he put his fortune boldly to the touch and jogged into the first little town before him.

Chapter Sixteen

It was just after the hot hour of the afternoon. The shadows from the hills to the west were beginning to drop across the village; people who had kept to their houses during the early afternoon now appeared on their porches. Small boys and girls, returning from school, were beginning to play. Their mothers were at the open doors exchanging shouted pieces of news and greetings, and Andrew picked his way with care along the street. It was a town flung down in the throat of a ravine without care or pattern. Houses appeared absurdly on sharp hilltops, and again in gullies, where the winter rains must threaten the foundations, at least once a year. There was not even one street, but rather a collection of straggling paths that met about a sort of open square, on the sides of which were the stores and the inevitable saloons and hotel.

But the narrow path along which Andrew rode was a gantlet to him. Before he came among the houses, he had rolled a cigarette, and now he smoked it with enforced carelessness, and, although his heart was thudding at his ribs painfully, he made the gelding move slowly. He was intent on appearing at all costs the casual traveler. And he could not know how completely he failed in his part. For the shop pallor, which years of work had given Andrew, was not yet gone. His was one of those white skins that never satisfactorily takes on a tan, and, to contrast with that skin, he had intense black eyes that, no matter how casual he attempted to make their glances, burned into the faces of passers-by. It was impossible for him to pass any man, woman, or child without searching the face. For all he knew, the placards might be already out. One of the least of those he passed might have recognized him. He noticed that one or two women, in their front doors, stopped in the midst of a word to watch him curiously. It seemed to Andrew that a buzz of comment and warning preceded him and closed behind him. He felt that the children stood and gaped at him from behind, but he dared not turn in his saddle to look back.

At all costs he must get into the heart of this place, hear men talk, learn if those placards were up, and discover if any posses were out to search the road for the wanderer. And he kept on, reining in the gelding, and probing every face with one swift, resistless glance that went to the heart. He had been accustomed, in the old days, to look straight before him, and see no one. He had been apt to pass even old acquaintances without noticing them, but those times were far in the past. Now it was a matter of necessity. He dared not let a single one go by. He found himself literally taking the brains and hearts of men into the palm of his hand and weighing them. Yonder old man, so quiet, with the bony fingers clasped around the bowl of his corncob, sitting with blank eyes under the awning by the watering trough—that would be an ill man to cross in a pinch—that hand would be steady as a rock on the barrel of a gun. But the big square man with the big square face who talked so loudly on the porch of yonder store—there was a bag of wind that could be punctured by one threat and turned into a figure of tallow by the sight of a gun. Here was a pair of honest eyes on which the glance of Andrew caught and clung a moment. Ah, those were the eyes that he must fear now. For they belonged to the side of law and order, and the owner of them would stamp him underfoot like a snake in the house. Yonder was a pair of small, bright, shifting eyes that Andrew was glad to see. A whispered word, a coin slipped into the palm of that man, and he might be made useful.

Andrew went on with his lightning summary of the things he passed. Human nature had been a blank to him before. Now he found it a crowded book, written in letters, sometimes so large and bold that the facts stared at him, and sometimes so small, an important thing was scrawled away in corners that he almost overlooked.

But he came to the main square, the heart of the town. It was quite empty. He went across to the hotel, tied the gelding at the rack, and sat down on the verandah. He wanted with all his might to go inside, to get a room, to be alone and away from this battery of searching eyes. But he dared not. He must mingle with these people and learn what they knew.

An old man beside him began talking—rambling on—asking questions. Was he out of the south? Had he come by Bill Jowett's place by any chance? Bill Jowett was an old friend. His wife was "took bad" a few weeks since with some heart trouble. The maundering voice droned on; the little dull eyes kept wandering about the square, and Andrew came to the verge of a mad explosion. That impulse alarmed him and taught him the guard that he must keep over his tongue. As it was, he turned and, with one angry glance, silenced the old man. Then, alarmed at what he had done, Andrew went in and sought the bar.

It should be there, if anywhere, the poster with the announcement of Andrew Lanning's outlawry and the picture of him. What picture would they take? The old snapshot of the year before, which Jasper had taken? No doubt that would be the one. But much as he yearned to do so, Andrew dared not search the wall. He stood up to the bar and faced the bartender. The latter favored him with one searching glance, and then pushed across the whiskey bottle.

How did he know that Andrew wanted whiskey? The

bartender knew at a glance he was not confronted with a government agent, but a regular fellow of the Western country.

"Do you know me?" asked Andrew with surprise. And then he could have cursed his careless tongue.

"I know you're safe and need a drink," said the bartender, looking at Andrew again. Suddenly he grinned. "When a man's been dry that long, he gets a hungry look around the eyes that I know. Hit her hard, boy."

Andrew brimmed his glass and tossed off the drink. And to his astonishment there was none of the shocking effect of his first drink of whiskey. It stung his throat, it burned in his stomach for a moment, but it was like a drop of water tossed on a huge blotter. To the tired nerves of Andrew the alcohol was a mere nothing. Besides, he dared not let it affect him. He filled a second glass, pushing across the bar one of the gold pieces of Henry Allister. Then, turning casually, he glanced along the wall. There were other notices up—many written ones—but not a single face looked back at him. All at once Andrew grew weak with relief. But in the meantime he must talk to this fellow.

"What's the news?"

"What kind of news?"

"Any kind. I've been talkin' more to coyotes than to men for a long spell."

Should he have said that? Was not that a suspicious speech? Did it not expose him utterly?

"Nothin' to talk about here much more excitin' than a coyote's yap. Not a damn' thing. Which way you come from?"

"South. The last I heard of excitin' news was this stuff about Lanning, the outlaw."

It was out, and he was glad of it. He had taken the bull by the horns.

"Lanning? Lanning? Never heard of him. Oh, yes, the gent that bumped off Bill Dozier. Between you and me, they won't be any sobbin' for that. Bill had it comin'. He's been huntin' trouble too long. But they've outlawed Lanning, have they?"

"That's what I hear."

But sweet beyond words had been this speech from the bartender. They had barely heard of Andrew Lanning in this town, they did not even know that he was outlawed. Andrew felt hysterical laughter bubbling in his throat. Now for one long sleep, then he would make the ride across the mountains and into safety. That sleep on a soft bed, he felt, would give him the strength of a Hercules.

He went out of the barroom, put the gelding away in the stables behind the hotel, and got a room. In ten minutes, pausing only to tear the boots from his feet, he was sound asleep under the very gates of freedom.

And while he slept, the gates were closing and barring the way. If he had wakened even an hour sooner, all would have been well and, although he might have dusted the skirts of danger, they could never have blocked his way. But, with seven days of exhausting travel behind him, he slept like one drugged, the clock around, and more. It was morning, mid-morning when he wakened.

Even then he was too late, but he wasted priceless minutes using the luxury of hot water to shave. He wasted more priceless minutes eating his breakfast, for it was delightful beyond words to have food served to him that he had not cooked with his own hands. And so, sauntering out onto the verandah of the hotel, he saw a compact crowd on the other side of the square, and the crowd focused on a man who was tacking up a sign. Andrew, still sauntering, joined the crowd, and, looking over their heads, he found his own face staring back at him, and, under the picture of that lean, serious face, in huge black type, *$5,000 reward for the capture, dead or alive. . . .*

The rest of the notice blurred before his eyes.

Someone was speaking. "You made a quick trip, Mister Dozier, and I expect if you send word up to Hallowell in the mountains they can. . . ."

So Hal Dozier had brought the notices himself.

Andrew, in that moment, became perfectly calm. And he felt that tingling nervousness in his knees, in his elbows, and thrilling into the tips of his fingers.

He went back to the hotel, and, resting one elbow on the desk, he looked calmly into the face of the clerk and the proprietor. Instantly he saw that the men did not suspect—as yet.

"I hear Mister Dozier's here?" he asked.

"Room Seventeen," said the clerk. "Hold on. He's out in the square now."

" 'S all right. I'll wait in his room."

He went to Room Seventeen. The door was unlocked. And drawing a chair into the farthest corner, Andrew sat down, rolled a cigarette, lighted it, drew his revolver, and waited.

Chapter Seventeen

He waited an eternity; in actual time it was exactly ten minutes. Then a cavalcade tramped down the hall. He heard their voices, and Hal Dozier was among them. About him flowed a babble of questions as the men struggled for the honor of a word from the great man. Perhaps he was coming to his room to form the posse and issue general instructions for the chase.

The door opened. Dozier entered, jerked his head squarely to one side, and found himself gazing into the muzzle of a revolver. The astonishment and the swift hardening of his face had begun and ended in a fraction of a second.

"It's you, eh?" he said, still holding the door.

"Right," said Andrew. "I'm here for a little chat about this Lanning you're after."

Hal Dozier paused another heartbreaking second, then he saw that caution was the better way. "I'll have to shut you out for a minute or two, boys. Go down to the bar and have a few on me." He turned, laughing and waving to them, and Andrew's heart went out to such consummate coolness, such remarkable nerve. Then the door closed, and Dozier turned slowly to face his hunted man. Their glances met, held, and probed each other deeply, and each of them recognized the man in the other. Into Andrew's mind came back the words of the great outlaw, Allister: *There's one man I'd think twice about meeting, and that. . . .*

"Sit down," said Andrew. "And you can take off your belt if you want to. Easy! That's it. Thank you."

The belt and the guns were tossed onto the bed, and Hal Dozier sat down. He reminded Andrew of a terrier, not heavy, but all compact nerve and fighting force—one of those rare men who are both solid and wiry. "I'm not going to frisk you for another gun," said Andrew.

"Thanks. I have one, but I'll let it lie." He made a movement.

"If you don't mind," said Andrew, "I'd rather that you don't reach into your pockets. Use my tobacco and papers, if you wish." He tossed them onto the table, and Hal Dozier rolled his smoke in silence. Then he tilted back in his chair a little. His hand with the cigarette was as steady as a vise, and Andrew, shrugging forward his own ponderous shoulders, dropped his elbows on his knees and trained the gun full on his companion.

"I've come to make a bargain, Dozier," he said.

The other made no comment, and the two continued that silent struggle of the eyes that was making Andrew's throat dry and his heart leap.

"Here's the bargain. Drop off this trail. Let the law take its own course through other hands, but you give me your word to keep off the trail. If you'll do that, I leave this country and stay away. Except for one thing, I'll never come back here. You're a proud man . . . you've never quit a trail yet before the end of it. But this time I only ask you to let it go with running me out of the country."

"What's the one thing for which you'd come back?"

"We're talking in confidence?"

"Certainly, Lanning."

That small thing made a vast deal of difference to Andrew. For ten years he had been Andy to this man; now he was Lanning. For the first time, probably, he felt the meaning of Bill's death to his brother.

"I'll come back . . . once . . . because of a girl."

He saw the eyes of Dozier widen and then contract again.

"You're not exactly what I expected to find," he said. "But go on. If I don't take the bargain, you pull that trigger?"

"Exactly."

"*Hmm.* You may have heard the voices of the men who came up the hall with me?"

"Yes."

"The moment a report of a gun is heard they'll swarm up to this room and get you."

"They made too much noise. Barking dogs don't bite. Besides, the moment I've dropped you, I go out that window."

"You'll break a leg with the drop."

"Get up and stand at that window and look down. No, keep both your hands at your sides, if you please. That's better."

Hal Dozier went obediently to the window and looked down to the saddled horse beneath. "You'd jump for that saddle and ride like the wind."

"Right again, Dozier."

"Suppose you missed the saddle?"

Andrew smiled, but his smile gradually went out before a gradual wrinkling around the eyes of the other.

"It's a good bluff, Lanning," said the other. "I'll tell you what . . . if you were what I expected you to be, a hysterical kid, who had a bit of bad luck and good rolled together, I'd take that offer. But you're different . . . you're a man. All in all, Lanning, I think you're about as much of a man as I've ever crossed before. No, you won't pull that trigger, because there isn't one deliberate murder packed away in your system. It's a good bluff, as I said before, and I admire the way you worked it. But it won't do. I call it. I won't leave your trail, Lanning. Now pull your trigger."

He smiled straight into the eye of the younger man. A flush jumped into the cheeks of Andrew, and, fading, left him by contrast paler than ever. "You were one-quarter of an inch from death, Dozier," he replied, "and I was the same distance from being a yellow cur."

"Lanning, with men like you . . . and like myself, I hope . . . there's no question of distance. It's either a miss or a hit. Here's a better proposition. Let me put my belt on again. Then put your own gun back in the holster. We'll turn and face the wall. And when the clock downstairs strikes ten . . . that'll be within a few minutes . . . we'll turn and blaze at the first sound."

He watched his companion eagerly, and he saw the face of Andrew work. "I can't do it, Dozier," said Andrew. "I'd like to. But I can't."

"Why not?" The voice of Hal Dozier was sharp with a new suspicion. "You say that the rest of these fellows are barking dogs, and that you don't fear 'em. Get me out of the way, and you're free to get across the mountains, and, once there, your trail will never be found. I know that . . . everyone knows that. That's why I hit up here after you."

"I'll tell you why," said Andrew slowly. "I've got the blood of one man on my hands already, but, so help me God, I'm not going to have another stain. I had to shoot once, because I was hounded into it. And, if this thing keeps on, I'm going to shoot again . . . and again. But as long as I can I'm fighting to keep clean, you understand?"

His voice became thin and rose as he spoke; his breath was a series of gasps, and Hal Dozier changed color.

"I think," said Andrew, regaining his self-control, "that I'd kill you. I think I'm just a split second surer and faster than you are with a gun. But don't you see, Dozier?" He cast out his left hand, but his right hand held the revolver like a rock. "Don't you see? I've got the taint in me. I've killed my man. If I kill another, I'll go bad. I know it. Life will mean nothing to me. I can feel it in me." His voice fell and became deeper. "Dozier, give me my chance. It's up to you. Stand aside now, and I'll get across those mountains and become a decent man. Keep me here, and I'll be a killer. I know it . . . you know it. Dozier, you can make me or break me. You can make me a good citizen, or you can turn me into something that people will remember around here for a long time. Why are you after me? Because your brother was killed by me. Dozier, think of your brother, and then look at me. Was his life worth my life? He was your brother, and that's the reason I say it. You're a cool-headed man. You knew him, and you knew what he was worth. A fighter, he loved fighting, and he picked his chances for it. His killings were as long as the worst bad man that ever stepped, except that he had the law behind him. When he got on my trail, he knew that I was just a scared kid who thought he'd killed a man. But he ran me down with his gang. Why didn't he give me a chance? Why didn't he let me run until I found out that I hadn't killed Buck Heath? Then he knew, and you know, that I'd have come back. But he wouldn't give me the chance. He ran me into the ground, and I shot him down. And that minute he turned me from a scared kid into an outlaw . . . a killer. Tell me, man to man, Dozier, if Bill hasn't already done me more wrong than I've done him."

As he finished that strange appeal, he noted that the famous fighter was white about the mouth and shaken. He added with a burst of appeal: "Dozier, if it's pride that holds you back, look at me. I'm not proud. I'll get down there on my knees. I'll beg you to let me go and give me a chance. You can open the door and let the others look in at me while I'm beggin'. That's how little pride I have. Do you think I'd let shame keep me out of heaven?"

For heaven was the girl, and Dozier, looking into that white face and those brilliant black eyes, knew it. If he had been shaken before, he was sunk in gloom now.

And then there was a last appeal, a last agony of appeal from

Andrew: "Hal, you know I'm straight. You know I'm worth a chance."

The older man lifted his head at last.

"Pride won't keep you out of heaven, Andy, but pride will keep me out. And pride will send me to perdition. Andy, I can't leave the trail."

At that sentence every muscle of Andrew's body relaxed, and he sat like one in a state of collapse, except that the right hand and the gun in it were steady as rocks.

"Here's something between you and me that I'd swear I never said if I was called in a court," went on Hal Dozier in a solemn murmur. "I'll tell you that I know Bill was no good. I've known it for years, and I've told him so. It's Bill that bled me, and bled me until I've had to soak a mortgage on the ranch. It's Bill that's spent the money on his cussed booze and gambling. Until now there's a man that can squeeze and ruin me any day, and that's Merchant. He sent me hot along this trail. He sent me, but my pride sent me, also. No, son, I wasn't bought altogether. And, if I'd known as much about you then as I know now, I'd never have started to hound you. But now I've started. Everybody in the mountains, every 'puncher on the range knows that Hal Dozier has started on a new trail, and every man of them knows that I've never failed before. Andy, I can't give it up. You see, I've got no shame before you. I tell you the straight of it. I tell you that I'm a bought man. But I can't leave this trail to go back and face the boys. If one of them was to shake his head and say on the side that I'm no longer the man I used to be, I'd shoot him dead as sure as there's a reckoning that I'm bound for. It isn't you, Andy . . . it's my reputation that makes me go on."

He stopped, and the two men looked sadly at each other.

"Andy, boy," said Hal Dozier, "I've no more bad feeling toward you than if you was my own boy." Then he added with a little ring to his voice: "But I'm going to stay on your trail till I kill you. You write that down in red."

And the outlaw dropped his gun suddenly into the holster. "That ends it then," he said slowly. "I don't feel the way you do, Hal. I'm beginning to hate you, because you stand between me and the girl. I'm as frank as you are, you see. And the next time we meet we won't sit down and chin friendly-like. We'll let our guns do our talking for us. And, first of all, I'm going to get across these mountains, Hal, in spite of you and your friends."

"You can't do it, Andy. Try it. I've sent the word up. The whole mountains will be alive watchin' for you. Every trail will be alive with guns."

But Andrew stood up, and, using always his left hand while the right arm hung with apparent carelessness at his side, he arranged his hat so that it came forward at a jaunty angle, and then hitched his belt around so that the holster hung a little more to the rear. The position for a gun when one is sitting is quite different from the proper position when one is standing. All these things Uncle Jasper had taught Andrew long and long before. He was remembering them in chunks.

"Give me three minutes to get my saddle on my horse and out of town," said Andrew. "Is that fair?"

"Considering that you could have filled me full of lead here," said Hal Dozier with a wry smile, "I think that's fair enough."

"Are you riding Grey Peter?" asked Andrew from the door, to which he backed with instinctive caution.

"Of course."

"He'll be safe, Hal. No matter how you press me, I'll never take a bead on that horse. Why, God bless him, I've ridden him myself."

"You didn't have to tell me that," said Hal. "Skunks that shoot horses don't look down their rifles with your kind of eyes, Andy."

There was a moisture in the eyes of Hal Dozier as the door closed, and Andrew's quick, light step went down the hall.

CHAPTER EIGHTEEN

As Andrew went down the stairs and through the entrance hall, he noticed it was filled with armed men. He saw half a dozen looking over the working parts of their rifles in the corners of the room. At the door he paused for the least fraction of a second, and during that breathing space he had seen every face in the room. Then he walked carelessly across to the desk and asked for his bill.

Someone, as he crossed the room, whirled to follow him with a glance. When Andy paid his bill, he heard, for his ears were sharpened: "I thought for a minute. . . . But it does look like him."

"Aw, Mike, I seen that gent in the barroom the other day. Besides, he's just a kid."

"So's this Lanning. I'm going out to look at the poster again. You hold this gent here."

"All right. I'll talk to him while you're gone. But be quick. I'll be holdin' a laugh for you, Mike."

Andrew paid his bill, but, as he reached the door, a short man with legs bowed by a life in the saddle waddled out to him and said: "Just a minute, partner. Are you one of us?"

"One of who?" asked Andrew.

"One of the posse Hal is getting together? Well, come to think of it, I guess you're a stranger around here, ain't you?"

"Me?" asked Andrew. "Why, I've just been talking to Hal."

"About young Lanning?"

"Yes."

"By the way, if you're out of Hal's country, maybe you know Lanning, too?"

"Sure. I've stood as close to him as I am to you."

"You don't say so. What sort of a looking fellow is he?"

"Well, I'll tell you," said Andrew, and he smiled in an embarrassed manner. "They say he's a ringer for me. Not much of a compliment, is it?"

The other gasped, and then laughed heartily. "No, it ain't, at that," he replied. "Say, I got a pal that wants to talk to you. Sort of a joke on him, at that."

"I'll tell you what," said Andy calmly. "Take him into the bar, and I'll come in and have a drink with him and you in about two minutes. S'long."

He was gone through the door, while the other half reached a hand toward him. But that was all.

In the stables he had the saddle on the chestnut in twenty seconds and brought him to the watering trough before the barroom.

He found his short, bow-legged friend in the barroom in the midst of excited talk with a big blond man. He looked German, with his parted beard and his imposing front, and he had the stern blue eye of a fighter. "Is this your friend?" asked Andrew, and walked straight up to them. He watched the eyes of the big man expand, and then narrow; his hand even fumbled at his hip, but then he shook his head. He was too bewildered to act.

"I was just telling Mike," said the short man, "that you told me yourself folks think you're a ringer for Lanning. As a matter of fact . . . get in on this . . . Mike thought you was Lanning himself." He began to laugh heartily.

"Can't you picture Lanning hangin' around the same hotel where Hal Dozier is?"

"Well, let's drink." Andy smiled. While the others were poising their glasses, he took a stub of a pencil out of his vest pocket and scribbled idly on the top of the bar. They drank, and Andy wandered slowly toward the door, waving his hand to the others. But the short man was busy trying to decipher the scribbled writing on the bar.

"It's words, Mike," he informed his companion. "But I can't get the light right for reading it."

At the same time there was a hubbub and an uproar from the upper part of the hotel. A dozen men were shouting from the lobby. And the men in the barroom started crowding toward the door.

"Wait!" cried the short man. "Mike, listen to what he wrote . . . 'Dear Mike, in a pinch always believe what your eyes tell you. Lanning.' Mike, it was him."

But Mike, with a roar, was already rushing for the street. Others were before him; a fighting mass jammed its way into the open, and there, in the middle of the square, sat Hal Dozier on his gray stallion. He was giving orders in a voice that rang above the crowd, and made voices hush to whispers as they heard him. Under his direction the crowd split into groups of four and five and six and rode at full speed in three directions out of the town. In the meantime, there were two trusted friends of Hal Dozier busy at telephones in the hotel. They were calling little towns among the mountains. The red alarm was spreading like wildfire, and faster than the fastest horse could gallop.

But Andrew, with the chestnut running like a red flash beneath him, shot down the tangle of paths on the same course as that by which he entered. He would have been interested had he heard the quiet remark of the very old man with the bony hands, who sat under the awning by the watering trough of the store.

"I knew that young gent was coming to town to raise blazes, and there he goes with blazes roarin' after him."

As the first rush of the pursuers came foaming around the nearest corner, the storekeeper darted out. "What's up?" he asked.

"Nothin'," said the very old man, "but times is pickin' up. Oh, times is pickin' up amazin'."

The first squadron went down the lanes, five men like five thunderbolts, but they took care not to exceed the speed of the slowest of their comrades, for it was suicide obviously to get into a lonely lead behind a man who could drop his man at five hundred yards from horseback—from running horseback, the story had it.

However, these five were only one unit among many. Two more were pushing up the ravine, making good time into the heart of the mountains; others were angling out to the right and left, always on the look-out, and always warning man, woman, and child to take up the alarm and spread it. And not only were the telephone lines working busily, but that strange and swift messenger, rumor, was instantly at work, buzzing in strange places. It stopped the cowpuncher on the range, it stopped the plowman with his team, and made him think what one slug of lead would mean to his farm; it set the boys in school drawing up schedules of how they would spend $5,000. And not $5,000 alone. There was talk that, besides the state, rich John Merchant, in the far south near Martindale, would contribute generously. The cattlemen, the poor farmers of the hills, every man and child in that region of mountains was ready to look and report, or look and shoot.

But Andrew Lanning, although he guessed at all this and more, kept straight on his course. He did not cut straight into the heart of the mountains, for he knew that the districts just above would be thoroughly alarmed. But he had a very good reason for making his strike for liberty in this direction, in spite of the fact that the mountains were lower and easier on either side.

Buried away in the mountains, one stiff day's march, was a trapper who Uncle Jasper had once befriended. That was many a day long since, but Uncle Jasper had saved the man's life, and he had often told Andrew that, sooner or later, he must come to that trapper's cabin to talk of the old times.

He was bound there now. For, if he could get shelter for three days, the hue and cry would subside. When the mountaineers were certain that he must have gone past them to other places and slipped through their greedy fingers he could ride on in comparative safety. It was an excellent plan. It gave Andrew such a sense of safety, as he trotted the chestnut up a steep grade, that he did not hear another horse, coming in the opposite direction, until the latter was almost upon him. Then, coming about a sharp shoulder of the hill, he almost ran upon a bare-legged boy who rode without saddle upon the back of a bay mare. The mare leaped cat-like to one side, and her little rider clung like a piece of her hide. "You might holler, comin' around a turn!" shrilled the boy. And he brought the mare to a halt by jerking the rope around her neck. He had no other means of guiding her, no sign of a bridle.

But Andrew looked with hungry eyes. He knew something of horses, and this bay fitted into his dreams of an ideal perfectly. She was beautiful, quite heavily built in the body, with a great spread of breast that surely told of an honest heart beneath a glorious head, legs that fairly shouted to Andrew of good blood, and, above all, she had that indescribable thing that is to a horse what personality is to a man. She did not win admiration, she commanded it. And she stood alert at the side of the road, looking at Andrew like a queen. Horse stealing is the last crime and the cardinal sin in the mountain desert, but Andrew felt the moment he saw her that she must be his. At least he would first try to buy her honorably.

"Son," he said to the urchin, "how much for that horse?"

"Why," said the boy, "anything you'll give."

"Don't laugh at me," said Andrew sternly. "I like her looks and I'll buy her. I'll trade this chestnut . . . and he's a fine traveler . . . with a good price to boot. If your father lives up the road and not down, turn back with me and I'll see if I can't make a trade."

"You don't have to see him," said the boy. "I can tell you that he'll sell her. You throw in the chestnut and you won't have to give any boot." And he grinned. "But there's the house." He pointed across the ravine at a little green-roofed shack buried in the rocks. "You can come over if you want to."

"Is there something wrong with her?"

"Nothin' much."

"She looks sound. She stands well."

"Sure. Pop says she's the best hoss that ever run in these parts. And he knows, I'll tell a man."

"Son, I've got to have that horse."

"She's yours."

"How much?"

"Mister," said the boy suddenly, "I know how you feel. Lots feel the same way. You want her bad, but she ain't worth her feed. A skunk put a bur under the saddle when she was bein' broke, and since then anybody can ride her bareback, but nothin' in the mountains can sit a saddle on her."

Andrew cast one more long sad look at the horse. He had never seen a horse that went so straight to his heart, and then he straightened the chestnut up the road and went ahead.

Chapter Nineteen

He had to be guided by what Uncle Jasper had often described—a mountain whose crest was split like the crown of a hat divided sharply by a knife, and the twin peaks were like the ears of a mule, except that they came together at the base. By the position of those distant summits he knew that he was in the ravine leading to the cabin of Hank Rainer, the trapper.

Presently the sun flashed on a white cliff, a definite landmark by which Uncle Jasper had directed him, so Andrew turned out of his path on the eastern side of the gully and rode across the ravine. The slope was steep on either side, covered with rocks, thick with slides of loose pebbles and sand. Altogether it was by no means favorable territory for an average horse, and, although Andrew felt that the cat-footed bay mare might have kept a fair rate of speed, even through these rocks and bushes, his own horse, accustomed to a more open country, was continually at fault. He did not like his work, and kept tossing his ugly head and champing the bit as they went down to the river bottom.

It was not a real river, but only an angry creek that went fuming and crashing through the cañon with a voice as loud as some great stream. Andrew had to watch with care for a ford, for, although the bed was not deep, the water ran like a rifle bullet over smooth places and was torn to a white froth when it struck projecting rocks. He found, at length, a place where it was backed up into a shallow pool, and here he rode across, hardly wetting the belly of the gelding. Then up the far slope he was lost at once in a host of trees. They cut him off from his landmark, the white cliff, but he kept on with a feel for the right direction, until he came to a sudden clearing, and in the clearing was a cabin. It was apparently just a one-room shanty with a shed leaning against it from the rear. No doubt the shed was for the trapper's horse. Also an ancient buckboard stood with sagging wheels near the cabin, and, if this were indeed the house of Hank Rainer, he used that wagon to carry his pelts to town. But Andrew was amazed at the sight of the buckboard. He did not see how it could be used in the first place, and in the second place he wondered how it was ever drawn to that place through the forest and over the rocks.

He had no time for further thought. In the open door of the cabin appeared a man so huge that he had to bend his head to look out, and Andrew's heart fell. It was not the slender, raw-boned youth of whom Uncle Jasper had told him, but a hulking giant. And then he remembered that twenty years had passed since Uncle Jasper rode that way, and in twenty years the gaunt body might have filled out, the shock of bright red hair of which Jasper spoke might well have been the original of the red flood that now covered the face and throat of the big man. Where his hat covered it from the sun the hair fairly flamed; where the beard and side whiskers had been reached it was a faded bronze. It was a magnificent beard, sweeping across the chest of the man, and Andrew wondered at it.

"Hello!" called the trapper. "Are you one of the boys on the trail? Well, I ain't seen anything. Been about six others here already."

The blood leaped in Andrew, and then ran coldly back to his heart. Could they have outridden the gelding to such an extent as that?

"From Tomo?" he asked.

"Tomo? No. They come down from Gunter City up yonder,

and Twin Falls."

And Andrew understood. Well indeed had Hal Dozier fulfilled his threat of rousing the mountains against his quarry. He glanced westward. It was yet an hour lacking of sundown, but since mid-morning Dozier had been able to send his messages so far and so wide. Andrew set his teeth. What did cunning of head and speed of horse count against the law when the law had electricity for its agent?

"Well," said Andrew, slipping from his saddle, "if he hasn't been by this way I may as well stay over for the night. If they've hunted the woods around here all day, no use in me doing it by night. Can you put me up?"

"Can I put you up? I'll tell a man. Glad to have you, stranger. Gimme your hoss. I'll take care of him. Looks like he was kind of ganted up, don't it? Well, I'll give him a feed of oats that'll thicken his ribs. Barley don't do nothin' but heat up a hoss . . . oats is the thing."

Still talking, he led the gelding into his shed. Andrew followed, took off the saddle, and, having led the chestnut out and down to the creek for a drink, he returned and tied him to a manger that the trapper had filled with a liberal supply of hay, to say nothing of a feed box stuffed with oats. A man who was kind to a horse could not be treacherous to a man, Andrew decided.

"You're Hank Rainer, aren't you?" he asked.

"That's me. And you?"

"I'm the unwelcome guest, I'm afraid," said Andrew. "I'm the nephew of Jasper Lanning. I guess you'll be remembering him?"

"I'll forget my right hand sooner," said the big red man calmly. But he kept on looking steadily at Andrew.

"Well," said Andrew, encouraged and at the same time repulsed by this calm silence, "my name is one you've heard. I am. . . ."

The other broke in hastily. "You are Jasper Lanning's nephew. That's all I know. What's a name to me? I don't want to know names." It puzzled Andrew, but the big man ran on smoothly enough: "Lanning ain't a popular name around here, you see? Suppose somebody was to come around and say . . . 'Seen Lanning?' What could I say, if you was here . . . 'I've got a Lanning here. I dunno but he's the one you want.' But suppose I don't know anything except you're Jasper's nephew? Maybe you're related on the mother's side. Eh?" He winked at Andrew. "You come along and don't talk too much about names."

He led the way into the house and picked up one of the posters, which lay on the floor.

"They've sent those through the mountains already?" asked Andrew gloomily.

"Sure. These come down from Twin Falls. Now a gent with special fine eyes might find that you looked like the gent on this poster. But my eyes are terrible bad mostly. Besides, I need to quicken up that fire." He crumpled the poster and inserted it beneath the lid of his iron stove. There was a rush and faint roar of the flame up the chimney as the cardboard burned. "And now," said Hank Rainer, turning with a broad smile, "I guess they ain't any reason why I should recognize you. You're just a plain stranger comin' along and you stop over here for the night. That all?"

Andrew had followed this involved reasoning with a rather bewildered mind, but he smiled faintly in return. He was bothered, in a way, by the extreme mental caution of this fellow. It was kindly enough, but it was not altogether honest. It was as if the keen-eyed trapper were more interested in his own foolish little subterfuge than in preserving Andrew.

"Now, tell me, how is Jasper?"

"I've got to tell you one thing first. Dozier has raised the mountains."

"He's done just that."

"And I could never cross 'em now."

"Going to turn back into the plains?"

"No. The ranges are wide enough, but they're a prison just the same. I've got to get out of 'em now or stay a prisoner the rest of my life, only to be trailed down in the end. No, I want to stay right here in your cabin until the men are quieted down again and think I've slipped away from 'em. Then I'll sneak over the summit and get away unnoticed."

"Man, man. Stay here? Why, they'll find you right off. I wonder you got the nerve to sit there now with maybe ten men trailin' you to this cabin. But that's up to you."

There was a certain careless calm about this that shook Andrew to his center again. But he countered: "No, they won't look, 'specially in houses. Because they won't figure that any man would toss up that reward. Five thousand is a pile of money."

"It sure is," agreed the other. He parted his red beard and looked up to the ceiling. "Five thousand is a considerable pile, all in hard cash. But mostly they hunt for this Andrew Lanning a dozen at a time. Well, you divide five thousand by ten, and you've got only five hundred left. That ain't enough to tempt a man to give up Lanning . . . so bad as all that."

"Ah"—Andrew smiled—"but you don't understand what a stake you could make out of me. If you were to give information about me being here, and you brought a posse to get me, you'd come in for at least half of the reward. Besides, the five thousand isn't all. There's at least one rich gent that'll contribute maybe that much more. And you'd get a good half of that. You see, Hal Dozier knows all that, and he knows there's hardly a man in the mountains who would be able to keep away from selling me. So that's why he won't search the houses."

"Not you," corrected the trapper sharply. "Andy Lanning is

the man Dozier wants."

"Well, Andrew Lanning, then." The guest smiled again. "It was just a slip of the tongue."

"Sometimes slips like that break a man's neck," observed the trapper, and he fell into a gloomy meditation.

And after that they talked of other things, until supper was cooked and eaten and the tin dishes washed and put away. Then they lay in their bunks and watched the last color in the west through the open door.

If a member of a posse had come to the door, the first thing his eyes fell upon would have been Andrew Lanning lying on the floor on one side of the room and the red-bearded man on the other. But, though his host suggested this, Andrew refused to move his blankets. And he was right. The hunters were roving the open, and even Hal Dozier was at fault.

"Because," said Andrew, "he doesn't dream that I could have a friend so far from home. Not five thousand dollars' worth of friend, anyway."

And the trapper grunted heavily.

Chapter Twenty

It was a truth long after wondered at, when the story of Andrew Lanning was told and retold, that he had lain in perfect security within a six-hour ride from Tomo, while Hal Dozier himself combed the mountains and hundreds more were out hunting fame and fortune. To be sure, when a stranger approached, Andrew always withdrew into the horse shed, but, beyond keeping up a steady watch during the day, he had little to do and little to fear.

Indeed, at night he made no pretense toward concealment, but slept quite openly on the floor on the bed of hay and blankets, just as Hank Rainer slept on the farther side of the room. And the great size of the reward was the very thing that kept him safe. For when men passed the cabin, as they often did, they were riding hard to get away from Tomo and into the higher mountains, where the outlaw might be, or else they were coming back to rest up, and their destination in such a case was always Tomo. The cabin of the trapper was just near enough to the town to escape being used as a shelter for the night by stray travelers. If they got that close, they went on to the luxurious beds of the hotel.

But often they paused long enough to pass a word with Hank, and Andrew, from his place behind the door of the horse shed, could hear it all. He could even look through a crack and see the faces of the strangers. They told how Tomo was wrought to a pitch of frenzied interest by this manhunt. For the story of how Andrew Lanning had written the message on the bar and drunk with the man who suspected him had gone the rounds. It had received an embroidery of delightful conversation, over which Andrew chuckled many a time behind the door. Besides, a dozen well-to-do citizens of Tomo, feeling that the outlaw had insulted the town by so boldly venturing into it, had raised a considerable contribution toward the reward. Other prominent miners and cattlemen of the district had come forward with similar offers. It was determined to crush this career of crime before it was well started, and every day the price on the head of Andrew mounted to a higher and more tempting figure.

It was a careless time for Andrew. After that escape from Tomo he was not apt to be perturbed by his present situation, but the suspense seemed to weigh more and more heavily upon the trapper. Hank Rainer was so troubled, indeed, that Andrew sometimes surprised a half-guilty, half-sly expression in the eyes of his host. He decided that Hank was anxious for the day to come when Andrew would ride off and take his perilous company elsewhere. He even broached the subject to Hank, but the mountaineer flushed and discarded the suggestion with a wave of his hand.

"But if a gang of 'em should ever hunt me down, even in your cabin, Hank," said Andrew one day—it was the third day of his stay—"I'll never forget what you've done for me, and one of these days I'll see that Uncle Jasper finds out about it."

The little pale-blue eyes of the trapper went swiftly to and fro, as if he sought escape from this embarrassing gratitude.

"Well," he said, "I've been thinkin' that the man that gets you, Andy, won't be so sure with his money, after all. He'll have your Uncle Jasper on his trail *pronto*, and Jasper used to be a killer with a gun in the old days."

"No more," Andrew said, and smiled. "He's still steady as a rock, but he hasn't the speed any more. He's over seventy, you see. And his muscles are shriveling up, and his joints sort of creak when he tries to move with a snap."

"Ah," muttered the trapper, and again, as he started through the open door: "Ah." Then he added: "Well, son, you don't need Jasper. If half what they say is true, you're a handy lad with the guns. I suppose Jasper showed you his tricks?"

"Yes, and we worked out some new ones together."

"Now you're in a pinch, ain't it a shame that you ain't got a chance to keep in practice?"

"To tell the truth . . . don't think I'm bragging . . . I don't need much practice. Uncle Jasper raised me with a gun in my hand, you might say, and I don't think I'll ever lose the feel of a gun. You know what I mean?"

"*Hmm*," said Hank Rainer.

When they were sitting at the door in the semi-dusk, he reverted to the idea. "You been seein' that squirrel that's been runnin' across the clearin'?"

"Yes."

"I'd like to see you work your gun, Andy. It was a sight to talk about to watch Jasper, and I'm thinkin' you could go him one better. S'pose you stand up there in the door with your back to the clearin'. The next time that squirrel comes scootin' across, I'll say 'now,' and you try to turn and get your gun on him before he's out of sight. Will you try that?"

"Suppose someone hears it?"

"Oh, they're used to me pluggin' away for fun over here. Besides, they ain't anybody lives in hearin'."

And Andrew, falling into the spirit of the contest, stood up in the door, and the old tingle of nerves, which never failed to come over him in the crisis, was thrilling through his body again. Then Hank barked the word—"Now!"—and Andrew whirled on his heel. The word had served to alarm the squirrel as well. As he heard it, he twisted about like the snapping lash of a whip and darted back for cover, three yards away. He covered that distance like a little gray streak in the shadow, but, before he reached it, the gun spoke, and the .45-cailber slug struck him in the middle and tore him in two. Andrew, hearing a sharp crackling, looked down at his host and observed that the trapper had bitten clean through the stem of his corncob.

"That," said the red man huskily, "is some shootin'."

But he did not look up, and he did not smile. And it troubled Andrew to hear this rather grudging praise. That moment he wanted very much to have a fair look into the eyes of his host. Afterward he remembered this.

In the meantime, three days had put the gelding in very fair condition. He was enough mustang to recuperate swiftly, and that morning he had tried with hungry eagerness to kick the head from Andrew's shoulders. This had decided the outlaw. Besides, in the last day there had been fewer and fewer riders up and down the ravine, and apparently the hunt for Andrew Lanning had journeyed to another part of the mountains. It seemed an excellent time to begin his journey again, and he told the trapper his decision to start on at dusk the next day.

The announcement brought with it a long and thoughtful pause.

"I wisht I could send you on your way with somethin' worthwhile," said Hank Rainer at length. "But I ain't rich. I've lived plain and worked hard, but I ain't rich. I've lived and worked hard, but I've got not so much as a wife nor a child. So what I can give you, Andy, won't be much."

Andrew protested that the hospitality had been more than a generous gift, but Hank Rainer, looking straight out the door, continued: "Well, I'm goin' down the road to get you my little gift, Andy. Be back in an hour maybe."

"I'd rather have you here to keep me from being lonely," said Andrew. "I've money enough to buy what I want, but money will never buy me the talk of an honest man, Hank."

The other started. "Honest enough maybe," he said bitterly. "But honesty don't get you bread or bacon."

And presently he stamped into the shed, saddled his pony, and after a moment was scattering the pebbles on the way down the ravine.

The dark and silence gathered over Andrew Lanning. He had little warmth of feeling for Hank Rainer, to be sure, but in the hush of the cabin he looked forward to many a long evening and many a long day in a silence like this, with no man near him. For the man who rides outside the law rides alone, and the thought of that loneliness made the heart of Andrew ache.

He could have embraced the big man, therefore, when Hank finally came back, and Andrew could hear the pony panting in the shed, a sure sign that it had been ridden hard.

"It ain't much," said Hank, "but it's yours, and I hope you get a chance to use it in a pinch." And he dumped down a case of .45 cartridges.

After all, there could have been no gift more to the point, but it gave Andrew a little chill of distaste, this reminder of the life that lay ahead of him. And in spite of himself he could not break the silence that began to settle over the cabin again. Finally Hank announced that it was bedtime for him, and, preparing himself for the blankets by the simple expedient of kicking off his boots and then drawing off his trousers, he slipped into his blankets, twisted them tightly around his broad shoulders with a single turn of his body, and was instantly snoring. Andrew followed that example more slowly.

Not since he left Martindale, however, had he slept soundly. Take a tame dog into the wilderness and he learns to sleep like a wolf quickly enough, and Andrew, with mind and nerve constantly set for action like a cocked revolver, had learned to sleep like a wild thing in turn. And accordingly, when he wakened in the middle of the night, he was alert on the instant. He had a singular feeling that someone had been looking at him while he slept.

Chapter Twenty-One

First of all, naturally, he looked at the door. It was now a bright rectangle, filled with moonshine, and quite empty. There might, of course, be something or someone just outside the door. It might even be that a wild animal had looked in. But Andrew knew that the mere falling of an eye upon him would not waken him. There must have been a sound, and he glanced over to the trapper for an explanation. But Hank Rainer lay twisted closely in his blankets.

Andrew raised up on one elbow and thought. It troubled him—the insistent feeling of the eyes that had been upon him. They had burned their way into his dreams with a bright insistence.

He looked again, and, having formed the habit of photographing things with one glance, he compared what he saw now with what he had last seen when he fell asleep. It tallied in every detail except one. The trousers that had lain on the floor beside Hank's bed were no longer there. It was a little thing, of course, but Andrew closed his eyes to make sure. Yes, he could even remember the gesture with which the trapper had tossed down the trousers to the floor.

Andrew sat up in bed noiselessly. He slipped to the door and flashed one glance up and down. Below him the hillside was bright beneath the moon. The far side of the ravine was doubly black in shadow.

But nothing lived, nothing moved. And then again he felt the eye upon him. He whirled. "Hank," he called softly. And he saw the slightest start as he spoke. "Hank," he repeated in the same tone, and the trapper stretched his arms, yawned heavily, and turned. "Well, lad?" he inquired.

But Andrew knew that he had been heard the first time, and he felt that this pretended slow awakening was too elaborate to be true. He went back to his own bed and began to dress rapidly. In a moment he was equipped. And the trapper was staring stupidly at him and asking what was wrong.

"Something mighty queer," said Andrew. "Must have been a coyote in here that sneaked off with your trousers, unless you have 'em on."

Just a touch of pause, then the other replied through a yawn: "Sure, I got 'em on. Had to get up in the night, and I was too plumb sleepy to take 'em off again when I come back."

"Ah," said Andrew, "I see."

He stepped to the door into the horse shed and paused; there was no sound. He opened the door and stepped in quickly. Both horses were on the ground, asleep, but he took the gelding by the nose, to muffle a grunt as he rose, and brought him to his feet. Then, still softly and swiftly, he lifted the saddle from its peg and put it on the back of the chestnut. One long draw made the cinches taut. He fastened the straps, and then went to the little window behind the horse, through which had come the vague and glimmering light by which he did the saddling. Now he scanned the trees on the edge of the clearing with painful anxiety. Once he thought that he heard a voice, but it was only the moan of one branch against another as the wind bent some tree. He stepped back from the window and rubbed his knuckles across his forehead, obviously puzzled. It might be that after all he was wrong. So he turned back once more toward the main room of the cabin to make sure. Instead of opening the door softly, as a suspicious man will, he cast it open with a sudden push of his foot; the hulk of Hank Rainer turned at the opposite door, and the big man staggered as though he had been struck.

It might have been caused by his swift right about face, throwing him off his balance, but it was more probably the shock that came from facing a revolver in the hand of Andrew. The gun was at his hip. It had come into his hand with a nervous flip of the fingers as rapid as the gesture of the card expert.

"Come back," said Andrew. "Talk soft, step soft. Now, Hank, what made you do it?"

The red hair of the other was burning faintly in the moonlight, and it went out as he stepped from the door into the middle of the room, his fingertips brushing the ceiling above him. And Andrew, peering through that shadow, saw two little bright eyes, like the eyes of a beast, twinkling out at him from the mass of hair. A twitch of cold went among the muscles of his back as he saw the thing.

"When you went after the shells for me, Hank," he stated, "you gave the word that I was here. Then you told the gent that took the message to spread it around . . . to get it to Hal Dozier if possible . . . to have the men come back here. You'd go out, when I was sound asleep, and tell them when they could rush me. Is that straight?"

There was no answer.

"Speak out! I feel like shovin' this gun down your throat, Hank, but I won't if you speak out and tell me the truth."

Whatever other failings might be his, there was no great cowardice in Hank Rainer. His arms remained above his head and his little eyes burned. That was all.

"Well," said Andrew, "I think you've got me, Hank. I suppose I ought to send you to death before me, but, to tell you the straight of it, I'm not going to, because I'm sort of sick. Sick, you understand? Tell me one thing . . . are the boys here yet?

Are they scattered around the edge of the clearing, or are they on the way? Hank, was it worth five thousand to double-cross a gent that's your guest . . . a fellow that's busted bread with you, bunked in the same room with you? And even when they've drilled me clean, and you've got the reward, don't you know that you'll be a skunk among real men from this time on? Did you figure on that when you sold me?"

The hands of Hank Rainer fell suddenly, but no lower than his beard. The fingers thrust at his throat—he seemed to be tearing his own flesh.

"Pull the trigger, Andy," he said. "Go on. I ain't fit to live. I don't want to live. But if I had it to do over again."

"Why did you do it, Hank?"

"I wanted a new set of traps, Andy . . . that was what I wanted. I'd been figurin' and schemin' all autumn how to get my traps before the winter come on. My own wasn't any good. Then I seen that fur coat of yours. It set me thinking about what I could do if I had some honest-to-goodness traps with springs in 'em that would hold . . . and . . . I stood it as long as I could."

While he spoke, Andrew looked past him, through the door. All the world was silver beyond. The snow had been falling, and on the first great peak there was a glint of the white, very pure and chill against the sky. The very air was keen and sweet. Ah, it was a world to live in, and he was not ready to die.

He looked back to Hank Rainer. "Hank, my time was sure to come sooner or later, but I'm not ready to die. I'm . . . I'm too young, Hank. Well, good bye."

He found gigantic arms spreading before him.

"Andy," insisted the big man, "it ain't too late for me to double-cross 'em. Let me go out first and you come straight behind me. They won't fire . . . they'll think I've got a new plan for givin' you up. When we get to the circle of 'em, because they're all 'round the cabin, we'll drive at 'em together. Come on."

"Wait a minute. Is Hal Dozier out there?"

"Yes. Oh, go on and curse me, Andy. I'm cursin' myself."

"If he's there, it's no use. But there's no use two dyin' when I try to get through. Only one thing, Hank . . . if you want to keep your self-respect don't take the reward money."

"I'll see it burn first, and I'm goin' with you, Andy."

"You stay where you are . . . this is my party. Before the finish of the dance I'm going to see if some of those sneaks out yonder, lyin' so snug, won't like to step right out and do a caper with me."

And before the trapper could make a protest, he had drawn back into the horse shed. There he led the chestnut to the door, and, looking through the crack, he scanned the surface of the ground. It was sadly broken and chopped with rocks, but the gelding might make headway fast enough. It was a short distance to the trees—twenty-five to forty yards perhaps. And if he burst out of that shed on the back of the horse, spurred to full speed, he might take the watchers, who perhaps expected a signal from the trapper before they acted, quite unawares, and he would be among the sheltering shadows of the forest while the posse was getting up its guns. There was an equally good chance that he would ride straight into a nest of the waiting men, and, even if he reached the forest, he would be shot.

Now all these thoughts and all this weighing of the chances occupied perhaps half a second, while Andrew stood looking through the crack. Then he swung into the saddle, leaning far over to the side so that he would have clearance under the doorway, kicked open the swinging door, and sent the chestnut leaping into the night.

Chapter Twenty-Two

If only the night had been dark, if the gelding had had a fair start, but the moon was bright, and in the thin mountain air it made a radiance almost as keen as day and just sufficiently treacherous to delude a horse, which had been sent unexpectedly out among rocks by a cruel pair of spurs. At the end of the first leap the gelding stumbled to his knees with a crash and snort among the stones. The shock hurled Andrew forward, but he clung with spurs and hand, and, as he twisted back into the saddle, the gelding rose valiantly and lurched ahead again.

Yet that double sound might have roused an army, and for the keen-eared watchers around the clearing it was more than an ample warning. There was a crash of musketry so instant and so close together that it was like a volley delivered by a line of soldiers at command. Bullets sang shrill and small around Andrew, but that first discharge had been a burst of snap-shooting, and by moonlight it takes a rare man indeed to make an accurate snap shot. The first discharge left both Andrew and the horse untouched, and for the moment the wild hope of unexpected success was raised in his heart. And he had noted one all-important fact—the flashes, widely scattered as they were, did not extend across the exact course of flight toward the trees. Therefore, none of the posse would have a pointblank shot at him. For those in the rear and on the sides the weaving course of the gelding, running like a deer and swerving agilely among the rocks, as if to make up for his first blunder, offered the most difficult of all targets.

All this in only the space of a breath, yet the ground was already crossed and the trees were before him when Andrew saw a ray of moonlight flash on the long barrel of a rifle to his right, and he knew that one man at least was taking a deliberate aim. He had his revolver on the fellow in the instant, and yet he held his fire. God willing, he would come back to Anne Withero with no more stains on his hands.

And that noble, boyish impulse killed the chestnut, for a moment later a stream of fire spouted out, long and thin, from the muzzle of the rifle, and the gelding struck at the end of a stride, like a ship going down in the sea; his limbs seemed to turn to tallow under him, and he crumpled on the ground.

The fall flung Andrew cleanly out of the saddle. He staggered from his knees and leaped for the woods, but now there was a steady roar of guns behind him. He was struck heavily behind the left shoulder, staggered. Something gashed his neck like the edge of a red-hot knife; his whole left side was numb.

And then the merciful dark of the trees closed around him.

For fifty yards he raced through an opening in the trees, while a yelling like wild Indians rose behind him, and then he leaped into cover and waited. One thing favored him still. They had not brought horses, or at least they had left their mounts at some distance for fear of the chance noises they might make when the cabin was stalked. And now, looking down the lane among the trees, he saw men boil into it.

All his left side was covered with a hot bath, but, balancing his revolver in his right hand, he felt a queer touch of joy and pride at finding his nerve still unshaken. He raised the weapon, covered their bodies, and then something like an invisible hand forced down the muzzle of his gun. He could not shoot to kill.

He did what was perhaps better; he fired at that mass of legs, and even a child could not have failed to strike the target. Once, twice, and again. The crowd melted to either side of the path, and there was a shrieking, and forms writhing on the ground.

Someone was shouting orders from the side; he was ordering them to the right and left to surround the fugitive; he was calling out that Lanning was hit. At least they would go with caution down his trail after that first check. He left his sheltering tree and ran again down the ravine.

By this time the first shock of the wounds and the numbness were leaving him, but the pain was terrible. It gathered in his shoulder and shot with hot and cold fingers up and down his side. Yet he knew that he was not fatally injured if he could stop that mortal drain of his wounds.

He heard the pursuit in the distance more and more. Every now and then there was a spasmodic outburst of shooting, and Andrew grinned in spite of his pain. They were closing around the place where they thought he was making his last stand, shooting at shadows that might be the man they wanted.

Then he stopped, tore off his shirt, and ripped it with his right hand and his teeth into strips. He tied one around his neck, knotting it until he could only draw his breath with difficulty. Several more strips he tied together and then wound the long bandage around his shoulder and pulled. The pain brought him close to a swoon, but, when his senses cleared, he found that the flow from his wounds had eased. But not entirely. There was still some of that deadly trickling down his side, and, with the chill of the night biting into him, he knew that it was life or death to him if he could reach some friendly house within the next two miles. Some friendly house—in two thousand miles even. There was only one dwelling straight before him, and that was the house of the owner of the bay mare. They would doubtless turn him over to the posse instantly. But there was one chance in a hundred that they would not break the immemorial rule of mountain hospitality. For Andrew there was no hope except that tenuous one.

The rest of that walk became a nightmare. Such was the singing in his ears that he was not sure whether he heard the yell of rage and disappointment behind him as the posse discovered that the bird had flown or whether the sound existed only in his own ringing head. But one thing was certain—they would not trail Andrew Lanning recklessly in the night, not even with the moon to help them.

So he plodded steadily on. If it had not been for that ceaseless drip he would have taken the long chance and broken for the mountains above him, trying through many a long day ahead to cure the wounds and in some manner sustain his life. But the drain continued. It was hardly more than drop by drop, but all the time a telltale weakness was growing in his legs, as if he were drunk, and making his knees buckle more and more at every step. In spite of the agony he was sleepy, and he would have liked to drop on the first mat of leaves that he found. That crazy temptation he brushed away and went on until surely, like a star of hope to Andrew, he saw the light winking feebly through the trees, and then came out on the cabin.

He remembered afterward that even in his dazed condition he was disappointed because of the neat, crisp appearance of the house. There must be women there, and women meant screams, horror, betrayal.

But there was no other hope for him now. Twice, as he crossed the clearing before he reached the door of the cabin, his foot struck a rock and he pitched weakly forward, with only the crumbling strength of his right arm to keep him from striking on his face. Then there was a furious clamor and a huge dog rushed at him.

It was like a picture of a dog rather than a reality to Andrew. He heeded it only with a glance from the corner of his eye. And then, his dull brain clearing, he realized that the dog no longer howled at him or showed his teeth, but was walking beside him, licking his hand and whining with sympathy.

Oh, Lord, thought Andrew, *if I could find one human being with a heart as kind as this dog's.*

He dropped again, and this time he could never have regained his feet had not his right arm flopped helplessly across the back of the big dog, and the beast cowered and growled, but it did not attempt to slide from under his weight.

He managed to get erect again, but, when he reached the low flight of steps to the front door, he was reeling drunkenly from side to side. He fumbled for the knob, and it turned with a grating sound.

"Hold on! Keep out!" shrilled a voice inside. "We got guns here. Keep out, you dirty bum!"

The door fell open, and he found himself confronted by what seemed to him a dazzling torrent of light and a host of human faces. He drew himself up beside the doorway.

"Gentlemen," said Andrew, "I am not a bum. I am worth five thousand dollars to the man who turns me over, dead or alive, to the sheriff. My name is Andrew Lanning."

At that the faces became a terrible rushing and circling flare, and the lights went out with equal suddenness. He was left in total darkness, falling through space, but, at his last moment of consciousness, he felt arms going about him, arms through which his bulk kept slipping down, and below him was a black abyss.

Chapter Twenty-Three

It was a very old man who held, or tried to hold, Andrew from falling to the floor. He was, in fact, the same man who had sat under the awning smoking the corncob pipe, some three days before. Now his old shoulders shook under the burden of the outlaw, and the burden, indeed, would have slumped brutally to the floor had not the small ten-year-old boy, who Andrew had seen on the bay mare, come running in under the arms of the old man. With his meager strength he assisted, and the two managed to lower the body gently. Andrew was struggling to the last, and there was a horror in his wide, blank eyes.

"Hold me," he kept saying. "Don't let me slip, or I'm done for. Hold me and the girl will come and save me. Anne. . . ."

The boy was frightened. He was white at the sight of the wounds, and the freckles stood out in copper patch from his pallor Now he clung to the old man. "What does he mean, Granddad?" he whispered. "What girl is comin' to save him?"

"When you get a pile older, Jud," said granddad, "you'll know what he means. You might even know the girl, or a dead ringer for her. I knew her kind once."

"Who was she?"

"Your grandma, you little fool. Now don't ask questions."

"Granddad, it's the gent that tried to buy Mary."

The old man had produced a murderous jackknife with a blade that had been ground away to the disappearing point by years of steady grinding. "Get some wood in the stove," he commanded. "Fire her up, quick. Put on some water. Easy, lad."

The room became a place of turmoil with the clatter of the stove lids being raised, the clangor of the kettle filled and put in place. By the time the fire was roaring and the boy had turned, he found the bandages had been taken from the body of the stranger and his grandfather was studying the smeared, naked torso with a sort of detached, philosophic interest. With the thumb and forefinger of his left hand he was pressing deeply into the left shoulder of Andrew.

"Now there's an arm for you, Jud," said the old man. "See them long, stringy muscles in the forearm? If you grow up and have muscles like them, you can call yourself a man. And you see the way his stomach caves in? Aye, that's a sign. And the way his ribs sticks out . . . and just feel them muscles on the point of his shoulder. . . . Oh, Jud, he would've made a prime wrestler, this fine bird of ours."

"It's like touchin' somethin' dead, Granddad," said the boy. "I don't dasn't to do it."

"Jud, they's some times when I just about want to give you up. Dead? He ain't nowhere near dead. Jest bled a bit, that's all. Two as pretty little wounds as was ever drilled clean by a powerful rifle at short range. Dead? Why, inside two weeks he'll be fit as a fiddle, and inside a month he'll be his own self. Dead! Jud, you make me tired. Gimme that water."

He went to work busily. Out of a sort of first-aid chest he took homemade bandages, and, after cleansing the wounds, he began to dress them carefully.

He talked with every movement.

"So this here is the lion, is it?" Granddad nodded. "This here is the ravenin', tearin', screechin' man-eater? Why, he looks mostly plain kid to me."

"He . . . he's been shot, ain't he, Granddad?" asked the child in a whisper.

"Well, boy, I'd say that the lion had been chawed up considerable . . . by dogs." He pointed. "See them holes? The big one in front? That means they sneaked up behind him and shot him while his back was turned." He sighed. "I've heard fine things and brave things about Hal Dozier, but mostly I begin to misdoubt 'em all. These ain't the days for a man-sized man to go cavortin' around. When he goes out to take a little exercise, they get a hundred of 'em together and put him in a cage and say he's broke the law. Oh, Jud, these ain't no days for a man to be livin' in."

"He's wakin' up, Granddad," said Jud more frightened than before.

The eyes of Andrew were opening, indeed. He smiled up at them. "Uncle Jas," he said, "I don't like to fight. It makes me sick inside, to fight." He closed his eyes again.

"Now, now, now," murmured Pop. "This boy has a way with him. And he killed Bill Dozier, did he? Son, gimme the whiskey."

He poured a little down the throat of the wounded man, and Andrew frowned and opened his eyes again. He was conscious at last.

"I think I've seen you before," he said. "Are you one of the posse?"

The old man stiffened a little. A spot of red glowed on his withered cheek and went out like a snuffed light.

"Young feller," said the old man, "when I go huntin', I go alone. You write that down in red, and don't forget it. I ain't ever been a member of no posse. Look around and see yourself to home."

Andrew raised his head a little and made out the neat room. It showed, as even his fading senses had perceived, when he saw the house first, a touch of almost feminine care. The floor was scrubbed to whiteness, the pans hanging on the wall flashed under the lamplight, the very stove was burnished.

"I remember," said Andrew faintly.

"You did see me before," said the other, "when you rode into Tomo. I seen you and you seen me. We changed looks, so to speak. And now you've dropped in to call on me. I'm goin' to put you up in the attic. Gimme a hand to straighten him up, Jud."

With Jud's help and the last remnant of Andrew's strength they managed to get him to his feet, and then he partly climbed, partly was pushed by Jud, and partly was dragged by the old man up a ladder to the loft. It was quite cool there, very dark, and the air came in through two windows.

"Ain't very sociable to put a guest in the attic," said Pop, between his panting breaths. "But I'll be the doctor, and I order quiet and rest. Ain't apt to have much rest downstairs, 'cause a public character like you, Lanning, will have a consid'able pile of callers askin' after you. Terrible jarrin' to the nerves when folks come in and call on a sick man. You lie here and rest easy."

He went down the ladder and came back dragging a mattress. There, by the light of a lantern, he and Jud made Andrew as comfortable as possible.

"You mean to keep me here?"

"Long as you feel like restin'," answered the old man.

"You can make about. . . ."

"Stop that fool talk about what I can make out of you. How come it you stayed so close to Tomo? Where was you lyin' low? In the hills?"

"Not far away."

"And they smelled you out?"

"A man I thought was my friend. . . ."

"You was sold, eh?"

"I made a mistake."

"*Hmm*," was the other's comment. "Well, you forget about that and go to sleep. I got a few little attentions to pay to that posse. It'll be here r'arin' before tomorrer. Sleep tight, partner."

He climbed down the ladder and looked around the room. Jud, his freckles still looking like spots of mud or rust, his eyes popping, stood silently.

"I'm glad of that," said the old man with a sigh.

"What, Granddad?"

"You're like a girl. Takes a sight to make you reasonable quiet. But look yonder. Them spots look tolerable like red paint, don't they? Well, we got to get 'em off."

"I'll heat some more water," suggested Jud.

"You do nothing of the kind. You get them two butcher knives out of the table drawer and we'll scrape off the wood, because you can't wash that stain outen a floor." He looked suddenly at Jud with a glint in his eyes. "I know, because I've tried it."

For several minutes they scraped at the floor until the last vestige of the fresh stains was gone. Then the old man went outside and, coming back with a handful of sand, rubbed it in carefully over the scraped places. When this was swept away, the floor presented no suspicious traces.

"But," he exclaimed suddenly, "I plumb forgot! I plumb forgot. He's been leakin' all the way here and, when the sun comes up, they'll foller him that easy by the sign. Jud, we're beat."

They dropped, as at a signal into two opposite chairs, and sat staring gloomily at one another. The old man looked simply sad and weary, but the color came and went in the face of Jud. And then, like a light, an idea dawned in the face of the child. He got up from his chair, lighted a lantern, and went outside. His grandfather observed this without comment or suggestion, but, when Jud was gone, he observed to himself: *Jud takes after me.*

He's got thoughts. And them was things his ma and pa was never bothered with.

Chapter Twenty-Four

The thought of Jud now took him up the back trail of Andrew Lanning. He leaned far over with the lantern, studying with intense interest every place where the wounds of the injured man might have left telltale stains on the rocks or the grass. When he had apparently satisfied himself of this, he turned and ran at full speed back to the house and went up the ladder to Andrew. There he took the boots—they were terribly stained, he saw—and drew them on.

The loose boots and the unaccustomed weights tangled his feet sadly, as he went on down the ladder, but he said not a word to his grandfather, who was far too dignified to make a comment on the borrowed footgear.

Again outside with his lantern, the boy took out his pocket knife and felt the small blade. It was of a razor keenness. Then he went through the yard behind the house to the big hen house where the chickens sat perched in dense rows. He raised his lantern; at once scores of tiny, bright eyes flashed back at him. It was an uncanny thing to see. But Jud, with a twisted face of determination, kept on with his survey until he saw the red comb and arched tail plumes of a large Plymouth Rock rooster.

It was a familiar sight to Jud. Of all the chickens on the place this was his peculiar property. He had helped the weakling out of the shell. He had fed him through all the fluffy and gaunt stages of a rooster's growth. He had watched with enormous pride the appearance of the big spurs. He had accompanied with a beating heart the progress of the rooster, as he fought his way against the older and wiser birds, until at length, by sheer strength of leg and length of spur, the Plymouth Rock was the undisputed cock of the walk. And now Jud had determined to sacrifice this dearest of pets. The bay mare herself was hardly possessed of a larger share of his heart.

The old rooster was so accustomed to his master, indeed, that he allowed himself to be taken from the perch without a single squawk, and there was no sound except the rushing of his wings as he regained his balance on the wrist of Jud. The boy took his captive beyond the pen. Once, when the big rooster canted his head and looked into his face with his courageous red eyes, the boy had to wink away the tears, but he thought of the man so near death in the attic, he felt the clumsy boots on his feet, and his heart grew strong again.

He went around to the front of the house and by the steps he fastened on the long neck of his prisoner a grasp strong enough to keep him silent for a moment. Then he cut the rooster's breast deeply, shuddering as he felt the knife take hold.

Something trickled warmly over his hands. Dropping his knife in his pocket, Jud started walking with steps as long as he could make them. He went, with the spurs chinking to keep time for each stride, straight toward a cliff some hundreds of yards away from the house. The blood ran freely. The old rooster, feeling himself sicken, sank weakly against the breast of the boy, and Jud thought that his heart would break. He reached the sharp edge of the cliff and heard the rush of the little river far below him. At the same time his captive gave one final flutter of the wings, one feeble crow, and was dead.

Jud waited until the tears had cleared from his eyes. Then he took off the boots, and, in bare feet that would leave no trace on the rocks, he skirted swiftly back to the house, put the dead body back in the chicken yard, and returned to his grandfather.

There was one great satisfaction for him that evening, one reward for the great sacrifice, and it came immediately. He saw his grandfather, who scorned shows of emotion, come from his chair with a groan.

"Suffering saints, boy, have you been playin' dead outlaw? Suffering saints, Jud, ain't you got no sense?"

While the old man stood trembling before him, Jud told his story.

It was a rich feast indeed to see the relief, the astonishment, the pride come in swift turns upon that grim old face. And yet in the end Pop was able to muster a fairly good imitation of a frown.

"And here you come back with a shirt and a pair of trousers plumb spoiled by all your gallivantin'," he said, "not speakin' of a perfectly good chicken killed. Ain't you never goin' to get grown up, Jud?"

"He was mine, the chicken I killed," said Jud, choking.

It brought a pause upon the talk. The other was forced to wink both eyes at once and sigh.

"The big speckled feller?" he asked more gently.

"The Plymouth Rock," said Jud fiercely. "He wasn't no speckled feller. He was the finest and the gamest. . . ."

"Have it your own way," said the old man. "You got your grandma's tongue when it comes to arguin' fine points. Now go and skin out of them clothes and come back and see that you've got all that . . . that stuff offen your face and hands."

Jud obeyed, and presently reappeared in a ragged outfit, his face and hands red from scrubbing.

"I guess maybe it's all right," declared the old man. "Only, they's risks in it. Know what's apt to happen if they was to find that you'd helped to get a outlaw off free?"

"What would it be?" asked the boy.

"Oh, nothin' much. Maybe they'd try you and maybe they

wouldn't. Anyways, they'd sure wind up by hangin' you by the neck, till you was as dead as the speckled rooster."

"The Plymouth Rock," insisted Jud hotly.

"All right, I don't argue none. But you just done a dangerous thing, Jud. And there'll be a consid'able pile of men here in the mornin', most like, to ask you how and why."

He was astonished to hear Jud break into a careless gale of laughter.

"Hush up," said Pop. "You'll be wakin' him up with all that noise. Besides, what d'you mean by laughin' at the law?"

"Why, Granddad," said Jud, "don't I know you wouldn't never let no posse take me from you? Don't I know maybe you'd clean 'em all up?"

"Pshaw," said Pop, and flushed with delight. "You was always a fool kid, Jud. Now you run along to bed."

It was a gloomy hour, always, with Jud, and now he regarded his grandfather with a wistful eye.

"Maybe," he suggested in the face of the other's frown, "I'd better stay up . . . in case the posse should come tonight?"

The hint of a smile twitched at the corners of the man's wide mouth. "Pull up a chair beside the stove, son," he said. "Next thing I know, you'll be sittin' up smokin' and swappin' lies with me, eh?"

"Oh," said Jud cheerily, "maybe it won't be so long."

He drew up his chair according to instructions and sat very stiffly and silently, fearful that this new liberty would be soon curtailed. Presently a long, bony arm went out and rested around his shoulders.

"I been thinkin'," observed his grandfather, and Jud was as still as a mouse. "I been thinkin'," went on the old man, "and I got an idea maybe you'd like to hear. They's a place in Tomo where they sell chickens and roosters and such. And the last time I was in town I seen some of these speckled chickens. I'll get you one when I go in next time, eh?"

"Oh, Granddad," said the boy, hurt, "I don't never want to see one of 'em again."

"I thought you liked 'em, Jud?"

"It wasn't the color. But him and me was pals."

"Pshaw," said the man. "Jud, you go for your bed now. Good night."

Jud went obediently to the corner of the room to his bunk, and his grandfather rose and stood before the open door. The moonlight was softening all the ragged outlines of the hills, as with a great mercy.

Chapter Twenty-Five

In Hal Dozier there was a belief that the end justified the means. When Hank Rainer sent word to Tomo that the outlaw was in his cabin, and, if the posse would gather, he, Hank, would come out of his cabin that night and let the posse rush the sleeping man who remained, Hal Dozier was willing and eager to take advantage of the opportunity. A man of action by nature and inclination, Dozier had built a great repute as a hunter of criminals, and he had been known to take single-handed chances against the most desperate, but, when it was possible, Hal Dozier played a safe game.

He understood the Napoleonic maxim that the side that puts the greatest number of units at the point of contact will be practically sure to win, and, when he could use two men to do the work of one man, Hal did it. And if he could get twenty, so much the better. In a crisis he was willing and able to do his work alone, but, by the time he had accumulated half a dozen scars representing half a dozen battles in his early life, he reached the conclusion that sooner or later one of his enemies was bound to kill him. The law of chance of itself condemned him. And although the people of the mountain desert considered him invincible, because he had run down some dozen notorious fighters, Hal himself felt that this simply increased the chances that the thirteenth man, by luck or by cunning, would strike him down.

Therefore he played safe always. On this occasion he made

surety doubly sure. He could have taken two or three known men, and they would have been ample to do the work. Instead, he picked out half a dozen. For just as Henry Allister had recognized that indescribable element of danger in the new outlaw, so the manhunter himself had felt it. On the one hand he knew the fighting qualities of the Lanning blood. On the other hand he had seen Andrew Lanning face to face and had watched both his eye and his hand. During that interview in the room of Hal Dozier, if there had been one instant during which both eye and hand had wavered, Andrew would have been a dead man, but, although the eye might change, the hand was never relaxed. Thinking of these things, Hal Dozier determined that he would not tempt Providence. He had his commission as marshal, and as such he swore in his men and started for the cabin of Rainer.

When the news had spread, others came to join him, and he could not refuse. Before the cavalcade entered the mouth of the cañon he had some thirty men about him. They were all good men, but in a fight, particularly a fight at night, Hal Dozier knew that numbers to excess are apt to simply clog the working parts of the machine. All that he feared came to pass. There was one breathless moment of joy when the horse of Andrew was shot down and the fugitive himself staggered under the fire of the posse. At that moment Hal had poised his rifle for a shot that would end this long trail, but at that moment a yelling member of his own group had come between him and his target, and the chance was gone. When he leaped to one side to make the shot, Andrew was already among the trees.

Afterward he had sent his men in a circle to close in on the spot from which the outlaw made his stand, but they had closed on empty shadows—the fugitive had escaped, leaving a trail of blood. However, it was hardly safe to take that trail in the night, and practically impossible until the sunlight came to follow the sign. So Hal Dozier had the three wounded men taken back to the cabin of Hank Rainer.

The stove was piled with wood until the top was white hot, and then the posse sat about on the floor, crowding the room, and waiting for the dawn. The three wounded men were made as comfortable as possible. One had been shot through the hip, a terrible wound that would probably stiffen his leg for life; another had gone down with a wound along the shin bone that kept him in a constant torture. The third man was hit cleanly through the thigh, and, although he had bled profusely for some time, he was now only weak, and in a few weeks he would be perfectly sound again. The hard breathing of the three was the only sound in that dim room during the rest of the night. The story of Hank Rainer had been told in half a dozen words. Lanning had suspected him, stuck him up at the point of a gun, and then—refused to kill him in spite of the fact that he knew he was betrayed. After his explanation Hank withdrew to the darkest corner of the room and was silent. From time to time looks went toward that corner, and one thought was in every mind. This fellow, who had offered to take money for a guest, was damned for life and branded. Thereafter no one would trust him, no one would change words with him; he was an outcast, a social leper. And Hank Rainer knew it as well as any man.

A cloud of tobacco smoke became dense in the room, and a halo surrounded the lantern on the wall. Then one by one men got up and muttered something about being done with the party, or having to be at work in the morning, and stamped out of the room and went down the ravine to the place where the horses had been tethered. The first thrill of excitement was gone. Moreover, it was no particular pleasure to close in on a wounded man who lay somewhere among the rocks, without a horse to carry him far, and too badly wounded to shift his position. Yet he could lie in his shelter, whatever clump of boulders he chose, and would make it hot for the men who tried to rout him out. The heavy breathing of the three wounded men gave point to these thoughts, and the men of family and the men of little heart got up and left the posse.

The sheriff made no attempt to keep them. He retained his first hand-picked group. In the gray of the morning he rallied these men again. They went first to the dead, stiff body of the chestnut gelding and stripped it of the saddle and the pack of Lanning. This, by silent consent, was the reward of the trapper. This was his in lieu of the money that he would have earned if they had killed Lanning on the spot. Hal Dozier stiffly invited Hank to join them in the manhunt; he was met by a solemn silence, and the request was not repeated. Dozier had done a disagreeable duty, and the whole posse was glad to be free of the traitor. In the meantime the morning was brightening rapidly, and Dozier led out his men.

They went to their horses, and, coming back to the place where Andrew had made his halt and fired his three shots, they took up the trail.

It was as easy to read as a book. The sign was never wanting for more than three steps at a time, and Hal Dozier, reading skillfully, watched the decreasing distance between heel indentations, a sure sign that the fugitive was growing weak from the loss of the blood that spotted the trail. Straight on to the doorstep of Pop's cabin went the trail. Dozier rapped at that door, and the old man himself appeared. The bony fingers of one hand were wrapped around the corncob, which was his inseparable companion, and in the other he held the cloth with which he had been drying dishes. Jud, standing on a box to bring him above the level of the sink, turned from his pan of dishwater to cast a frightened glance over his shoulder. Pop did not wait for explanations.

"Come in, Dozier," he invited. "Come in, boys. Glad to see you. I know what you're after, and it's pretty good to see you here. Ain't particular comfortable for an oldster like me when they's a full-grown, man-eatin' outlaw lyin' about the grounds. This Lanning come to my door last night. Me and Jud was sittin' by the stove. He wanted to get us to bandage him up, but I yanked my gun offen the wall and ordered him away."

"You got your gun on Lanning . . . off the wall . . . before he had you covered?" asked Hal Dozier with a singular smile.

"Oh, I ain't so slow with my hands," declared Pop. "I ain't half so old as I look, son. Besides, he was bleedin' to death and crazy in the head. I don't figure he even thought about his gun just then?"

"Why didn't you shoot him down, Pop? Or take him? There's money in him."

"Don't I know it? Ain't I seen the posters? But I wasn't for pressin' things too hard. Not me at my age, with Jud along. I ordered him away and let him go. He went down yonder. Oh, you won't have far to go. He was about all in when he left. But I ain't been out lookin' around yet this morning. I know the feel of a Forty-Five slug in your innards."

He placed a hand upon his stomach, and a growl of amusement went through the posse. After all Pop was a known man. In the meantime someone had picked up the trail to the cliff, and Dozier followed it. They went along the heel marks to a place where blood had spurted liberally over the ground. "Must have had a hemorrhage here," said Dozier. "No, we won't have far to go. Poor devil."

And then they came to the edge of the cliff where the heel marks ended. "He walked straight over," said one of the men. "Think o' that."

"No," exclaimed Dozier, who was on his knees examining the marks, "he stood here a minute or so! First he shifted one foot, and then he shifted his weight to the other. And his boots were turning in. Queer. I suppose his knees were buckling. He saw he was due to bleed to death and he took a shorter way. Plain suicide. Look down, boys. See anything?"

There was a jumble of sharp rocks at the base of the cliff, and the water of the stream very close. Nothing on the rocks; nothing showed on the sharp face of the cliff. They found a place a short distance to the right and lowered a man down with the aid of a rope. He looked about among the rocks. Then he ran down the stream for some distance. He came back with a glum face.

There was no sign of the body of Andrew Lanning among the rocks. Looking up to the top of the cliff, from the place where he stood, he figured that a man could have jumped clear of the rocks by a powerful leap and might have struck in the swift current of the stream. There was no trace of the body in the waters, no drop of blood on the rocks. But then the water ran here at a terrific rate; the scout had watched a heavy boulder moved while he stood there. He went down the bank and came at once to a deep pool, over which the water was swirling. He sounded that pool with a long branch and found no bottom.

"And that makes it clear," he said, "that the body went down the water, came to that pool, was sucked down, and got lodged in the rocks. Anybody differ? No, gents, Andrew Lanning is food for the trout. And I say it's the best way out of the job for all of us." But Hal Dozier was a man full of doubts. "There's only one other thing possible," he said. "He might have turned aside at the house of Pop. He may be there now."

"But don't the trail come here? And is there any back trail to the house?" one of the men protested.

"It doesn't look possible," Hal Dozier agreed, nodding, "but queer things happen. Let's go back and have a look."

CHAPTER TWENTY-SIX

He dismounted and gave his horse to one of the others, telling them that he would do the scouting himself this time, and he went back on foot to the house of Pop. He made his steps noiseless as he came closer, not that he expected to surprise Pop to any purpose, but the natural instinct of the trailer made him advance with caution, and, when he was close to the door he heard: "Oh, he's a clever gent, well enough, but they ain't any of 'em so clever that they can't learn somethin' new." Hal Dozier paused with his hand raised to rap at the door and he heard Pop say in continuation: "You write this down in red, sonny, and don't you never forget it. The wisest gent is the gent that don't take nothin' for granted."

It came to Hal Dozier that, if he delayed his entrance for another moment, he might hear something distinctly to his advantage, but his rôle of eavesdropper did not fit with his broad shoulders, and, after knocking on the door, he stepped in. Pop was putting away the dishes, and Jud was scrubbing out the sink.

"The boys are working up the trail," said Hal Dozier, "but they can do it by themselves. I know that the trail ends at the cliff. I'll tell you that poor kid walked to the edge of the cliff, stopped there a minute, made up his mind that he was bleeding to death, and then cut it short. He jumped, missed the rocks underneath, and was carried off by the river." Dozier followed up his statement with some curse words.

He watched the face of the other keenly, but the old man was busy filling his pipe. His eyebrows, to be sure, flicked up as he heard this tragedy announced, and there was a breath from Jud. "I'll tell you, Dozier," said the other, lighting his pipe and then tamping the red-hot coals with his calloused forefinger, "I'm kind of particular about the way people cusses around Jud. He's kind of young, and they ain't any kind of use of him litterin' up his mind with useless words. Don't mean no offense to you, Dozier."

The deputy officer took a chair and tipped it back against the wall. He felt that he had been thoroughly checkmated in his first move, and yet he sensed an atmosphere of suspicion in this little house. It lingered in the air. No doubt it was all created by the words he had overheard before he entered. Also, he noted that Jud was watching him with rather wide eyes and a face of unhealthy pallor, but that might very well be because of the awe that the youngster felt in beholding Hal Dozier, the manhunter, at close range. All these things were decidedly small clues, but the marshal was accustomed to acting on hints.

Pop, having put away the last of the dishes in a cupboard, whose shelves were lined with fresh white paper, offered Dozier a cup of coffee. While he sipped it, the marshal complimented his host on the precision with which he maintained his house.

"It looks like a woman's hand had been at work," concluded the marshal.

"Something better'n that," declared the other. "A man's hand, Dozier. People has an idea that because women mostly do housework, men are out of place in a kitchen. It ain't so. Men just got somethin' more important on their hands most of the time." His eyes glanced sadly toward his gun rack. "Women is a pile overpraised, Dozier. The point is, they chatter a consid'able lot about how hard they work, and they all got a favorite way of making jelly, or bakin' bread, or sewin' calico.

But I ask you . . . man to man . . . did you ever see a cleaner floor'n than that in a woman's kitchen?"

The marshal admitted that he never had. "But you're a rare man," he said.

Pop shook his head. "When I was a boy like you," he said, "I wasn't nothin' to be passed up too quick. But a man's young only once, and that's a short time . . . and he's old for years and years and years, Dozier." He added for fear that he might have depressed his guest: "But me and Jud team it, you see. I'm extra-old and Jud's extra-young . . . so we kind of hit an average."

He touched the shoulder of the boy and there was a flash of eyes between them, the flicker of a smile.

Hal Dozier drew a breath. "I got no kids of my own," he declared. "You're lucky, friend. And you're lucky to have this neat little house."

"No, I ain't. They's no luck to it, because I made every sliver of it with my own hands."

An idea came to the deputy marshal.

"There's a place up in the hills behind my house, a day's ride," he said, "where I go hunting now and then, and I've an idea a little house like this would be just the thing for me. Mind if I look it over?"

Pop tamped his pipe. "Sure thing," he said. "Look as much as you like." He stepped to a corner of the room and by a ring he raised a trap door. "I got a cellar 'n' everything. Take a look at it below."

He lighted the lantern, and Hal Dozier went down the steep steps, humming. "Look at the way that foundation's put in," said the old man in a loud voice. "I done all that, too . . . with my own hands."

His voice was so unnecessarily loud, indeed, just as if the deputy were already underground, that it occurred to Dozier

161

that, if a man were lying in that cellar, he would be amply warned. And going down he walked with the lantern held to one side, to keep the light off his own body as much as possible; his hand kept at his hip.

But, when he reached the cellar, he found only some boxes and canned provisions in a rack at one side, and a various litter all kept in close order. Big stones had been chiseled roughly into shape to build the walls, and the flooring was as dry as the floor of the house. It was, on the whole, a very solid bit of work. A good place to imprison a man, for instance. At this thought Dozier glanced up sharply and saw the other holding the trap door ajar. Something about that implacable, bony face made Dozier turn and hurry back up the stairs to the main floor.

"Nice bit of work down there," he said. "I can use that idea very well. Well," he added carelessly, "I wonder when my fool posse will get through hunting for the remains of poor Lanning? Come to think of it"—for it occurred to him that, if the old man were indeed concealing the outlaw, he might not know the price that was on his head—"there's a pretty little bit of coin connected with Lanning. Too bad you didn't drop him when he came to your door."

"Drop a helpless man . . . for money?" asked the old man. "Never, Dozier."

"He hadn't long to live, anyway," answered the marshal in some confusion. Those old, straight eyes of Pop troubled him. He fenced with a new stroke for a confession. "For my part, I've never had much heart in this work of mine."

"He killed your brother, didn't he?" asked Pop with considerable dryness.

"Bill made the wrong move," replied Hal instantly. "He never should have ridden Lanning down in the first place. Should have let the fool kid go until he found out that Buck Heath wasn't killed. Then he would have come back of his own accord."

"That's a good idea," remarked the other, "but sort of late, it strikes me. Did you tell that to the sheriff?"

"Late it is," remarked Dozier, not following the question. "Now the poor kid is outlawed. Well, between you and me, I wish he'd gotten away clean-handed. As I said before, my heart isn't in this trail. But too late now."

"Who had him outlawed? Who put it up to the governor?" asked Pop shrewdly.

Hal Dozier had to turn his head and cough, for he found his stroke parried and the point placed at his own breast. "By the way," he went on, "I'd like to take a squint at your attic, too. That ladder goes up to it, I guess."

"Go ahead," said Pop. And once more he tamped his pipe.

There was a sharp, shrill cry from the boy, and Dozier whirled on him. He saw a pale, scared face, with the freckles standing out more rusty than ever, and the eyes painfully wide.

"What's the matter?" he asked sharply. "What's the matter with you, Jud?" And he fastened his keen glance on the boy.

Vaguely, from the corner of his eye, he felt that Pop had taken the pipe from his mouth. There was a sort of breathless touch in the air of the room.

"Nothin'," said Jud. "Only . . . you know the rungs of that ladder ain't fit to be walked on, Granddad."

"Jud," said the old man with a strained tone, "it ain't my business to give warnin's to an officer of the law . . . not mine. He'll find out little things like that for himself."

For one moment Dozier remained looking from one face to the other. He would have given a great deal if he could have made the child meet his glance at that moment, but the boy was looking steadily at his grandfather. Then he shrugged his shoulders and went slowly up the ladder. It squeaked under his weight, he felt the rungs bow and tremble. Halfway up he turned suddenly, but Pop was sitting, as old men will, humming a tune and keeping time to it by patting the bowl of his pipe with a forefinger. And Dozier made up his mind.

He turned and came down the ladder.

"I guess there's no use looking in the attic," he said. "Same as any other attic, I suppose, Pop?"

"The same?" asked Pop, taking the pipe from his mouth. "I should tell a man it ain't. It's my work . . . that attic is . . . and it's different. But seein' it's you, Dozier, I'll let you copy it. Better go up and see how it's done. I handled the joinin' of them joists pretty slick, but you better go and see for yourself." And he smiled at the deputy from under his bushy brows.

Hal Dozier grinned broadly back at him. "I've seen your work in the cellar, Pop," he said.

"But nothin' to compare to the work you'd see in the attic. That'll give you somethin' worth talkin' about. Ain't you goin' to go up?"

"I don't want to risk my neck on that ladder, for one thing. No, I'll have to let it go. Besides, I'll have to round up the boys."

He waved farewell, stepped through the door, and closed it behind him.

"Granddad," whispered Jud in a gasp.

The old man silenced him with a raised finger and a sudden frown. He slipped to the door in turn with a step so noiseless that even Jud wondered. Years seemed to have fallen from the shoulders of his grandfather. He opened the door quickly, and there stood the deputy. His back, to be sure, was turned to the door, but he hadn't moved.

"Think I see your gang over yonder," said Pop. "They seem to be sort of waitin' for you, Dozier?"

The other turned and twisted one glance up at the old man.

"Thanks," he said shortly, and strode away.

Pop closed the door and sank into a chair. He seemed suddenly to have aged again.

"Oh, Granddad," said Jud, "how'd you guess he was there all the time?"

"I dunno," said Pop. "Don't bother me."

"But why'd you beg him to look into the attic? Didn't you know he'd see him right off?"

"Because he goes by contraries, Jud. He wouldn't've started for the ladder at all, if you hadn't told him he'd probably break his neck on it. Only when he seen I didn't care, he made up his mind he didn't want to see that attic."

"And if he'd gone' up?" whispered Jud.

"Don't ask me what would've happened," said Pop. All his bony frame was shaken by a shiver.

"Is he such a fine fighter?" asked Jud.

"Fighter?" echoed Pop. "Oh, lad, he's the greatest hand with a gun that ever shoved foot into stirrup. He . . . he was like a bulldog on a trail . . . and all I had for a rope to hold him was just a little spider thread of thinking. Gimme some coffee, Jud. I've done a day's work."

CHAPTER TWENTY-SEVEN

The bullets of the posse had neither torn a tendon nor broken a bone. Striking at close range and driven by high-power rifles, the slugs had whipped cleanly through the flesh of Andrew Lanning, and the flesh closed again, almost as swiftly as ice freezes firm behind the wire that cuts it. In a very few days he could sit up, and finally came down the ladder with a rather tottering step—Pop beneath him and Jud steadying his shoulders from above. That was a gala day in the house. Indeed, they had lived well ever since the coming of Andrew, for he had insisted that he bear the household expense while he remained there, since they would not allow him to depart.

"I'll let you pay for things, Andrew," Pop had said, "if you won't say nothing about it, ever, to Jud. He's a proud kid, is Jud, and he'd bust his heart if he thought I was lettin' you spend a cent here."

But this day they had a fine steak, brought out from Tomo by Pop the evening before, and they had French-fried potatoes and store candy and beans with plenty of pork and molasses in them, cream biscuits, which Pop could make delicious beyond belief, to say nothing of canned tomatoes with bits of dried bread in them, and coffee as black as night. Such was the celebration when Andrew came down to join his hosts, and so high did all spirits rise that even Jud, the resolute and the alert, forgot his watch. Every day from dawn to dark he was up at the door or at the rear window, keeping the landscape under a sweeping observance every few moments, lest some chance traveler—all search for Andrew Lanning had, of course, ceased with the moment of his disappearance—should happen by and see the stranger in the household of Pop. But during these festivities all else was forgotten, and in the midst of things a decided, rapid knock was heard at the door.

Speech was cut off at the root by that sound. For whoever the stranger might be, he must certainly have heard three voices raised in that room.

It was Andrew who spoke. And he spoke in only a whisper. "Whoever it may be, let him in," said Andrew, "and, if there's any danger about him, he won't leave till I'm able to leave. Open the door, Jud."

Jud, with a stricken look, crossed the floor with trailing feet. The knock was repeated; it had a metallic clang, as though the man outside were rapping with the butt of a gun in his impatience, and Andrew, setting his teeth, laid his hand on the handle of his revolver. Here Jud cast open the door, and, standing close to it with her forehoofs on the top step, was the bay mare. She instantly thrust in her head and snorted in the direction of the stranger.

"Thank heaven," said Andrew. "I thought it was the guns again." And Jud, shouting with delight and relief, threw his arms around the neck of the horse. "It's Sally," he said. "Sally, you rascal."

"That good-for-nothing hoss Sally," complained the old man. "Shoo her away, Jud."

But Andrew himself protested at that, and Jud cast him a glance of gratitude. Andrew himself got up from the table and went across the room with feeble steps, half of an apple in his hand. He sliced it into bits, and she took them daintily from between his fingers. And when Jud reluctantly ordered her away, she did not blunder down the steps, but threw her weight back on her haunches and swerved lightly away. It fascinated Andrew; he had never seen so much of feline control in the muscles of a horse. He felt that the animal, if she chose, could walk across gravel without making any more sound than a mountain lion. When he turned back to the table, he announced: "Pop, I've got to ride that horse. I've got to have her. How does she sell?"

"She ain't mine," said Pop. "You better ask Jud."

Jud was at once white and red. In the long hours during which he had sat beside the bunk of Andrew in the room above, the outlaw had come to fill his mind as a perfect specimen of what a man should be. He looked at his hero, and then he looked into his mind and saw the picture of Sally. A way out occurred to him. "You can have her when you can ride her," he said. "She ain't much use except to look at. But if you can saddle her and ride her before you leave . . . well, you can leave on her, Andy."

It was the beginning of busy days for Andrew. The cold weather was coming on rapidly. Now and then they had a flurry of snow, and, although it melted as soon as it reached the ground, the higher mountains above them were swiftly whitening, while the line of the snow was creeping nearer and nearer. The sight of it alarmed Andrew, and, with the thought of being snowbound in these hills, his blood turned cold. What he yearned for were the open spaces of the mountain desert, where he could see the enemy approach. But every day in the cabin the terror grew that someone would pass, someone, unnoticed, would observe the stranger. The whisper would reach Tomo— the posse would come again, and the second time the trap was sure to work. He must get away, but no ordinary horse would do for him. If he had had a fine animal under him, Bill Dozier would never have run him down, and he would still be within the border of the law. A fine horse—such a horse as Sally.

Once he had connected her with his hope of freedom, he felt

a tremendous urge to back her, and, besides, she had fitted into his mind the first moment he saw her, as a girl's face fits into the mind of an impressionable boy—there was Andrew's idea of a horse. No matter what experts may say men are born with prejudices in horseflesh.

If he had been strong, he would have attempted to break her at once, but he was not strong. He could barely support his own weight during the first couple of days after he left the bunk, and he had to use his mind. He began, then, at the point where Jud had left off.

Jud could ride Sally with a scrap of cloth beneath him; Andrew started to increase the size of that cloth. He did it very gradually. But he was with Sally every waking moment. He barely snatched time for his meals. Pop encouraged him, not with any hope that he would ever be able to ride an unrideable horse, but because the chilly air of the outdoors rapidly began to whip the color back into Andrew's face and brighten his eye.

Half a dozen times a day Andrew changed the pad on Sally's back. To keep it in place he made a long strip of sacking to serve as a cinch, and before the first day was gone she was thoroughly used to it. With this great step accomplished, Andrew increased the burden each time he changed the pad. He got a big tarpaulin and folded it many times; the third day she was accepting it calmly and had ceased to turn her head and nose it. Then he carried up a small sack of flour and put that in place upon the tarpaulin. She winced under the dead-weight burden; there followed a full half hour of frantic bucking that would have pitched the best rider in the world out of a saddle, but the sack of flour was tied on, and Sally could not dislodge it. When she was tired of bucking, she stood still, and then discovered that the sack of flour was not only harmless but that it was good to eat. Andrew was barely in time to save the contents of the sack from her teeth.

It was another long step forward in the education of Sally. Next he fashioned clumsy imitations of stirrups, and there was a long fight between Sally and the stirrups, but the stirrups, being inanimate, won, and Sally submitted to the bouncing wooden things at her sides. And still, day after day, Andrew built his imitation saddle closer and closer to the real thing, until he had taken a real pair of cinches off one of Pop's saddles and had taught her to stand the pressure without flinching.

There was another great return from Andrew's long and steady intimacy with the mare. She came to accept him absolutely. She knew his voice; she would come to his whistle. And, finally, when every vestige of unsoundness had left his wounds, he climbed into that improvised saddle and put his feet in the stirrups. Sally winced down in her cat-like way and shuddered, but she straightened again, and, by the quiver of her muscles, the rider knew that she was hesitating between bolting and standing still. He began to talk to her, and the familiar voice decided Sally. She merely turned her head and rubbed his knee with her nose. The battle was over and won. Ten minutes later Andrew had cinched a real saddle in place, and she bore the weight of the leather without a stir. The memory of that first saddle and the biting of the bur beneath it had been gradually wiped from her mind, and the new saddle was connected indissolubly with the voice and the hand of the man. At the end of that day's work Andrew carried the saddle back into the house with a happy heart.

And the next day he took his first real ride on the back of the mare.

Only a lover of horseflesh can dream what the gait of a new mount may mean—the length of stride, the suppleness that comes of flexible fetlock joints and hind legs, angling well out, and there is the swing of the gallop, during which one must watch the shoulders and the forelegs, and be watchful of the least sign of pounding with the front hoofs, since that tells soonest that a horse cannot stand a long ride, and, above all, there is the run, with the long drives coming from the hindquarters, a succession of smooth, swift impulses. A man who rides for pleasure will note such things as these, but to Andrew his horse meant life and death as well as companionship. And he leaned to hear her breathing after he had run her; he noted how easily she answered the play of his wrist, how little her head moved in and out, so that he seldom had to sift the reins through his fingers to keep in touch with the bit. It was a plain bar bit, but she came about on it as though it had been armed with a murderous Spanish curb. He could start her from a stand into a full gallop with a touch of his knees, and he could bring her to a sliding halt with the least pressure on the reins. He could tell, indeed, that she was one of those rare possessions, a horse with a wise mouth.

And yet he had small occasion to keep up on the bit as he rode her. She was no colt that hardly knew its own paces. She was a stanch five-year-old, and she had roamed the mountains about Pop's place at will. She went like a wild thing over the broken going. The loose stones and the gravel, which had turned the chestnut gelding into a clumsy blunderer, were nothing to her. She seemed to have a separate brain in each foot, telling her how to handle her ground. And always there was that catlike agility with which she wound among the rocks, hardly impairing her speed as she swerved. Andrew found her a book whose pages he could turn forever and always find something new.

He forgot where he was going. He only knew that the wind was clipping his face and that Sally was eating up the ground, and he came to himself with a start, after a moment, realizing that his dream had carried him perilously out of the mouth of the ravine. He had even allowed the mare to reach a bit of winding road, rough indeed, but cut by many wheels and making a white streak across the country. Andrew drew in his breath anxiously and turned her back for the cañon.

Chapter Twenty-Eight

It was, indeed, a grave moment, yet the chances were large that even if he met someone on the road he would not be recognized, for it had been many days since the death of Andrew Lanning was announced through the countryside. He gritted his teeth when he thought that this single burst of childish carelessness might have imperiled all that he and Jud and Pop had worked for so long and so earnestly—the time when he could take the bay mare and start the ride across the mountains to the comparative safety on the other side.

That time, he made up his mind, would be the next evening. He was well and Sally was thoroughly mastered and, with a horse beneath him that, he felt, could give even the gray stallion of Hal Dozier hard work, and therefore show her heels to any other animal on the mountain desert, he looked forward to the crossing of the mountains as an accomplished fact. Always supposing that he could pass Twin Falls and the fringe of towns in the hills, without being recognized and the alarm sent out.

Going back up the road toward the ravine at a brisk canter, he pursued the illuminating comparison between Sally and Dozier's famous Gray Peter. Of course, nothing but a downright test of speed and weight-carrying power, horse to horse, could decide which was the superior, but Andrew had ridden Gray Peter many times when he and Uncle Jasper went out to the Dozier place, and he felt that he could sum up the differences between the two beautiful animals. Sally was the smaller of the two, for instance. She could not stand more than fifteen hands, or fifteen-one at the most. Gray Peter was a full sixteen hands of strong bone and fine muscle, a big animal—almost too big for some purposes. Among these rocks, now, he would stand no chance with Sally. Gray Peter was a picture horse. When one looked at him, one felt that he was a standard by which other animals should be measured. He carried his head loftily, and there was a lordly flaunt to his tail. On the other hand, Sally was rather long and low. Her back, indeed, was comparatively short, as the back of a good saddle horse must be, but she had a long line underneath, so long that one felt at first glance that she would be apt to break down under a hard ride and a big burden. There was something subtly deceptive about her—she got that impression of length not so much out of her coupling as from the great slope and length of her shoulders and the length of the straight croup. Furthermore, her neck, which was by no means the heavy neck of the gray stallion, she was apt to carry stretched rather straight out and not curled proudly up as Gray Peter carried his. Neither did she bear her tail so proudly. Some of this, of course, was due to the difference between a mare and a stallion, but still more came from the differing natures of the two animals. In the head lay the greatest variation. The head of Gray Peter was close to perfection, light, compact, heavy of jowl, a great distance from the eye to the angle of the jaw, and well set upon his neck; his eye at all times was filled with an intolerable brightness, a keen flame of courage and eagerness. But one could find a fault with Sally's head. In general, it was very well shaped, with the wide forehead and all the other good points that invariably go with that feature, but her face was just a trifle dished; her ears, although of an almost transparently delicate tissue, were a bit too long, but very thin and tapering. Moreover, her eye was apt to be a bit dull. She had been a pet all her life, and, like most pets, her eye partook of the human quality. It had a conversational way of brightening and growing dull. On the whole, the head of Sally had a whimsical, inquisitive expression, and by her whole carriage she seemed to be perpetually putting her nose into other business than her own. A horseman would have wished to send her to school, where she would have been taught to cock up her tail and bend her neck.

But the gait was the main difference. Riding Gray Peter, one felt an enormous force urging at the bit and ready and willing to expend itself to the very last ounce, with tremendous courage and good heart; there was always a touch of fear that Gray Peter, plunging unabated over rough and smooth, might be running himself out. But Sally would not maintain one pace. She was apt to shorten her stride for choppy going, and she would lengthen it like a witch on the level. She kept changing the elevation of her head. She ran freely, looking about her and taking note of what she saw, so that she gave an indescribable effect of enjoying the gallop just as much as her rider, but in a different way. When Andrew spoke to her, she would flick an ear back as though she listened to him with half her mind, and, if she approved of his order, both ears were pricking at once, but, if she did not like the direction, her ears went back and she ran sullenly. All in all, Gray Peter was a glorious machine; Sally was a tricky intelligence. Gray Peter's heart was never in doubt, but what would Sally's courage be in a pinch?

Full of these comparisons, studying Sally as one would study a friend, Andrew forgot again all around him, and so he came suddenly, around a bend in the road, upon a buckboard with two men in it. He went by the buckboard with a wave of greeting and a side glance, and it was not until he was quite around the elbow turn that he remembered that one of the men in the wagon had looked at him with a strange intentness. It was a big man with a great blond beard, parted as though with a comb by the wind. Andrew stopped Sally with a word and thought. Then it rushed back on him. That was Mike, who had drunk with him at the bar. Had he also been recognized?

He rode back around the bend, and there, down the road, he saw the buckboard bouncing, with the two horses pulling it at a dead gallop and the driver leaning back in the seat.

But the other man, the big man with the beard, had picked a rifle out of the bed of the wagon, and now he sat turned in the seat, with his blond beard blown sidewise as he looked back. Beyond a doubt Andrew had been recognized, and now the two were speeding to Tomo to give their report and raise the alarm a second time. Andrew, with a groan, shot his hand to the long holster of the rifle that Pop had insisted he take with him if he rode out. There was still plenty of time for a long shot. He saw the rifle jerk up to the shoulder of Mike; something hummed by him, and then the report came barking up the ravine.

But Andrew turned Sally and went around the bend; that old desire to rush on the men and shoot them down, that same cold tingling of the nerves, which he had felt when he faced the posse after the fall of Bill Dozier, was on him again, and he had to fight it down. He mastered it, and galloped with a heavy heart up the ravine and to the house of Pop. The old man saw him; he called to Jud, and the two stood in front of the door to admire the horseman and his horse. But Andrew flung himself out of the saddle and came to them sadly. He told them what had happened, the meeting, the recognition. There was only one thing to do—make up the pack as soon as possible and leave the place, for they would know where he had been hiding. Sally was famous all through the mountains; she was known as Pop's outlaw horse, and the searchers would come straight to his house.

Pop took the news philosophically, but Jud became a pitiful figure of stone in his grief. He came to life again to help in the packing. They worked swiftly, and Andrew began to ask the final questions about the best- and least-known trails over the mountains. Pop discouraged the attempt.

"You seen what happened before," he said. "They'll have learned their lesson from Hal Dozier. They'll take the telephone and rouse the towns all along the mountains. In two hours, Andy, two hundred men will be blocking every trail and closin' in on you."

And Andrew reluctantly admitted the truth of what he said. Even if he had started before any warning had been given, it would have been perilous work to get across the belt of towns and mountain grazing lands unrecognized, but, now that the warning would go out from Tomo in a few hours, it would be a manifest folly. He resigned himself gloomily to turning back onto the mountain desert, and now he remembered the warning of failure that Henry McAllister had given him. He felt, indeed, that the great outlaw had simply allowed him to run on a long rope, knowing that he must travel in a circle and eventually come back to the band.

Now the pack was made—he saw Jud covertly tuck some little mementoes into it—and he drew Pop aside and dropped a weight of gold coins into his pocket.

"You tarnation scoundrel . . . ," began Pop huskily.

"Hush," said Andrew, "or Jud will hear you and know that I've tried to leave some money. You don't want to ruin me with Jud, do you?"

Pop was uneasy and uncertain.

"I've had your food these weeks and your care, Pop," said Andrew, "and now I walk off with a saddle and a horse and an outfit all yours. It's too much. I can't take charity. But suppose I accept it as a gift . . . I leave you an exchange . . . a present for Jud that you can give him later on. Is that fair?"

"Andy," said the old man, "you've double-crossed me, and

you've got me where I can't talk out before Jud. But I'll get even yet. Good bye, lad, and put this one thing under your hat ... it's the loneliness that's goin' to be the hardest thing to fight, Andy. You'll get so tired of bein' by yourself that you'll risk murder for the sake of a talk. But then hold hard. Stay by yourself. Don't trust to nobody. And keep clear of towns. Will you do that?"

"That's plain common sense, Pop."

"Aye, lad, and the plain things are always the hardest things to do."

Next came Jud. He was very white, but he approached Andrew with a careless swagger and shook hands firmly. "When you bump into that Dozier, Andy," he said, "get him, will you? S'long."

He turned sharply and sauntered toward the open door of the house. But before he was halfway to it, they heard a choking sound. Jud broke into a run, and, once past the door, slammed it behind him.

"Don't mind him," said Pop, clearing his throat violently. "He'll cry the sick feelin' out of his insides. God bless you, Andy. And remember what I say ... the loneliness is the hard thing to fight, but keep clear of men, and after a time they'll forget about you. You can settle down and nobody'll rake up old scores. I know."

"D'you think it can be done?"

There was a faint, cold twinkle in the eyes of Pop. "I'll tell a man it can be done," he said slowly. "When you come back here, I may be able to tell you a little story, Andy. Now climb on Sally and don't hit nothin' but the high spots."

Chapter Twenty-Nine

Even in his own lifetime a man in the mountain desert passes swiftly from the fact of history into the dream of legend. The telephone and the newspaper cannot bring that lonely region into the domain of cold truth. In the time that followed, people seized on the story of Andrew Lanning and embroidered it with rare trimmings. It was told over and over again in saloons and around family firesides and at the general merchandise stores and in the bunkhouses of many ranches. Each retelling emphasized something new and added to the vividness of the yarn. They not only squeezed every available drop of interest out of the facts, but they added quite imaginary details, for Andrew had done what many men failed to do in spite of a score of killings—he struck the public fancy. People realized, however vaguely, that here was a unique story of the making of a desperado, and they gathered the story of Andrew Lanning to their hearts.

On the whole, it was not an unkindly interest. In reality the sympathy was with the outlaw. For everyone knew that Hal Dozier was on the trail again, and everyone felt that in the end he would run down his man, and there was a general hope that the chase might be a long one. For one thing, the end of that chase would have removed one of the few vital current bits of news. Men could no longer open conversations by asking the last tidings of Andrew. Such questions were always a signal for an unlocking of tongues around the circle.

Many untruths were told. For instance, the blowing of the safe in Allertown was falsely attributed to Andrew, while in reality he knew nothing about soup and its uses. And the running of the cows off the Circle O Bar range toward the border was another exploit that was wrongly checked to his credit or discredit. Also the brutal butchery in the night at Buffalo Head was sometimes said to be Andrew's work, but in general the men of the mountain desert came to know that the outlaw was not a red-handed murderer, but simply a man who fought for his own life.

The truths in themselves were enough to bear telling and retelling. The tale of how he wrote the message on the bar in Tosco was a dainty bit for spinners of yarns, and the breaking through the circle around Hank Rainer's cabin was another fine section, to say nothing of that historic occasion when he routed the posse and killed Bill Dozier. Yet these things were nothing to what had followed. Andrew's Thanksgiving dinner at William Foster's house, with a revolver on the table and a smile on his lips, was a pleasant tale and a thrilling one as well, for Foster had been able to go to the telephone and warn the nearest officer of the law. There was the incident of the jammed rifle at The Crossing. And the tale of how a youngster at Tomo decided that he would rival the career of the great man—how he got a fine bay mare and started a blossoming career of crime by sticking up three men on the road and committing several depredations that were all attributed to Andrew, until Andrew himself ran down the foolish fellow, shot the gun out of his hand, gave him a talking that recalled his lost senses, and then turned him gently over to his family. Out of his own pocket he made a contribution so that young Lasker could return to the victims the money he had stolen. The Lasker family had tried to hush up the tale, but it had leaked out and gone the rounds, and it made a famous yarn.

All these and other things would make volumes and volumes if they were narrated in full. Particularly there was the story of Sandy Macintosh. He came from the far south with a reputation as a manhunter that chilled the blood even of the lawful. His list of victims was as long as a man's arm, and Sandy determined to finish the job that was apparently too big for even the capable hands and the fast horse of Hal Dozier. Hal took a vacation and left an empty stage for the celebrated Sandy. And Sandy Macintosh established relays of horses and ran the bay mare in a circle, but, after thirty-six hours of furious riding, the outlaw broke out of the circle and cantered away, and Sandy rode back, leaving three dead horses behind him. Then, frantic with shame, he issued a challenge to Andrew Lanning, and Andrew Lanning came out of the hills and met Sandy and beat him to the draw and shot him twice through the right shoulder. This story of Sandy Macintosh became an epic; men were never tired of retelling it. Go out into the mountain desert today, and in any of a hundred villages broach the name of Lanning, and nine chances out of ten some man will say: "I suppose you know how Sandy Macintosh came up to get Andy?" In such a case it is always wise to pretend ignorance and listen, for the tale is sure to be interesting—and new.

But all other details fell into insignificance compared with the general theme, which was the mighty duel between Andrew and Hal Dozier—the inescapable manhunter and the trap-wise outlaw. Hal did not lose any reputation because he failed to take Andrew Lanning at once. The very fact that he was able to keep close enough to make out the trail at all increased his fame. He had been a household word in the mountain desert before; he became a daily topic of conversation now. He did not even lose his high standing because he would not hunt Andrew alone. He always kept a group with him, and people said that he was wise to do it. Not because he was not a match for Andrew

Lanning single-handed, but because it was folly to risk life when there were odds that might be used against the desperado. But everyone felt that eventually Lanning would draw the deputy marshal away from his posse, and then the outlaw would turn, and there would follow a battle of the giants. The whole mountain desert waited for that time to come and bated its breath in hope and fear of it.

But if the men of the mountain desert considered Hal Dozier the greatest enemy of Andrew, he himself had quite another point of view. It was the loneliness, as Pop had promised him. It was the consuming loneliness that ate into his heart. There were days when he hardly touched food, such was his distaste for the ugly messes that he had to cook with his own hands; there were days when he would have risked his life to eat a meal served by the hands of another and cooked by another man. That was the secret of that Thanksgiving dinner at the Foster house, although others put it down to sheer, reckless mischief. And today, as he made his fire between two stones—a smoldering, evil-smelling fire of sagebrush—the smoke kept running up his clothes and choking his lungs with its pungency. And the fat bacon that he cut turned his stomach. At last he sat down, forgetting the bacon in the pan, forgetting the long fast and the hard ride that had preceded this meal, and stared at the fire.

Rather, the fire was the thing that he kept chiefly in the center of his vision, but his glances went everywhere, to all sides, up and down. Hal Dozier had hunted him hotly down the valley of the Little Silver River, but near the village of Los Toros the fagged posse and Hal himself had dropped back and once more given up the chase. No doubt they would rest for a few hours in the town, change horses, and then come after him again.

It was a new Andrew Lanning that sat there by the fire. He had left Martindale, a clear-faced boy; the months that followed had changed him to a man; the boyhood had been literally burned out of him. The skin of his face, indeed, refused to tan, but now, instead of a healthy and crisp white, it was a colorless sallow. The rounded cheeks were now straight and sank in sharply beneath his cheek bones, with a sharply incised line beside the mouth. And his expression at all times was one of quivering alertness—the mouth a little compressed and straight, the nostrils seeming a trifle distended, and the eyes as restless as the eyes of a hungry wolf. The old blank, dull look was gone from them; the uneasy glitter that had come into them when he fled from Martindale on that age-long day had never died from them since. Sometimes, when his glance steadied on one object, the light became a point, but usually it was a continual shifting. Take a candle and pass it from side to side before the eyes of a man, and the same gleam will come into them that was never out of the eyes of Andrew Lanning. Two things might have been said about that expression of his eyes—that it was the glimmer of danger or the light of fear that turns into danger.

Moreover, all of Andrew's actions had come to bear out this same expression of his face. If he sat down, his legs were gathered, and he seemed about to stand up. If he walked, he went with a nervous step, rising a little on his toes as though he were about to break into a run or as though he were poising himself to whirl at any alarm. He sat in this manner even now, under that dead gray sky of sheeted clouds, and in the middle of that great rolling plain, lifeless and colorless—lifeless except for the wind that hummed across it, pointed with cold. Andrew, looking from the dull glimmer of his fire to that dead waste, sighed. He whistled, and Sally came instantly to the call and dropped her head beside his own. She, at least, had not changed in the long pursuits and the hard life. It had made her gaunt. It had hardened and matured her muscles so that now along the shoulders there were ridges and ripples, iron hard, and her thighs were twining masses of strength, but her head was the same, and her changeable, human eyes, the eyes of a pet, had not altered.

She stood there with her head down, silently, and Andrew, his hands locked around his knees, neither spoke to her nor stirred. But by degrees the pain and the hunger went out of his face, and, as though she knew that she was no longer needed, Sally tipped his sombrero over his eyes with a toss of her head, and, having given this signal of disgust at being called without a purpose, she went back to her work of cropping the grama grass, which of all grasses a horse loves best. Andrew straightened his hat and cast one glance after her. Words, indeed, were almost unnecessary between them now. By a pressure of his knees he could guide her, by a gesture he could call her.

A shade of thought passed over his face as he looked at her. By this time the posse was probably once more starting on out of Los Toros and taking his trail. It would mean another test; he did not fear for her, but he pitied her for the hard work that was coming, and he looked almost with regret over the long racing lines of her body. And it was then, coming out of the sight of Sally, the thought of the posse, and the disgust for the greasy bacon in the pan, that Andrew received a quite new idea. It was to stop his flight, turn about, and double like a fox straight back toward Los Toros, making a detour to the left. The posse would plunge ahead, and he could cut in toward Los Toros. For he had determined to eat once again, at least, at a table covered with a white cloth, food prepared by the hand of another. Sally was known; he would leave her in the grove beside the Little Silver River. For himself, weeks had passed since any man had seen him, and certainly no one in Los Toros had met him face to face. He would be unknown except for a general description. And to disarm suspicion entirely he would leave his cartridge belt and his revolver with Sally in the woods. For what human being, no matter how imaginative, would possibly dream of

Andrew Lanning going unarmed into a town and sitting calmly at a table to order a meal?

CHAPTER THIRTY

People in telling that story long afterward, and it became one of the favorite tales connected with Andrew Lanning, attributed the whole maneuver to an outbreak of madness. Just as there seemed to be madness in the campaign of Napoleon when he dropped over the Alps into Italy. While Melas was taking Genoa, heroic Masséna, appeared quietly on that unfortunate general's communications and then blotted him out at Marengo. And that campaign would have been judged madness instead of genius if it had not worked.

Retrospection made Andrew Lanning's coming to Los Toros a mad freak, whereas it was in reality a very clever stroke. Hal Dozier would have been on the road five hours before if he had not been held up in the matter of horses, but this is to tell the story out of turn.

Andrew saddled the mare and sent her back swiftly out of the plain, over the hills, and then dropped her down into the valley of the Little Silver River until he reached the grove of trees just outside Los Toros—some four hundred yards, say, from the little group of houses. He then took off his belt, hung it over the pommel, fastened the reins to the belt, and turned away. Sally would stay where he left her—unless someone else tried to get to her head, and then she would fight like a wildcat. He knew that, and he therefore started for Los Toros with his line of communications sufficiently guarded.

He instinctively thought first of drawing his hat low over his eyes and walking swiftly; a moment of calm figuring told him that the better way was to push the hat to the back of his head, put his hands in his pockets, and go whistling through the streets of the town. And this was actually the manner in which he made his entry to Los Toros. It was not much of a place—say five hundred people—but its single street looked as large and as long as a great avenue to Andrew as he sauntered carelessly toward the restaurant. It was the middle of the gray afternoon; there were few people about, and the two or three who Andrew passed nodded a greeting. Each time they raised their hands the fingers of Andrew twitched, but he made himself smile back at them and waved in return.

He went on until he came to the restaurant. It was a long, narrow room with a row of tables down each side, a little counter and cash register beside the door, some gaudy posters on the wall, a screen at the rear to hide the entrance to the kitchen, faded green sackcloth tacked on the ceiling to cover the bare boards, and a ragged strip of linoleum on the narrow passage between the tables.

These things Andrew saw with the first flick of his eyes as he came through the door; as for people, there was a fat old man sitting behind the cash register in a dirty white apron and two men in greasy overalls and black shirts, perhaps from the railroad. There was one other thing that immediately blotted out all the rest; it was a big poster, about halfway down the wall, on which appeared in staring letters: *$10,000 reward for the apprehension, dead or alive, of Andrew Lanning.* Above this caption was a picture of him, and below the big print appeared the body of smaller type that named his particular features. Straight to this sign Andrew walked and sat down at the table beneath it.

It was no hypnotic attraction that took him there. He knew perfectly well that, if a man noticed that sign, he would never dream of connecting the man for whom, dead or alive, $10,000 was to be paid, with the man who sat underneath the picture calmly eating his lunch in the middle of a town. And a town from which a posse pursuing the man had just ridden.

Andrew was sure they had gone. Even if some super-curious person should make a comparison, he would not proceed far with it, Andrew was sure, for the picture represented the round, young face of a person who hardly existed now; the hardened features of Andrew were now only a skinny caricature of what they had been.

At any rate, Andrew sat down beneath the picture, and, instead of resting one elbow on the table and partially veiling his face with his hand, as he might most naturally have done, he tilted back easily in his chair and looked up at the poster. The fat man from behind the register had come to take his order. He noted the direction of Andrew's eyes while he jotted down the items.

"You ain't the first," he said, "that's looked at that. Think of the gent that'll get ten thousand dollars out of a single slug?"

"I can name the man who'll get it," said Andrew, "and his name is Hal Dozier."

"I guess you ain't far wrong," replied the other. "For that matter, the folks around here would mostly make the same guess. But maybe Hal's luck will take a turn."

"Well," said Andrew, "if he gets the money, I'll say that he's earned it. And rush in some bread first, captain. I'm two-thirds starved."

It was a historic meal in more than one way. The size of it was one notable feature, and even Andrew had to loosen his belt when he came to attack the main feature, which was a vast steak with fried eggs scattered over the top of it. The proprietor, admiring such gastronomic prowess, hung about Andrew and made suggestions of side dishes—corn, tomatoes, and canned fish. The suggestions were added; the table groaned, for a diet of beans and bacon leaves vast holes that take much filling.

The steak had been reduced to a meager rim before Andrew had any attention to pay to the paper that had been placed on his table. It was an eight-page sheet entitled *The Granville Bugle,* and a subhead announced that it was *the greatest paper on the ranges and the cattleman's guide.* It was devoted strictly to news of the mountain desert. Andrew found a picture on the first page, a picture of Hal Dozier, and over the picture the following caption: *Watch this column for news of the Andrew Lanning hunt.*

The article in this week's issue contained few facts. It announced a number of generalities: *Marshal Hal Dozier, when interviewed, said*—and a great many innocuous things that he was sure that grim manhunter could not have spoken. He passed over the rest of the column in careless contempt. On the second page, in a muddle of short notices, one headline caught his eye and held it: *Charles Merchant to Wed Society Belle.*

The editor had spread his talents for the public eye in doing justice to it:

> *On the Fifteenth of the month will be consummated a romance that began last year, when Charles Merchant, son of the well-known cattle king, John Merchant, went East and met Miss Anne Withero. It is Miss Withero's second visit in the West, and it is now announced that the marriage. . . .*

Andrew crumpled the paper and let it fall. He glanced at a calendar on the wall opposite him. There remained six days before the wedding. And he was still so stunned by the announcement that, raising his head slowly, his thoughts spinning, he looked up and encountered the eyes of Hal Dozier as the latter sank into a chair.

He did not complete the act, but was arrested in mid-air, one hand grasping the back of the chair, the other hand at his hip.

Andrew, in the space of an instant, thought of three things—to kick the table from him and try to get to the side door of the place, to catch up the heavy sugar bowl and attempt to bowl over his man with a well-directed blow, or to simply sit and look Hal Dozier in the eye.

He had thought of the three things in the space that it would take a dog to snap at a fly and look away. He dismissed the first alternatives as absurd, and, picking up his cup of coffee, he raised his eyes slowly toward the ceiling, after the time-honored fashion of a man draining a glass, let his glance move gradually up and catch on the face of Dozier, and then, without haste, lowered the cup to its saucer.

The flush of his own heavy meal kept his pallor from showing. As for Dozier, there was a succession of changes in his features, and then he concluded by lowering himself heavily the rest of the way into his chair. He gave his order to the proprietor in a dazed fashion, looking straight at Andrew, and the latter knew perfectly that the deputy marshal felt that he was in a dream. He was seeing what was not possible to see; his eyes were telling his brain in definite terms: *There sits Andrew Lanning and $10,000.* But the reason of Dozier was speaking no less decidedly: *There sits a man without a weapon at his hip and actually beneath the poster that offers a reward for the capture of the person he resembles. Also, he is in a restaurant in the middle of a town. I have only to raise my voice in order to surround him.*

And reason gained the upper hand, although Dozier continued to look at Andrew in a fascinated manner.

Suddenly the outlaw knew that it would not do to disregard that glance so long continued. To disregard it would be to start the suspicions of Dozier as soon as his brain cleared, and the least spark would at once send the manhunter into a flame of conviction.

"Hello, stranger," said Andrew, and he merely made his voice a trifle husky and deep. "D'you know me?"

The eyes of Dozier widened, there was a convulsive motion of his arm, and then his glance wandered slowly away.

"Excuse me," he said. "I thought I remembered your face."

Should he let it rest at that? No, better risk a finishing touch. "No harm done," he said in the same loud voice. "Hey, captain, another cup of coffee, will you? And a cigar." He tilted back in his chair. He was about to begin whistling, but, feeling that this would be a trifle too brazen, he merely folded his hands behind his head and began to hum. And all the time his nerves were jumping, and that old frenzy was taking him by the throat, that bulldog eagerness for the fight. But fight empty-handed—and against Hal Dozier?

The restaurant owner brought Dozier's order, and then the coffee and the cigar to Andrew, and, while the deputy continued to look with dumb fascination at Andrew with swift side glances, Andrew finished his second cup. He bit off the end of his cigar, asked for his check, and paid it, and then felt his nerves crumble and go to pieces.

It was not Hal Dozier who sat there, but death itself that looked him in the face. One false move, one wrong gesture, would betray him. How could he tell? That very moment his expression might have altered into something that the marshal could not fail to recognize and the moment that final touch came there would be a gun play swifter than the eye could follow—simply a flash of steel and a simultaneous explosion.

Even now, with the cigar between his teeth, he knew that if he lighted a match the match would tremble between his fingers, and that trembling would betray him to Dozier. Was he wrong? Was there not even now a tightening of the jaw muscles of the marshal, a clearing and narrowing of his eyes, such as preceded action?

Yet he must not sit there, either, with the cigar between his teeth, unlighted. It was a little thing, but the weight of a feather would turn the balance and loose on him the thunderbolt of Hal Dozier in action.

But what could he do?

He found a thing in the very deeps of his despair. He got up from his chair, pushed his hat calmly upon his head—although that surely must complete Dozier's picture—and walked straight to the deputy. He dropped both hands upon the edge of Hal's table and leaned across it.

"Got a light, partner?" he asked. And standing there over the table, he knew that Dozier had at length finally and definitely recognized him, but that the numbed brain of the marshal refused to permit him to act. He believed, and yet he dared not believe his belief. Andrew saw the glance of Dozier go to his hip—his hip that the holster had rubbed until it gleamed. But no matter—the gun was not there—and stunned again by that impossible fact, Dozier reached back and brought up his hand bearing a matchbox. He took out a match. He lighted it, his brows drawing together and slackening all the time, and then he looked up, his eyes rising with the lighted match, and stared fully into the eyes of Andrew.

It was discovery undoubtedly—and how long would that mental paralysis last?

Andrew looked straight back into those eyes. His cigar took the fire and sucked in the flame. A cloud of smoke puffed out and rolled toward Hal Dozier, and Andrew turned leisurely and walked toward the door. He was a yard from it.

"Lanning!" came a voice behind him, terrible, like a scream of pain.

As he leaped forward a gun spoke heavily in the room. He heard the bullet crunch into the frame of the door; the door itself was split by the second shot as Andrew slammed it shut. Then he raced around the corner of the restaurant and made for the grove.

There was not a sound behind him for a moment. Then a roar rose from the village and rushed after him. It gave him wings. And, looking back, he saw that Hal Dozier was not among the pursuers. No, half a dozen men were running, and firing as they ran, but there was not a rifle in the lot, and it takes a good man to land a bullet on the run when he is firing at a dodging target. The pursuers lost ground; they stopped and yelled for horses.

But that was what Hal Dozier was doing now. He was jerking a saddle on the back of Gray Peter, and in sixty seconds he would be tearing out of Los Toros. In the same space Andrew was in his own saddle with a flying leap and spurring out of the trees.

Chapter Thirty-One

By one thing he knew the utter desperation of Hal Dozier. For the man had fired while Andrew's back was turned. The bullet had followed the warning cry as swiftly as the strike of a snake follows its rattle. Luck and his sudden leap forward had unbalanced the nice aim of Dozier, and perhaps his mental agitation had contributed to it. But, at any rate, Andrew was troubled as he cleared the edge of the trees and cantered Sally not too swiftly along the Little Silver River toward Las Casas Mountains, a little east of south.

He did not hurry her, partly because he wished to stay close and make sure of the number and force of his pursuers, and partly because he already had a lead sufficient to keep out of any but chance rifle shots.

He had not long to wait. Men boiled out of the village like hornets out of a shaken nest. He could see them buckling on belts while they were riding with the reins in their teeth. And they came like the wind, yelling at the sight of their quarry. Who would not kill a horse for the sake of saying that he had been within pistol range of the great outlaw? But, fast as their horses ran, Dozier, on Gray Peter, was able to keep up with them and also to range easily from group to group. Truly Gray Peter was a glorious animal. For the hundredth time Andrew admitted it. If he were allowed to stretch out after the mare, what would the result be?

The pursuers, under the direction of Dozier, spread across

the river bottom, and, having formed so that no tricky doubling could leave them in the lurch on a blind trail, they began to use a new set of tactics. It was new to Hal Dozier, but it was the old trick of his dead brother.

Dozier kept Gray Peter at a steady pace, never varying his gait. But, on either side of him, groups of his followers urged their horses forward at breakneck speed. Three or four would send home the spurs and rush up the river bottom after Andrew. If he did not hurry on, they opened fire with their rifles from a short distance and sent a hail of random bullets, but Andrew knew that a random bullet carries just as much force as a well-aimed one, and chance might be on the side of one of those shots. He dared not allow them to come too close. Yet his heart rejoiced as he watched the manner in which Sally accepted these challenges. She never once had to lurch into her racing gait; she took the rushes of the cow ponies behind her by merely lengthening her stride until she seemed to be settling closer and closer to the ground, and always the horses behind her were winded and had to fall back.

Yet they included some fine strains of blood in that bunch; only there was lacking the difference between a good animal and a fine one, in addition to the fact that Sally was long since hardened to just such races as this one.

If Andrew had let out Sally, she would have walked away from them all, but he dared not do that. For, after he had run the heart out of the commoner ones, there remained Gray Peter in reserve, never changing his pace, never hurrying, falling often far back, as the groups one after another pushed close to Sally and made her spurt, gaining again when the spurts ended one by one.

After all, there was nothing very new in these tactics. It was the fashion that a team of runners use against one dangerous opponent, challenging him one after the other and running him out, so that the best in the team can come through with a spurt at the end and pass the flagging enemy.

There were two hours of daylight; there was one hour of dusk, and all that time the crowd kept thrusting out its small groups, one after the other, reaching after Sally like different arms, and each time she answered the spurt, and always slipped away into a greater lead at the end of it. And then, while the twilight was turning into dark, Andrew looked back and saw the whole crowd rein in their horses and turn back. There remained a single figure following him, and that figure was easily seen, because it was a man on a gray horse. And then Andrew grasped the plan fully. The posse had played its part; the thing for which the mountain desert had waited was come at last, and Hal Dozier was going on to find his man single-handed and pull him down.

Twice, before complete darkness set in, Andrew drew Sally back to a gentler gait, and twice he sent her on again. And each time he had been on the verge of turning and going back to accept the challenge of Hal Dozier. Always two things stopped him. There was first the fear of the man which he frankly admitted, and more than that was the feeling that one thing lay before him to be done before he could meet Dozier and end the long trail. He must see Anne Withero. She was about to be married and be drawn out of his world and into a new one. He felt it was more important than life or death to see her before that transformation took place. They would go East, no doubt. Two thousand miles, the law, and the mountains would fence him away from her after that.

During the last months he had accepted her as he accepted the stars—something far away from him, and yet something that he knew was there and that he could look at perhaps out of his night. And now, by some pretext, by some wile, he must live to see her once more. After that let Hal Dozier meet him when he would.

But with this in mind, as soon as the utter dark shut down, he swerved Sally to the right and worked slowly up through the mountains, heading due southwest and out of the valley of the Little Silver. He kept at it, through a district where the mare could not even trot a great deal of the time, for two or more hours. Then he found a little plateau thick with good grazing for Sally and with a spring near it. There he camped for the night, without food, without fire.

And not once during the hours before morning did he close his eyes. When the first gray touched the sky he was in the saddle again; before the sun was up he had crossed the Las Casas and was going down the great shallow basin of the Roydon River. A fine, drizzling rain was falling, and Sally, tired from her hard work of the day before and the long duels with the horses of the posse, went even more down-heartedly moody than usual, shuffling wearily, but recovering herself with her usual cat-like adroitness whenever her footing failed on the steep downslope.

For all her dullness, it was a signal from Sally that saved Andrew. She jerked up her head and turned; he looked in the same direction and saw a form like a gray ghost coming over the hills to his left, a dim shape through the rain. Gloomily Andrew watched Hal Dozier come. Gray Peter had been fresher than Sally at the end of the run of the day before. He was fresher now. Andrew could tell that easily by the stretch of his gallop and the evenness of his pace as he rushed across the slope. He gave the word to Sally. She tossed up her head in mute rebellion at this new call for a race, and then broke into a canter whose first few strides, by way of showing her anger, were as choppy and lifeless as the stride of a plow horse.

That was the beginning of that famous ride from the Las Casas Mountains to the Roydon range, and all the distance across the Roydon valley. As a bird flies, it was a full seventy miles; as the horses galloped, winding to and fro to find the easier footing, it must have been a full eighty miles. That distance the gray horse and the bay ran in exactly nine hours and fifty-five minutes. To this time Hal Dozier swore in after days, and, although many a man has shaken his head over the tale, this is the story as it now runs current in the mountain desert, and this is the tale that two big stone pillars confirm. For Hal Dozier put them up to commemorate the run of great Gray Peter on this day—a pillar to mark the start and a pillar to mark the finish. The time is inscribed on the finish post.

It started with a five-mile sprint—literally five miles of hot racing in which each horse did its best. And in that five miles Gray Peter would most unquestionably have won had not one bit of luck fallen to the mare. A hedge of young evergreens streaked before Sally, and Andrew put her at the mark; she cleared it like a bird, jumping easily and landing in her stride. It was not the first time she had jumped with Andrew.

But Gray Peter was not a steeplechaser. He had not been trained to it, and he refused. His rider had to whirl and go up the line of shrubs until he found a place to break through. Then he was after Sally again. But the moment that Andrew saw the marshal had been stopped, he did not use the interim to push the mare and increase her lead. Very wisely he drew her back to the long, rocking canter that was her natural gait, and Sally got the breath that Gray Peter had run out of her. She also regained priceless lost ground, and, when the gray came in view of the quarry again, his work was all to do over again.

Hal Dozier tried again in straightaway running. It had been his boast that nothing under the saddle in the mountain desert could keep away from him in a stretch of any distance, and he rode Gray Peter desperately to make his boast good. He failed. If that first stretch had been unbroken—but there his chance was gone, and, starting the second spurt, Andrew came to re-alize one greatly important truth—Sally could not sprint for any distance, but up to a certain pace she ran easily and without labor. That was the meaning of those comparatively short forelegs and the high croup that gave the slight and awkward downpitch to her figure—she was essentially a distance horse. Gray Peter could outhoof her by many seconds in a mile sprint, but, kept inside a certain maximum, she ran tirelessly. He made it his point to see that she was never urged beyond that pace. He found another thing—that she took a hill in far better style than Peter, and she did far better in the rough, but on the level going he ate up her handicap swiftly.

With a strength of his own found, and a weakness in his pursuer, Andrew played remorselessly to that weakness with his strength. He sought the choppy ground as a preference and led the stallion through it wherever he could; he swung to the right, where there was a stretch of rolling hills, and once more Gray Peter had a losing space before him.

So they came to the river itself, with Gray Peter comfortably in the rear, but running well within his strength. Andrew paused in the shallows to allow Sally one swallow, then he went on. But Dozier did not pause for even this. It was a grave mistake.

And so the miles wore on. Sally was still running like a swal-low for lightness, but Andrew knew by her breathing that she was giving vital strength to the effort. He talked to her constantly. He told her how Gray Peter ran behind them. He encouraged her with pet words. And Sally seemed to under-stand, for she flicked one ear back to listen, and then she pricked them both and kept at her work. It was a heart-tearing thing to see her run to the point of lather, and then keep on.

They were in low hills, and Gray Peter was losing steadily. They reached a broad flat, and the stallion gained with terrible insistence. Looking back, Andrew could see that the marshal had stripped away every vestige of his pack. He followed that example with a groan. And still Gray Peter gained. He went forward in the stirrups to ease the mare by putting more weight on her forehand, and still Gray Peter gained.

It was the last great effort for the stallion. Before them rose the foothills of the Roydon Mountains; behind them the Las Casas range was lost in mist. It seemed that they had been galloping like this for an infinity of time, and Andrew was numb from the shoulders down. If he reached those hills, Gray Peter was beaten. He knew it; Hal Dozier knew it, and the two great horses gave all their strength to the last duel of the race.

The ears of Sally no longer pricked. They lay flat on her neck. The amazing lift was gone from her gait, and she pounded heavily with the forelegs. And still she struggled on. He looked back, and Gray Peter still gained, an inch at a time, and his stride did not seem to have abated. The one bitter question now was whether Sally would not collapse under the effort. With every lurch of her body, with every impact of her hoofs, Andrew expected to feel her crumble beneath him. And yet she went on. Courage? She was all courage. She was all heart, all nerve, and running on it. Behind her came Gray Peter, and he also ran with his head stretched out.

He was within rifle range now. Why did not Dozier fire? Perhaps he had set his heart on actually running Sally down, not dropping his prey with a distant shot.

And still they flew across the flat. The hills were close by and sometimes, when the drizzling rain that had wet Andrew to the skin and chilled him to the bone lifted, it seemed that the Roydon Mountains were exactly above them, leaning out over him like a shadow. He called on Sally again and again. He touched her for the first time in her life with spurs, and she found something in the depths of her heart and her courage to answer with. She ran again with a ghost of her former buoyancy, and

Gray Peter was held even.

Not an inch could he gain after that. Andrew saw his pursuer raise his quirt and flog. It was useless. Each horse was running itself out, and no power could get more speed out of the pounding limbs.

With his head still turned, Andrew felt a shock and flounder. Sally had almost fallen. He jerked sharply up on the reins, and she broke into a staggering trot. Then Andrew saw that they had struck the slope of the first hill, a long, smooth rise that she would have taken at full speed in the beginning of the race, but now it broke her heart to make it. He called to her; he spurred again; the trot quickened, but, although she labored bitterly, she could not raise a gallop. The trot was her best effort.

There was a shrill yelling behind, and Andrew saw Dozier, a hand brandished above his head. He had seen Sally break down; Gray Peter would catch her; his horse would win that famous duel of speed and courage. Rifle? He had forgotten his rifle. He would go in, he would overhaul Sally, and then finish the chase with a play of revolvers. And in expectation of that end, Andrew drew his revolver. It hung the length of his arm; he found that his muscles were numb from the cold and the cramped position from the elbow down. Shoot? He was as helpless as though he had no gun at all. His hand shook crazily under the strain. And in the meantime, flogging with his quirt, no doubt the marshal had kept his blood in circulation.

It gave Andrew a nightmare sensation, as of one fleeing in his sleep up a long stairs—only a step to gain safety, and yet his feet are turned to lead, and the horror rushes like the wind upon him from behind. He beat his hands together to bring back the blood. He bit the cold fingers. He thrashed his arms against the pommel of the saddle. There was only a dull pain; it would take long minutes to bring those hands back to the point of service, and Gray Peter galloped upon him from behind!

Well, he would let Sally do her best. For the last time he called on her; for the last time she struggled to respond, and Andrew looked back and grimly watched the stallion sweeping across the last portion of the flat ground, closer, closer, and then, at the very base of the slope, Gray Peter tossed up his head, floundered, and went down. And as he went, he hurled his rider over his head.

Andrew, fascinated, let Sally fall into a walk, while he watched. He was now in pointblank range of that deadly rifle, but he forgot his own danger in watching the singular convulsive struggles of Gray Peter to gain his feet. Hal Dozier was up again; he ran to his horse, caught his head, and at the same moment the stallion grew suddenly limp. The weight of his head dragged the marshal down, and then Andrew saw that Dozier made no effort to rise again.

He sat with the head of the horse in his lap, his own head buried in his hands, and Andrew knew then that Gray Peter was dead.

CHAPTER THIRTY-TWO

The mare herself was in a far from safe condition. And if the marshal had roused himself from his grief and hurried up the slope on foot he would have found the fugitive out of the saddle and walking by the side of the played-out Sally, forcing her with slaps on the hip to keep in motion. She went on, stumbling, her head down, and the sound of her breathing was a horrible thing to hear. But she must keep in motion, for, if she stopped in this condition, Sally would never run again.

Andrew forced her relentlessly on.

At length her head came up a little and her breathing was easier and easier. Before dark that night he came on a deserted shanty, and there he took Sally under the shelter, and, tearing up the floor, he built a fire that dried them both. The following day he walked again, with Sally following like a dog at his heels. One day later he was in the saddle again, and Sally was herself once more. Give her one feed of grain, and she would have run again that famous race from beginning to end.

But Andrew, stealing out of the Roydon Mountains into the lower ground, had no thought of another race. He was among a district of many houses, many men, and, for the final stage of his journey, he waited until after dusk had come, and then saddled Sally and cantered into the valley. It was late on the fourth night after he left Los Toros that Andrew came again to the house of John Merchant and left Sally in the very place among the trees where the pinto had stood before. There was no danger of a discovery on his approach, for it was a wild night of wind and rain. The drizzling mists of the last three days had turned into a steady downpour, and rivers of water had been running from his slicker on the way to the ranch house. Now he put the slicker behind the saddle, and from the shelter of the trees surveyed the house.

It was bursting with music and light; every moment or so automobiles, laboring through the mud, hummed up to the house or left it, bringing guests and taking them away; it must be the reception before the wedding. For some reason he had always imagined the house wrapped in black night as it was the time of his first coming, and it baffled him, this music, this noise, this radiance behind every window. Sometimes the front door was opened and voices stole out to him; sometimes even through the closed door he heard the ghostly tinkling of some girl's laughter.

And that was to Andrew the most melancholy sound in the world.

The rain, trickling even through the foliage of the evergreen, decided him to act at once. It might be that all the noise and light were, after all, an advantage to him, and, running close to the ground, he skulked across the dangerous open stretch and came into the safe shadow of the wall of the house.

Once there, it was easy to go up to the roof by one of the rain pipes, the same low roof from which he had escaped on the time of his last visit. On the roof the rush and drumming of the rain quite covered any sound he made, but he was drenched before he reached the window of Anne's room. Could he be sure that on her second visit she would have the same room? He settled that by a single glance. The curtain was not drawn, and a lamp, turned low, burned on the table beside the bed. The room was quite empty. The lamp reassured him, for the first person to enter the apartment would be sure to turn up the wick.

The window was fastened, but he worked back the fastening iron with the blade of his knife and raised himself into the room. He closed the window behind him. At once the noise of rain and the shouting of the wind faded off into a distance, and the voices of the house came more clearly to him. But he dared not stay to listen, for the water was dripping around him; he must move before a large dark spot showed on the carpet, and he saw, moreover, exactly where he could best hide. There was a heavily curtained alcove at one end of the room, and behind this shelter he hid himself. In case of a crisis the window was straight ahead of him; also, he could watch the door into the hall by pushing back the curtain.

Here he waited. How would she come? Would there be someone with her? Would she come laughing, with all the triumph of the dance bright in her face?

Behind him and about him he touched silken things, a mingling of fragrances reached him; apparently he had found the closet she used as a dressing room and every sight and scent—for a twilight came from the lamp and stole through above the curtain—spoke of Anne Withero and of her gentleness and all that nameless purity that he connected with her. He fell into a sort of sad-happy dream behind the curtain. Vaguely he heard the shrill droning of the violins die away beneath him, and the slipping of many dancing feet on a smooth floor fell to a whisper, and then ceased. Voices sounded in the hall, but he gave no heed to the meaning of all this. Not even the squawking of horns, as automobiles drove away, conveyed any thought to him; he wished that this moment could be suspended to an eternity.

Parties of people were going down the hall; he heard soft flights of laughter and many young voices. People were calling gaily to one another, and then, by an inner sense rather than by a sound, he knew that the door was opened into the room. He leaned and looked, and he saw Anne Withero close the door behind her and lean against it. In the joy of her triumph that evening?

No, her head was fallen, and he saw the gleam of her hand at her breast. He could not see her face clearly, but the bent head spoke eloquently of defeat. She came forward at length.

Thinking of her as the reigning power in that dance and all the merriment below him, Andrew had been imagining her tall, strong, with compelling eyes commanding admiration. He found all at once that she was small, very small, and her hair was not that keen fire that he had pictured. It was simply a coppery glow, marvelously delicate, molding her face. She went to a great full-length mirror; he had not seen it until her reflection suddenly flashed out at him from it with a touch of dull green fire at her throat. Was that a jewel?

He had not time to see. She had raised her head for one instant to look at her image, and then she bowed her head again and placed her hand against the edge of the mirror for support. Little by little, through the half light, he was making her out, and now the curve of her arm, from wrist to shoulder, went through Andrew like a phrase of music. He stepped out from behind the curtain, and, at the sound of the cloth swishing back into place, she whirled on him.

If he could have had a picture of her as she stood there with the first fear parting her lips and darkening her eyes, I suppose that Andrew Lanning would have parted with the rest of Anne Withero with small pain indeed.

"I've come to do no harm," he said hastily. "Do not be afraid."

She was speechless; her raised hand did not fall; it was as if she were frozen where she stood.

"I shall leave you at once," said Andrew quietly, "if you are badly frightened. You have only to tell me."

He had come closer. Now he was astonished to see her turn swiftly toward the door and touch his arm with her hand. "Hush," she said. "Hush. They may hear you." She glided to the door into the hall and turned the lock softly and came to him again.

It made Andrew weak to see her so close, and he searched her face with a hungry and jealous fear, lest she should be different from his dream of her. "You are the same," he said with a sigh of relief. "And you are not afraid of me?"

"Hush . . . hush," she repeated. "Afraid of you? Don't you see that I'm happy, happy, happy to see you again?" She drew him forward a little, and her hand touched his as she did so. She turned up the lamp, and a flood of strong yellow light went over the room. "But you have changed," said Anne Withero with a little cry. "Oh, you have changed. What have they been doing to you?"

He was dumb. Something cold that had been forming about his heart was breaking away and crumbling, and a strange warmth and weakness was coming in his blood. She was answering her own question.

"I know. They've been hounding you . . . the cowards."

"Does it make no difference to you . . . all that I've done?" asked Andrew.

"What is it that should make a difference?"

"I have killed a man."

"Ah, it was that brother to the Dozier man. But I've learned about him. He was a bloodhound like his brother, but treacherous. I've learned everything about him, and people say it was a good thing that he died. Besides, it was in fair fight. Fair fight? It was one against six."

"Don't," said Andrew, breathing hard, "don't say that. You make me feel that it's almost right to have done what I've done.

But besides him . . . all the rest . . . do they make no difference?"

"All of what?"

"People say things about me. They even print them." He
winced as he spoke.

But she was fierce again; her passion made her tremble.
"When I think of it . . . ," she murmured. "When I think of it,
the rotten injustice makes me want to choke them all. Why,
today I heard . . . I can't repeat it. It makes me sick . . . sick.
And you're only a boy, Andrew Lanning."

It was a staggering blow. He was not altogether sure that he
was glad to hear this statement. He made himself his full height.

"Some people would smile if they heard you say that," said
Andrew.

"If you draw yourself up like that again, I'll laugh at you.
Andrew Lanning, I say, you're just a boy. You're not two years
older than I am. Why, they've hounded you and bullied you
until they've made you think you are bad, Andrew. They've even
made you a little bit proud of the hard things people say about
you. Isn't that true?"

Was it any wonder that Andrew could not answer? He felt all
at once so supple that he was hot tallow that those small fingers
would mold and bend to suit themselves.

"Sit down here," she commanded. Meekly he obeyed. He sat
on the edge of his chair, with his hat held with both hands, and
his eyes widened as he stared at her—like a person coming out
of a great darkness into a great light.

Tears came into the eyes of the girl. "You're as thin as a
starved . . . wolf," she said, and closed her eyes and shuddered.
"And all the time I've been thinking of you as you were when I
saw you here before . . . the same clear, steady eyes and the
same direct smile. Oh, you see I've never forgotten that night.
What girl would? It was like something out of a play . . . but so

much finer. But they've made you older . . . they've burned the boy out of you with pain. And I've been thinking about you just cantering through wild, gay adventures. Are you ill now?"

He had leaned back in the chair and gathered his hat close to his breast, crushing it.

"I'm not ill," said Andrew. His voice was hoarse and thick. "I'm just listening to you. Go on and talk."

"About you?" asked the girl.

"I don't hear your words . . . hardly. I just hear the sound you make." He leaned forward again and cast out his arm so that the palm of his hand was turned up beneath her eyes. She could see the long, lean fingers. It suddenly came home to her that every strong man in the mountain desert was in deadly terror of that hand. Anne Withero was shaken for the first time, and her smile went out.

"Listen to me," he was saying in that tense whisper that was oddly like the tremor of his hand. "I've been hungry for that voice all these weeks . . . and months . . . and thousands of years. Go on and talk."

"I'll tell you what I'm going to do," said the girl, very grave. "I'm going to break up this cowardly conspiracy against you. I've written to my father to get the finest lawyer in the land and send him out here to make you . . . legal . . . again. Oh, I wrote a letter that'll make Dad's blood boil. You'll have to meet Dad, Andrew Lanning."

He began to smile, and shook his head. "It's no use," he said. "Perhaps your lawyer could help me on account of Bill's death, but he couldn't help me with Hal."

"Are you . . . do you mean you're going to fight the other man, too?"

"He killed his horse chasing me," said Andrew. "I couldn't stop to fight him because I was comin' down here to see you. But when I go away, I've got to find him and give him a chance back at me. It's only fair."

"Because he killed a horse trying to get you . . . you're going to give him a chance to shoot you?" Her voice had become shrill. She lowered it instinctively toward the end and cast a glance of apprehension toward the door. "You are quite mad," said the girl.

"You don't understand," said Andrew. "His horse was Gray Peter . . . the stallion."

The simple sentence seemed to mark the vast gulf of difference between them. She only stared at Andrew, and for the first time she grew aware of the fact that he was dripping on her carpet and that his clothes were tattered—remarkably ragged, in fact—and that he was by no means clean.

"I've ridden Gray Peter myself," went on Andrew. "And I would rather have killed a man than have seen Gray Peter die. Hal had Peter's head in his arms," he added softly. "And he'll never give up the trail until he's had it out with me. He wouldn't be half a man if he let things drop now."

And she forgot the dripping, the ragged clothes, the dirt. In some manner she saw the whole picture of the death of Gray Peter in the saddened face of Andrew. If she had felt above him the moment before, she now felt infinitely beneath him.

"So you have to fight Hal Dozier?"

"Yes."

"But when that's done . . . ?"

"When that's done one of us will be dead. If it's me, of course, there's no use worryin' . . . if it's Hal, of course, I'm done in the eyes of the law. Two . . . murders."

His eyes glinted and his fingers quivered. It sent a cold thrill through the girl.

"But they say he's a terrible man, Andrew. You wouldn't let him catch you?"

"I won't stand and wait for him," said Andrew gravely. "But

if we fight I think I'll kill him."

It was said with perfect lack of braggadocio.

"What makes you think that?" She was more curious than shocked.

"It's just a sort of feeling that you get when you look at a man . . . either you're his master or you aren't. You see it in a flash."

"Have you ever seen your master?" asked the girl slowly.

"I'll want to die when I see that," he said simply.

Suddenly she clenched her hands and sat straight up. "It's got to be stopped," she said hotly. "It's all nonsense, and I'm going to see that you're both stopped."

"You can't stop me."

She was not angry, but very curious. It was, in fact, difficult to be angry with a man who kept his eyes upon her with a look of mortal hunger, mortal stillness.

"Of course," she said, without smiling, "I'm not a fighting man."

It was as though, when words failed him, he relied upon a gesture to take their place. She followed the glint of his eyes and the movement of his hand, and was sorry she had made that last remark. Too late she knew she had precipitated the trouble. She would have stopped him, but it was like raising a hand to halt an avalanche. She felt lost, as though a horse had taken the bit in his teeth and was whirling her on into danger, out of control. The emotion that had been in the quivering gesture of his hand and in the glint of his eyes was stamped freely on his whole face now. It was in his pallor, in the deep lines beside the mouth, in his very breathing, and, above all, it flowed into the quality of his voice, which did not rise in pitch or in volume, but which took on a peculiar edge—something that went to her heart.

"Four days ago," he said, "you could have taken me in the

hollow of your hand. I would have come to you and gone from you at a nod. That time is about to end."

He paused a little, and looked at her in such a manner that she was frightened, but it was a pleasant fear. It made her interlace her fingers with nervous anxiety, but it set a fire in her eyes.

"That time is ending," said Andrew. "You are about to be married."

"And after that you will never look at me again, never think of me again?"

"I hope not," he answered. "I strongly hope not. I shall make myself busy with that purpose."

"But why? Is a marriage a blot or a stain?"

"It is a barrier," he answered.

"Even to thoughts? Even to friendship?"

"Yes."

A very strange thing happened in the excited mind of Anne Withero. It seemed to her that Charles Merchant sat, a filmy ghost, beside this tattered fugitive. He was speaking the same words that Andrew spoke, but his voice and his manner were to Andrew Lanning what moonshine is to sunlight. She had looked upon marriage simply as an acquisition, a gain, an inevitable event toward which all woman must move. And now a new point of view was opened to her, and she saw marriage as a bitter loss, a great gain, and a great sacrifice, a chance for joy, and a certainty for aching sorrow, inevitable trial by fire to which all womankind moves. She had been thinking of Charles Merchant as a social asset; she began to think of him now as a possessing force. Anne Withero possessed by Charlie Merchant. A faded smile came and went on her lips.

"What you have told me," she said, "means more than you may think to me. Have you come all this distance to tell me?"

"All this distance to talk?" he said. He seemed to sit back and wonder. "Have I traveled for four days?" he went on. "Has Gray Peter died, and have I been under Hal Dozier's rifle only to speak to you?" He suddenly recalled himself. "No, no. I have come to give you a wedding present."

He watched her color change. "Are you angry? Is it wrong to give you a present?"

"No," she answered in a singular, stifled voice.

"It is this watch." It was a large gold watch and a chain of very old make that he put into her hand. "It is for your son," said Andrew.

She stood up; he rose instinctively. "When I look at it I'm to remember that you are forgetting me?"

A little hush fell upon them.

"Are you laughing at me, Anne?"

He had never called her by her name before, and yet it came as naturally upon his lips as a child's name, say, comes upon the tongue of its playmate.

She stood, indeed, with the same smile upon her lips, but her eyes were fixed and looked straight past him. They were dim and obscured by moisture. And presently he saw a tear pass slowly down her face. Her hand remained without moving, with the watch in it exactly as he had placed it there. A great awe came upon Andrew. All before he had felt that he was the master with the upper hand while they talked together.

But now she wept, and his heart was humbled. It shocked him and crushed him with a feeling that in her were motives so deeply drawn, flowing from sources so remote that he could never have understood her even if she were to speak. All that mysterious power that is womanhood came upon him and about him like still and holy things—the whisper of rain in the evening when it is easiest to die, the pure and melancholy cold of autumn, the fragrance of a garden passed unknown in the night.

It became impossible for him to bear the sight of her eyes. If he remained she might speak, and he feared to hear her. A sense of a third presence, of another soul in the room overwhelmed him; he could not give it a name, and therefore he called it God.

She had not stirred when he slipped without a noise through the window and was instantly swallowed in the rushing of the wind and rain.

CHAPTER THIRTY-THREE

There was, as Andrew had understood for a long time, a sort of underground world of criminals even here on the mountain desert. Otherwise the criminals could not have existed for even a moment in the face of the organized strength of lawful society. Several times in the course of his wanderings Andrew had come in contact with links of the underground chain, and he learned what every fugitive learns—the safe stopping points in the great circuit of his flight.

Three elements went into the making of that hidden society. There was first of all the circulating and active part, and this was composed of men actually known to be under the ban of the law and openly defying it. It was the smallest component part of the whole, and yet it was the part with which law-abiding society occupied itself mostly. Beneath this active group lay a stratum much larger that served as a base for the operating criminals. This stratum was built entirely of men who had at one time been incriminated in shady dealings of one sort and another. It included lawbreakers from every part of the world, men who had fled first of all to the shelter of the mountain desert and who had lived there until their past was even forgotten in the lands from which they came. But they had never lost the inevitable sympathy for their more active fellows, and in this class there was included a meaner element—men who had in the past committed crimes in the mountain desert itself and who, from time to time, when they saw an absolutely safe opportunity, were perfectly ready and willing to sin again.

The third and largest of all the elements in the criminal world of the desert was a shifting and changing class of men who might be called the paid adherents of the active order. The longriders, acting in groups or singly, fled after the commission of a crime and were forced to find places of rest and concealment along their journey. Under this grave necessity they quickly learned what people on their way could be hired as hosts and whose silence and passive aid could be bought. Such men were secured in the first place by handsome bribes. And very often they joined the ranks unwillingly. But when some peaceful householder was confronted by a desperate man, armed, on a weary horse—perhaps stained from a wound—the householder was by no means ready to challenge the man's right to hospitality. He never knew when the stranger would take by force what was refused to him freely, and, if the lawbreaker took by force, he was apt to cover his trail by a fresh killing.

Of course such killings took place only when the longrider was a desperate brute rather than a man, but enough of them had occurred to call up vivid examples to every householder who was accosted. As a rule he submitted to receive the unwelcome guest. Also, as a rule, he was weak enough to accept a gift when the stranger parted. Once such a gift was taken, he was lost. His name was instantly passed on by the fugitive to his fellows as a *safe* man; other longriders were sure to come to his door quietly and ask shelter or food or some trifle in equipment. They always paid handsomely for what they received, and, if they had to take on credit, they were certain to pay doubly when they were again in funds. It was a point of honor. And so the innocent householder, drawn into the underground circle by force and retained there by bribes, was kept in the new world. Once fairly in, he could not withdraw. Before long he became, against or with his will, a depository of secrets—banned faces became known to him. And if he suddenly decided to withdraw from that criminal world, his case was most precarious.

The longriders admitted no neutrals. If a man had once been with them, he could only leave them to become an enemy. He became open prey. His name was published abroad. Then his cattle were apt to disappear. His stacks of hay might catch fire unexpectedly at night. His house itself might be plundered, and, in not infrequent cases, the man himself was brutally murdered. It was part of a code no less binding because it was unwritten.

All of this Andrew was more or less aware of, and scores of names had been mentioned to him by chance acquaintances of the road. Such names he stored away, for he had always felt that time impending of which Henry Allister had warned him, the time when he must openly forget his scruples and take to a career of crime. That time, he now knew, was come upon him.

It would be misrepresenting Andrew to say that he shrank from the future. Rather he accepted it with a fierce joy. It offered him a swift life of action, an all-absorbing career, a chance for forgetfulness of the one thing that, before this, had held him back with a meager leash. He accepted everything that lay before him wholeheartedly, and, with the laying aside of his scruples, there was an instant lightening of the heart, a fierce keenness of mind, a contempt for society, a disregard for life beginning with his own. One could have noted it in the recklessness with which he sent Sally up the slope away from the ranch house this night.

He had made up his mind immediately to hunt out a safe man, recently mentioned to him by that unconscionable scapegrace Harry Woods, crooked gambler, thief of small and large, and whilom murderer. The man's name was Garry Baldwin, a small rancher, some half day's ride above Sullivan's place in the valley. He was recommended as a man of silence. In that direction Andrew took his way, but, coming in the hills to a dished-out place on a hillside, where there was a natural shelter from both wind and rain, he stopped there for the rest of the night, cooked a meal, rolled himself in his blankets, and slept into the gray of the morning.

No sooner was the first light streaking the horizon to the east than Andrew wakened, and wakened in instant possession of all his faculties; he had gained a Napoleonic power to take his sleep whenever and wherever he chose, and wake refreshed and ready for a new start. He could sleep as a camel eats. If opportunity offered, he could spend a dozen hours wrapped in oblivion and then go freshly forty-eight hours without a new rest. Of all the rare qualities of hand and eye and mind that equipped Andrew Lanning for his hard life, there was nothing half so valuable as this command over sleep. The heart-breaking ride from Los Toros, which would have reduced another man to a tangle of nerves and weariness, left him as fresh as a bird. One sleep was all he needed to wipe his mind clean of the past.

He saddled Sally this morning, and, after a leisurely breakfast, started at a jog trot through the hills, taking the upslope with the utmost care. For nothing so ruins a horse as hard work uphill at the very beginning of the day. He gave Sally her head, and she went along in her own capricious manner, walking at a snail's pace here, trotting there, breaking into a wild gallop now and again to stretch her muscles, and on the whole behaving like some irresponsible boy turned loose for the first time on the road. But by letting her go as she pleased, she topped the divide, breathing as easily as if she had been walking on the flat; she gave one toss of her head as she saw the long, smooth slope ahead of her, breaking into a tumble of rolling ground beyond, and then, without a word from Andrew or a touch of her heels, she gave herself up to the long, rocking canter that she could maintain so tirelessly for hour on hour.

A clear cold morning came on; the wind, changing from

southwest to north, whipped the sky clear in a few moments; a rout of clouds piled away in storage to the south, and the sun came over the tips of the eastern mountains, dazzling bright and without a particle of warmth. Indeed, it was rarely chill for the mountain desert, with a feel of coming snow in the wind. Sally pricked one ear as she looked into the north, and Andrew knew that was a sign of trouble coming.

He came in the middle of the morning to the house of Garry Baldwin. It was a wretched shack. The roof sagged in the middle, and the building had been held from literally falling apart by bolting an iron rod through the length of it.

A woman who fitted well into such a background kicked open the door and looked up to Andrew with the dishwater still dripping from her red hands. He asked for her husband. He was gone from the house. Where, she did not know. Somewhere yonder, and her gesture included half the width of the horizon to the west. There was his trail, if Andrew wished to follow it. For her part, she was busy and could not spare time to gossip. At that she stepped back and kicked the door shut with a slam that set the whole side of the shack shivering.

At that moment Andrew wondered what he would have done those few months—those few lifetimes—when he lived in Martindale if he had been treated in such a manner. He would have crimsoned to the eyes, no doubt, and fled from the virago. But now he felt neither embarrassment nor fear or anger. He drew his revolver, and with the heavy butt banged loudly on the door. It left three deep dents in the wood, and the door was kicked open again. But this time he saw only the foot of the woman clad in a man's boot. The door remained open, but the hostess kept out of view.

"You be ridin' on, friend!" she called in her harsh voice. "Bud, keep outen the kitchen. Stranger, you be ridin' on. I don't know you and I don't want to know you . . . a man that beats on doors with his gun!"

Andrew laughed, and the sound brought her into view, a furious face, but a curious face as well. She carried a long rifle slung easily under her stout arm. There was the strength of a man in her shoulders and the readiness of a man about her hands.

"What d'you want with Garry?" she asked.

And he replied with a voice equally hard: "I want direction for finding scar-faced Allister." He watched that shot shake her.

"You do? You got a hell of a nerve askin' around here for Allister. Slope, kid, slope. You're on a cold trail."

"Wait a minute," protested Andrew. "You need another look at me."

"I can see all there is to you the first glance," said the woman calmly. "Why should I look again?"

"To see the reward," said Andrew bitterly. He laughed again. "I'm Andrew Lanning. Ever hear of me?"

It was obvious that she had. She blinked and winced as though the name stunned her. "Lanning?" she said. "Why, you ain't much more'n a kid. Lanning. . . . And you're him?" All at once she melted. "Slide off your hoss and come in, Andy," she said. "Dogged if I knew you at all."

"Thanks. I want to find Allister and I'm in a hurry."

"So you and him are goin' to team it? That'll be high times. Come here, Bud. Look at Andy Lanning. That's him on the horse right before you."

A scared, round face peered out at Andrew from behind his mother.

"All right, partner. I'll tell you where to find him pretty close. He'll be up the gulch along about now. You know the old shack up there? You can get to him inside three hours . . . with that hoss." She stopped and eyed Sally. "Is that the one that run Gray Peter to death? She don't look the part, but them long, low hosses is deceivin'. Can't you stay, Andy? Well, s'long. And give Allister a good word from Bess Baldwin. Luck!"

He waved, and was gone at a gallop.

CHAPTER THIRTY-FOUR

It was not yet noon when he entered the gulch. The sun, although it was almost directly at the zenith, gave but a mild warmth, and all the ravine was full of that hushing sound that comes after a heavy rain, when the earth is drinking the water out of myriad little pools. There was no creekbed in the cañon, but an impromptu rivulet was now running down over the gravel, winding foolishly into blind pools and cutting a crazy, ragged path down to the mouth of the gulch. It kept a faint tinkling sound over the murmur of the soaking water—two whispers, one barely louder than the other, and both making Andrew merely feel the weight of the silence.

He was not halfway up the gulch when something moved at the top of the high wall to his right. He guessed at once that it was a look-out signaling the main party of the approach of a stranger, so Andrew stopped Sally with a word and held his hands high above his head, facing the point from which he had seen the movement. There was a considerable pause, and then a man showed on the top of the cliff, and Andrew recognized Jeff Rankin by his red hair. Yet they were at too great a distance for conversation, and, after waving a greeting, Rankin merely beckoned Andrew on his way up the valley. Around the very next bend of the ravine he found the camp. It was of the most impromptu character, and the warning of Rankin had caused them to break it up precipitately, as Andrew could see by one length of tarpaulin tossed, without folding, over a saddle. Each of the four was ready, beside his horse, for flight or for attack, as their look-out on the cliff should give signal. But at sight of Andrew and the bay mare a murmur, then a growl of interest went among them. Even Larry la Roche grinned a skull-like welcome, and Henry Allister actually ran forward to receive the newcomer. Andrew dropped out of the saddle and shook hands with him.

"I've done as you said I would," said Andrew. "I've run in a circle, Allister, and now I'm back to make one of you, if you still want me."

Allister, laughing joyously, turned to the other three and repeated the question to them. There was only one voice in answer.

"Want you?" said Allister, and his smile made Andrew almost forget the scar that twisted the otherwise handsome face. "Want you? Why, man, if we've been beyond the law up to this time, we can laugh at the law now. You're worth a host, Lanning. As soon as it's known you're with me, the bumpkins will want a hundred men before they take our trails. Sit down. Hey, Scottie, shake up the fire and put on some coffee, will you? We'll take an hour off."

Larry la Roche was observed to make a dour face. "Who'll tell me it's lucky," he said, "to have a gent that starts out by makin' us all stop? Is that a good sign?"

But Scottie Macdougal, with laughter, hushed him. Yet Larry la Roche remained of all the rest quite silent during the making of the coffee and the drinking of it. The others kept up a running fire of comments and questions, but Larry la Roche, as though he had never forgiven Andrew for their first quarrel, remained with his long, bony chin dropped upon his breast and followed the movements of Andrew Lanning with restless eyes.

The others were glad to see him, as Andrew could tell at a glance, but also they were a bit troubled, and by degrees he made out the reason. Strange as it seemed, they regretted that he had not been able to make his break across the mountains. His presence made them more impregnable than they had ever been under the indomitable Allister, and yet, more than the aid of his fighting hand, they would have welcomed the tidings of a man who had broken away from the shadow of the law and made good. It was the first time that Andrew observed this quality among the outlaws, yet, he learned later, that even the tramps of the cross-continental road do not welcome recruits to their ranks. Once a man has taken the long step that places him beyond the reach of good society, he is received with open arms, but, as long as there is a chance of putting him back on his feet again, there are few, indeed, that will not contribute money and cunning to that purpose. There is, of course, a shade of selfishness in it. For each of the fallen wishes to feel that his exile is self-terminable, and the most notorious criminal will thrill to a story of regeneration.

Therefore, Andrew, telling his story to them in brief, found that they were not by any means filled with unmixed pleasure. Joe Clune, with his bright brown hair of youth and his lined, haggard face of worn middle-age, summed up their sentiments at the end of Andrew's story: "You're what we need with us, Lanning. You and Allister will beat the world, and it means high times for the rest of us, but God pity you . . . that's all."

The pause that followed this solemn speech was to Andrew like an amen. He glanced from face to face, and each stern eye met his in gloomy sympathy.

Then something shot through him that was to his mind what red is to the eye; it was a searing touch of reckless indifference, defiance.

"Forget this prayer-meeting talk," said Andrew. "I came up here for action, not mourning. I want something to do with my hands, not something to think about with my head."

Something to think about. It was like a terror behind him. If he should have long quiet, it would steal on him and look at him over his shoulder like a face. A little of this showed in his face, enough to make the circle flash significant glances at one another.

"You got something behind you, Andy," said Scottie. "Come out with it. It ain't too bad for us to hear."

"There's something behind me," said Andrew. "It's the one really decent part of my life. And I don't want to think about it. Allister, they say you never let the grass grow under you. What's on your hands now?"

"Somebody has been flattering me," said the leader quietly, and all the time he kept studying the face of Andrew. "We have a little game ahead, if you want to come in on it. We're short-handed, but I'd try it with you. That makes us six all told. Six enough, boys?"

"Count me half of one," said Larry la Roche. "I don't feel lucky about this little party."

"We'll count you two times two," replied the leader calmly, and he began to outline his plans to Andrew.

It developed, before he had been talking for five minutes, that the plans were as extraordinary as the man himself. He treated crime as any progressive businessman treats his business. He looked upon himself and his small band as a great capital investment, on which the money they secured was the interest. And accordingly he seldom risked the band in action.

"Tempt Providence once too much and the best-laid plan in the world will break down," he said, "as long as the other side has the same caliber guns we have. Who is the winning gambler? Jeff Rankin, who plunges every time he sees a three of a kind, or Larry there, who plunges once in an evening for everything he has? He makes more in that plunge than Jeff Rankin makes in a month's play. It's the same with this business of mine, Lanning.

I show my hand once in every six or eight months, but, when I strike, I strike hard and I strike for big stakes." He added: "You boys play a game. I'm going to break in Lanning to our job."

Taking his horse, he and Andrew rode at a walk up the ravine. On the way the leader explained his system briefly and clearly. Told in short, he worked somewhat as follows. Instead of raiding blindly right and left, he only moved when he had planned every inch of ground for the advance and the blow and the retreat. To make sure of success and the size of his stakes he was willing to invest heavily.

"Big businessmen sink half a year's income in their advertising. I do the same."

It was not public advertising; it was money cunningly expended where it would do most good. Fifty percent of the money the gang earned was laid away to make future returns surer. In twenty places Allister had his paid men who, working from behind the scenes, gained priceless information and sent word of it to the outlaw. Trusted officials in great companies were in communication with him. When large shipments of gold were to be made, for instance, he was often warned beforehand. Every dollar of the consignment was known to him—the date of its shipment, its route, and the hands to which it was supposed to fall. Or, again, in many a bank and prosperous mercantile firm in the mountain desert he had inserted his paid spies, who let him know when the safe was crammed with cash and when the way would be fairly open and by what means the treasure was guarded.

Not until he had secured such information did the leader move. And he still delayed until every possible point of friction had been noted, every danger considered, and a check appointed for it, every method of advance and retreat gone over.

"A good general," Allister was fond of saying, "plans in two ways . . . for an absolute victory and for an absolute defeat. The one enables him to squeeze the last ounce of success out of a triumph . . . the other keeps a failure from turning into a catastrophe."

With everything arranged for the stroke, he usually posted himself with the band as far as possible from the place where the actual work was to be done. Then he made a feint in the opposite direction—he showed himself or a part of his gang recklessly. The moment the alarm was given—even at the risk of having an entire hostile countryside around him—he started a whirlwind course in the opposite direction from which he was generally supposed to be traveling. If possible, at the ranches of adherents, or at out-of-the-way places where confederates could act, he secured fresh horses and dashed on at full speed all the way.

Then, at the very verge of the place for attack, he gathered his men, rehearsed in detail what each man was to do, delivered the blow, secured the spoils, and each man of the party split away from the other and fled in scattering directions, to assemble again at a distant point on a comparatively distant date. There they sat down around a council table, and there they divided the spoils. No matter how many were employed, no matter how vast a proportion of the danger and scheming had been borne by the leader, he took no more than two shares. Fifty percent of the prize was set aside. The rest was divided with an exact care among the remaining members of the gang. The people who had supplied the requisite information for the coup were always given their share. If anything happened to them, if their deceit was discovered, their heirs received every scruple of the money. More than that, excellent sources of information were kept fattened with bribes even when they were turning in no useful news. One man had only sent in two short bits of advice in three years, but each of those notes had meant many thousands of dollars.

From this general talk Allister descended to particulars. He talked of the gang itself. They were quite a fixed quantity. In the last half dozen years there had not been three casualties. For one thing, he chose his men with infinite care; in the second place, he saw to it that they remained in harmony, and to that end he was careful never to be tempted into forming an unwieldy crew, no matter how large the prize. Of the present organization each was an expert. Larry la Roche had been a counterfeiter and was a consummate penman. His forgeries were works of art. "Have you noticed his hands?"

Scottie Macdougal was an eminent advance agent, whose smooth tongue was the thing for the very dangerous and extremely important work of trying out new sources of information, noting the dependability of those sources and understanding just how far and in what line the tools could be used. Joe Clune was a past expert in the blowing of safes. Not only did he know everything that was to be known about means of guarding money and how to circumvent them, but he was an artist with the soup, as Allister called nitroglycerin.

Jeff Rankin, without a mental equipment to compare with his companions, was often invaluable on account of his prodigious strength. Under the strain of his muscles iron bars bent like hot wax. In addition he had more than his share of an ability that all the members of the gang possessed—an infinite cunning in the use of weapons and a star-storming self-confidence.

"And where," said Andrew at the end of this long recital, "do I fit in?"

"You begin," said Allister, "as the least valuable of my men . . . before six months you will be worth the whole set of 'em. You'll start as my lieutenant, Lanning. The boys expect it. You've built up a reputation that counts. They admit your superiority without question. Larry la Roche squirms under the weight of it, but he admits it like the rest of 'em. In a pinch they would obey you nearly as well as they obey me. It means that, having you to take charge, I can do what I've always wanted to do . . . I can give the main body a slip and go off for advance-guard and rear-guard duty. I don't dare to do it now.

"Do you know why? Those fellows yonder, who seem so chummy, would be at each other's throat in ten seconds if I weren't around to keep them in order. I know why you're here, Lanning. It isn't the money. It's the cursed fear of loneliness and the fear of having time to think. You want action, action to fill your mind and blind you. That's what I offer you. You're the keeper of the four wildcats you see over there. You start in with their respect. Let them lose their fear of you for a moment and they'll go for you. Treat them like men . . . think of them as wild beasts. That's what they are. The minute they know you're without your whip, they go for you like tigers at a wounded trainer. One taste of meat is all they need to madden them. It's different with me. I'm wild, too." His eyes gleamed at Andrew. "And, if they raise you, I think they'll find you've more iron hidden away in you than I have. But the way they'll find it out will be in an explosion that will wipe them out. You've got to handle them without that explosion, Lanning. Can you do it?"

The younger man moistened his lips. "I think this job is going to prove worthwhile," he returned.

"Very well, then. But there are penalties in your new position. In a pinch, you've got to do what I do . . . see that they have food enough . . . go without sleep if one of them needs your blankets . . . if any of 'em gets in trouble, even into a jail, you've got to get him out."

"Better still." Andrew smiled.

"And now," said the leader, "I'll tell you about our next job as we go back to the boys."

Chapter Thirty-Five

It was ten days later when the band dropped out of the mountains into the Murchison Pass—a singular place for a train robbery, Andrew could not help thinking. They were at the southwestern end of the pass, where the mountains gave back in a broad gap. Below them, not five miles away, was the city of Gidding Creek; they could see its buildings and parks tumbled over a big area, for there was a full 25,000 of inhabitants in Gidding Creek. Indeed, the whole country was dotted with villages and towns, for it was no longer a cattle region, but a semi-farming district cut up into small tracts. One was almost never out of sight of at least one house.

It worried Andrew, this closely built country, and he knew that it worried the other men as well, yet there had not been a single murmur from among them as they jogged their horses on behind Allister. Each of them was swathed from head to heels in a vast slicker that spread behind, when the wind caught it, as far as the tail of the horse. And the rubber creaked and rustled softly. Whatever they might have been inclined to think of this daring raid into the heart of a comparatively thickly populated country, they were too accustomed to let the leader do their thinking for them to argue the point with him. And Andrew followed blindly enough. He saw, indeed, one strong point in their favor. The very fact that the train was coming out of the heart of the mountains, through ravines that afforded a thousand places for assault, would make the guards relax their attention as they approached Gidding Creek. And, although there were many people in the region, they were a fat and inactive populace, not comparable with the lean fellows of the north.

There was bitter work behind them. Ten days before they had made a feint to the north of Martindale that was certain to bring out Hal Dozier, and then they doubled about and had plodded steadily south, choosing always the most desolate ground for their travel. There had been two changes of horses for the others, but Andrew kept to Sally. To her that journey was play after the labor she had passed through before; the iron dust of danger and labor was in her even as it was in Andrew. Three in all that party were fresh at the end of the long trail. They were Allister, Sally, and Andrew. The others were poisoned with weariness, and their tempers were on edge; they kept an ugly silence, and, if one of them happened to jostle the horse of the other, there was a flash of teeth and eyes—a silent warning. The sixth man, was Scottie, who had long since been detached from the party. His task was one that, if he failed in it, would make all that long ride go for nothing. He was to take the train far up, ride down as blind baggage to the Murchison Pass, and then climb over the tender into the cab, stick up the fireman and the engineer, and make them bring the engine to a halt at the mouth of the pass, with Gidding Creek and safety for all that train only five minutes away. There was a touch of the Satanic in this that pleased Andrew and made Allister show his teeth in self-appreciation.

So perfectly had their journey been timed that the train was due in a very few minutes. They disposed their horses in the thicket, and then went back to take up their position in the ambush. The plan of work was carefully divided. To Jeff Rankin, that nicely accurate shot and bulldog fighter, fell what seemed to be a full half of the total risk and labor. He was to go to the blind side of the job. In other words, he was to guard the opposite side of the train to that on which the main body advanced. It was always possible that, when a train was held up, the passengers—at least the unarmed portion, and perhaps even some of the armed men—would break away on the least threatened side. Jeff Rankin on that blind side was to turn them back with a hurricane of bullets from his magazine rifle. Firing from ambush and moving from place to place, he would seem more than one man. Probably three or four shots would turn back the mob. In the meantime, having made the engineer and fireman stop the train, Scottie would be making them continue to flood the firebox. This would delay the start of the engine on its way and gain precious moments for the fugitives. Two of the band were thus employed while Larry la Roche went through the train and turned out the passengers. There was no one like Larry for facing a crowd and cowing it. His spectral form, his eyes burning through the holes in his mask, stripped them of any idea of resistance. And to aid him, there was always the impression that this one robber was only a prelude to the scores surrounding the train on the outside. Even if he were shot down, there would be no hope; it might simply bring on a general massacre.

While the crowd turned out, Andrew, standing opposite the middle of the train, rifle in hand, lined them up, while Allister and Joe Clune attended to overpowering the guards of the safe. While Larry la Roche came out and went through the line of passengers for personal valuables, Clune and Allister fixed the soup to blow the safe. Last of all, there was the explosion, the carrying off of the coin in its canvas sacks to the horses. Each man was to turn his horse in a direction carefully specified, and, riding in a roundabout manner, which was also named, he was to keep on until he came, five days later, to a deserted, ruinous shack far up in the mountains on the side of the Twin Eagles peaks.

These were the instructions that Allister went over carefully with each member of his crew before they went to their posts. There had been twenty rehearsals before, and each man was letter perfect. They took their posts, and Allister came to the side of Andrew among the trees.

"How are you?" he asked.

"Scared to death," said Andrew truthfully. "I'd give a thousand dollars, if I had it to be free of this job." Andrew saw that hard glint come in the eyes of the leader.

"You'll do . . . later." Allister nodded. "But keep back from the crowd. Don't let them see you get nervous when they turn out of the coaches. If you show a sign of wavering, they might start something. Of course, if they did, I know that you'd come through in great style in the fight, but the thing to do with a crowd is to keep 'em from ever starting a fight. Once they make a surge, shooting won't stop 'em."

Andrew nodded. There was more practical advice on the heels of this. Then they stood quietly and waited.

For days and days a northeaster had been blowing; it had whipped little drifts of rain and mist that stung the face and sent a chill to the bone, and, although there had been no actual downpour, the cold and the wet had never broken since the journey started. Now the wind came like a wolf down the Murchison Pass, howling and moaning. Andrew, closing his eyes, felt that the whole thing was dream-like. Presently he would open his eyes and find himself back beside the fire in the house of Uncle Jasper, with the old man prodding his shoulder and telling him that it was bedtime. When he opened his eyes, in fact, they fell upon a solitary pine high up on the opposite slope, above the thicket where Jeff Rankin was hiding. It was a sickly tree, half naked of branches, and it shivered like a wretched animal in the wind. Then a new sound came down the pass, wolf-like, indeed. It was repeated more clearly—the whistle of a train.

It was the signal arranged among them for putting on the masks, and Andrew hastily adjusted his.

"Did you hear that?" asked Allister as the train hooted in the distance again.

Andrew turned and started at the ghostly thing that had been the face of the outlaw a moment before; he himself must look like that, he knew. "What?" he asked.

"That voice-like whistle," said Allister. "There's no luck in this day . . . for me."

"You've listened to Larry la Roche too much," said Andrew. "He's been growling ever since we started on this trail."

"No, no," returned Allister. "It's another thing, an older thing than Larry la Roche. My mother. . . ." He stopped.

Whatever it was that he was about to say, Andrew was never to hear it. The train had turned the long bend above, and now the roar of its wheels filled the cañon and covered the sound of the wind.

It looked vast as a mountain as it came rocking perceptibly on the uneven roadbed. It rounded the curve, the tail of the train flicked around, and it shot at full speed straight for the mouth of the pass. How could one man stop it? How could five men attack it after it was stopped? It was like trying to storm a medieval fortress with a popgun.

The great black front of the engine came rocking toward them, gathering impetus on the sharp grade. Had Scottie missed his trick? But when the thunder of the iron on iron was deafening Andrew and the engine seemed almost upon them, there was a cloud of white vapor that burst out on either side of it and a great whistling and breathing sound, as of an animal giving up life in an agony. The brakes were jumped on; the wheels skidded, screaming on the tracks. The engine lurched past; Andrew caught a glimpse of Scottie, a crouched, masked form

in the cab of the engine, with a gun in either hand. For Scottie
was one of the few natural two-gun men that Andrew was ever
to know. The engineer and the fireman he saw only as two
shadows before they were whisked out of his view. The train
rumbled on, and then it went from half speed to a stop with
one jerk that brought a cry from the coaches. During the next
second there was the successive crashing of couplings as the
coaches took up their slack.

Andrew, stepping out with his rifle balanced in his hands,
saw Larry la Roche whip into the rear car. Then he himself
swept the windows of the train, blurred by the mist, with the
muzzle of his gun, keeping the butt close to his shoulder, ready
for a swift snap shot in any direction. In fact, his was that very
important post, the reserve force, that was to come instantly to
the aid of any overpowered section of the active workers. He
had rebelled against this minor task, but Allister had assured
him that, in former times, it was the place that he took himself
to meet crises in the attack.

The leader had gone with Joe Clune straight for the front car.
How would they storm it? Two guards, armed to the teeth,
would be in it, and the door was closed.

But the guards had no intention to remain like rats in a trap,
while the rest of the train was overpowered and they themselves
were blasted into small bits with a small charge of soup. The
door jerked open, the barrels of two guns protruded. Andrew,
thrilling with horror, recognized one as a sawed-off shotgun. He
saw now the meaning of the manner in which Allister and Clune
made their attack. For Allister had run slowly straight for the
door, while Clune skirted in close to the cars, going more swiftly.
As the gun barrels went up, Allister plunged headlong to the
ground, and the volley of shot missed him cleanly, but Clune
the next moment leaped out from the side of the car, and,
thereby getting himself to an angle from which he could deliver

a crossfire, pumped two bullets through the door. Andrew saw a figure throw up its arms, a shadow form in the interior of the car, and then a man pitched out headlong through the doorway and flopped with horrible limpness on the roadbed. While this went on, Allister had snapped a shot, while he still lay prone, and his single bullet brought a scream. The guards were done for.

Two deaths, Andrew supposed. But presently a man was sent out of the car at the point of Clune's revolver. He climbed down with difficulty, clutching one hand with the other. He had been shot in the most painful place in the body—the palm of the hand. Allister turned over the other form with a brutal carelessness that sickened Andrew. But the man had been only stunned by a bullet that plowed its way across the top of his skull. He sat up now with a trickle running down his face. A gesture from Andrew's rifle made him and his companion realize that they were covered, and, without attempting any further resistance, they sat side-by-side on the ground and tended to each other's wounds—a ludicrous group for all their suffering.

In the meantime, Clune and Allister were at work in the car; the water was hissing in the firebox as a vast cloud of steam came rushing out around the engine; the passengers were pouring out of the cars. They acted like a group of actors, carefully rehearsed for the piece. Not once did Andrew have to speak to them, while they ranged in a solid line, shoulder to shoulder, men, women, children. And then Larry la Roche went down the line with a saddlebag and took up the collection.

"Passin' the hat so often has give me a religious touch, ladies and gents," Andrew heard the ruffian say. "Any little contributions I'm sure grateful for, and, if anything's held back, I'm apt to frisk the gent that don't fork over. Hey, you, what's that lump inside your coat? Lady, don't lie. I seen you drop it inside your dress. Why, it's a nice little set o' sparklers. That ain't nothin' to be ashamed of. Come on, please . . . a little more speed. Easy there, partner . . . don't take both them hands down at once. You can peel the stuff out of your pockets with one hand, I figure. Conductor, just lemme see your wallet. Thanks. Hate to bother you, ma'am, but you sure ain't traveling on this train with only eighty-five cents in your pocketbook. Just lemme have a look at the rest. See if you can't find it in your stocking. No, they ain't anything here to make you blush. You're among friends, lady . . . a plumb friendly crowd. Your poor old pa give you this to go to school on, did he? Son, you're gettin' a pile more education out of this than you would in college. No, honey, you just keep your locket. It ain't worth five dollars. Did you? That jeweler ought to have my job, 'cause he sure robbed you. You call that watch an heirloom? Heirloom is my middle name, miss. Just get them danglers outen your ears, lady. Thanks. Don't hurry, mister . . . you'll bust the chain."

His monologue was endless; he had a comment for every person in the line, and he seemed to have a seventh sense for concealed articles. The saddlebag was bulging before he was through. At the same time Allister and Clune jumped from the car and ran. Larry la Roche gave the warning. Everyone crouched or lay down. The soup exploded. The top of the car lifted. It made Andrew think, foolishly enough, of someone tipping a hat. It fell slowly, with a crash that was like a faint echo of the explosion. Clune ran back, and they could hear his shrill yell of delight. "It ain't a safe!" he exclaimed. "It's a baby mint!"

And a baby mint it was. It was a gold shipment. Gold coin runs about ninety pounds to $10,000, and there was close to a hundred pounds apiece for each of the bandits. It was the largest haul Allister's gang had ever made. Larry la Roche left the pilfering of the passengers and went to help carry the loot. They brought it out in little, loose canvas bags and went on the run with it to the horses.

Someone was speaking. It was the gray-headed man with the glasses and the kindly look about the eyes: "Boys, it's the worst little game you've ever worked. I promise you we'll keep on your trail until we've run you all into the ground. That's really something to remember. I speak for Gregg and Sons."

"Partner," said Scottie Macdougal from the cab, where he still kept the engineer and fireman covered, "a little hunt is like an after-dinner drink to me."

To the utter amazement of Andrew the whole crowd—the crowd that had just been carefully and systematically robbed—burst into laughter. But this was the end. There was Allister's whistle; Jeff Rankin ran around from the other side of the train; the gang faded instantly into the thicket. Andrew, as the rear guard—his most ticklish moment—backed slowly toward the trees. Once there was a waver in the line, such as precedes a rush. He stopped short, and a single twitch of his rifle froze the waverers in their tracks.

Once inside the thicket a yell came from the crowd, but Andrew had whirled and was running at full speed. He could hear the others crashing away at full speed. Sally, as he had taught her, broke into a trot as he approached, and the moment he struck the saddle she was in full gallop. Guns were rattling behind him; random shots cut the air sometimes close to him, but not one of the whole crowd dared venture beyond that unknown screen of trees.

Chapter Thirty-Six

To Andrew the last danger of the hold-up had been assigned as the rear guard, and he was the last man to pass Allister.

The leader had drawn his horse to one side a couple of miles down the valley, and, as each of his band passed him, he raised his hand in silent greeting. It was the last Andrew saw of him, a ghostly figure sitting his horse with his hand above his head. After that his mind was busied by his ride, for, having the finest mount in the crowd, to him had been assigned the longest and the most roundabout route to reach the Twin Eagles.

Yet he covered so much ground with Sally that, instead of needing the full five days to make the rendezvous, he could afford to loaf the last stage of the journey. Even at that, he camped in sight of the cabin on the fourth night, and on the morning of the fifth he was the first man at the shack.

Jeff Rankin came in next. To Jeff, on account of his unwieldy bulk, had been assigned the shortest route, yet, even so, he dismounted, staggering and limping from his horse, and collapsed on the pile of boughs that Andrew had spent the morning cutting for a bed. As he dropped, he tossed his bag of coins to the floor. It fell with a melodious jingling that was immediately drowned by Jeff's groans; the saddle was torture to him, and now he was aching in every joint of his enormous body.

"A nice haul . . . nothin' to kick about," was Jeff's opinion. "But Cæsar's ghost . . . what a ride. The chief makes this thing too hard on a gent that likes to go easy, Andy."

Andrew said nothing; silence had been his cue ever since he began acting as lieutenant to the chief. It had seemed to baffle the others; it baffled the big man now. Later on Joe Clune and Scottie came in together. That was about noon—they had met each other an hour before. But Allister had not come in, although he was usually the first at a rendezvous. Neither did Larry la Roche come. The day wore on; the silence grew on the group. When Andrew, proportioning the work for supper, sent Joe to get wood, Jeff for water, and began himself to work with Scottie on the cooking, he was met with ugly looks and hesitation before they obeyed. Something, he felt most decidedly, was in the air. And when Joe and Rankin came back slowly, walking side-by-side and talking in soft voices, his suspicions were given an edge.

They wanted to eat together, but he forced Scottie to take post on the high hill to their right to keep look-out, and for this he received another scowl. Then, when supper was half over, Larry la Roche came into camp. News came with him, an atmosphere of tidings around his gloomy figure, but he cast himself down by the fire and ate and drank in silence, until his hunger was gone. Then he tossed his tin dishes away.

"Pick 'em up," said Andrew quietly. "We'll have no litter around this camp." Larry la Roche stared at him in hushed malevolence. "Stand up and get 'em," repeated Andrew. As he saw the big hands of Larry twitching, he smiled across the fire at the tall, bony figure. "I'll give you two seconds to get 'em," he said.

One deadly second pulsed away, then Larry crumpled. He caught up his tin cup and the plate. "We'll talk later about you," he said ominously.

"We'll talk about something else first," said Andrew. "You've seen Allister?"

At first it seemed that la Roche would not speak, then his wide, thin lips writhed back from his teeth. "Yes."

"Where is he?"

"Gone to the happy hunting grounds."

The silence came, and the pulse in it. One by one, by a natural instinct, the men looked about them sharply into the night and made sure of their weapons. It was the only tribute to the memory of Allister from his men, but tears and praise could not have been more eloquent. He had made these men fearless of the whole world. Now were they ready to jump at the passage of a shadow. They looked at each other with strange eyes.

"Who? How many?" asked Jeff Rankin.

"One man done it."

Jeff Rankin's mouth had fallen ajar. He brushed his fist across his loosely trembling lips.

"Hal Dozier?" said Andrew.

"Him," said Larry la Roche. He went on, looking gloomily down at the fire. "He got me first. The chief must've seen him get me by surprise, while I was down off my hoss, lying flat and drinking out of a creek." He closed his great, bony fist in unspeakable agony at the thought. "Dozier come behind and took me. Frisked me. Took my guns . . . not the coin. We went down through the hills. Then the chief slid out of a shadow and come at us like a tiger. I sloped."

"You left Allister to fight alone?" said Scottie Macdougal quietly, for he had come from his look-out to listen.

"I had no gun," said Larry, without raising his eyes from the fire. "I sloped. I looked back and seen Allister sitting on his hoss, dead still. Hal Dozier was sittin' on his hoss, dead still. Five seconds, maybe. Then they went for their guns together. They was two bangs like one. But Allister slid out of his saddle and Dozier stayed in his. I come on here."

The quiet covered them. Joe Clune, with a shudder and

another glance over his shoulder, cast a branch on the fire, and the flames leaped.

"Dozier knows you're with us," added Larry la Roche, and he cast a long glance of hatred at Andrew. "He knows you're with us, and he knows our luck left us when you come."

Andrew looked about the circle, and not an eye met his. The talk of Larry la Roche during the days of the ride was showing its effect now. After all, they were only superstitious children, with the destructive power of giants. But the gauge had been thrown down to Andrew, and he dared not pick it up.

"Boys," he said, "I'll say this. Are we going to bust up and each man go his way?"

There was no answer.

"If we do, we can split the profits over again. I'll take no money out of a thing that cost Allister's death. There's my sack on the floor of the shack. Divvy it up among you. You fitted me out when I was broke. That'll pay you back. Do we split up?"

"They's no reason why we should . . . and be run down like rabbits," said Joe Clune, with another of those terrible glances over his shoulder into the night.

The others assented with so many growls.

"All right," said Andrew, "we stick together. And, if we stick together, I run this camp."

"You?" asked Larry la Roche. "Who picked you? Who 'lected you, son? Why, you unlucky. . . ."

"Ease up," said Andrew softly.

The eyes of la Roche flicked across the circle and picked up the glances of the others, but they were not yet ready to tackle Andrew Lanning. The hand that had been sliding back along the ground ceased its retrograde motion, and he watched Andrew like a cat.

"The last thing Allister did," said Andrew, "was to make me his lieutenant. It's the last thing he did, and I'm going to push it through. Not because I like the job." He raised his head, but not his voice. "They may run down the rest of you. They won't run down me. They can't. They've tried, and they can't. And I might be able to keep the rest of you clear. I'm going to try. But I won't follow the lead of any of you. If there'd been one that could keep the rest of you together, d'you think Allister wouldn't have seen it? Don't you think he would've made that one leader? Why, look at you. Jeff, you'd follow Clune. But would Larry or Scottie follow Clune? Look at 'em and see."

All eyes went to Clune, and then the glances of Scottie and la Roche dropped.

"Nobody here would follow la Roche. He's the best man we've got for some of the hardest work, but you're too flighty with your temper, Larry, and you know it. We respect you just as much, but not to plan things for the rest of us. Is that straight?"

They could not face this direct talk. Each of them was beginning to understand that the kid had looked through his eyes and into his heart.

"And you, Scottie," said Andrew, "you're the only one I'd follow. I say that freely. But who else would follow you? You're the best of us all at head work and planning, but you don't swing your gun as fast, and you don't shoot as straight as Jeff or Larry or Joe. Is that straight?"

"What's leading the gang got to do with fighting?" asked Scottie harshly. "And who's got the right to the head of things but me?"

"Ask Allister what fighting had to do with the running of things," said Andrew calmly.

The moon was sliding up out of the east; it changed the faces of the men and made them oddly animal-like; they stared, fascinated, at Andrew.

"There's two reasons why I'm going to run this job, if we

stick together. Allister named them once. I can take advice from any one of you . . . I know what each of you can do . . . I can plan a job for you . . . I can lead you clear of the law . . . and there's not one of you that can bully me or make me give an inch . . . no, nor all of you together . . . la Roche, Macdougal, Clune, Rankin."

It was like a roll call, and at each name a head was jerked up in answer, and two glittering eyes flashed at Andrew—flashed, sparkled, and then became dull. The moonlight had made his pale skin a deadly white, and it was a demoniac face they saw.

The silence was his answer.

"Jeff," he commanded, "take the hill. You'll stand the watch tonight. And look sharp. If Dozier got Allister, he's apt to come at us. Step on it."

And Jeff Rankin rose without a word and lumbered to the top of the hill. Larry la Roche suddenly filled his cup with boiling hot coffee, regardless of the heat, regardless of the dirt in the cup. His hand shook when he raised it to his lips.

Chapter Thirty-Seven

There was no further attempt at challenging his authority. When he ordered Clune and la Roche to bring in boughs for bedding—since they were to stop in the shack overnight—they went silently. But it was such a silence as comes when the wind falls at the end of a day and in a silent sky the clouds pile heavily, higher and higher. Andrew took the opportunity to speak to Scottie Macdougal. He told Scottie simply that he needed him, that with him at his back, he could handle the others, and more, too. He was surprised to see a twinkle in the eye of the Scotsman.

"Why, Andy," said the canny fellow, "didn't you see me pass you the wink? I was with you all the time."

Andrew thanked him and went into the cabin to arrange for lights. He had no intention of shirking a share in the actual work of the camp, even though Allister had set that example for his following. He took some lengths of pitchy pine sticks and arranged them for torches. One of them alone would send a flare of yellow light through the cabin; two made a comfortable illumination. But he worked cheerlessly. The excitement of the robbery and the chase was over, and then the conflict with the men was passing. He began to see things truly by the drab light of retrospection. The bullets of Allister and Clune might have gone home—they were intended to kill, not to wound. And if there had been two deaths he, Andrew Lanning, would have been equally guilty with the men who handled the guns, for he had been one of the forces that made that shooting possible.

It was an ugly way to look at it—very ugly. It kept a frown on Andrew's face while he arranged the torches in the main room of the shack, and then put one for future reference in the little shed that leaned against the rear of the main structure. He had piled the boughs for four bunks in the first room; he arranged his own bed in this second room, where the saddles and other accouterments were piled. It was easily explainable, since there was hardly room for five men in the first room. But he had another purpose. He wanted to separate himself from the others, just as Allister always did. Even in a crowded room Allister would seem aloof, and Andrew determined to make the famous leader his guide.

Above all, he was troubled by what Scottie had said. He would have felt easy at heart if the Scotsman had met him with an argument or with a frown or honest opposition or with a hearty handshake, to say that all was well between them. But this cunning lie—this cunning protestation that he had been with the new leader from the first, put Andrew on his guard, for he knew perfectly well that Scottie had not been on his side during the crisis with la Roche.

Macdougal sat before the door, his metal flask of whiskey beside him. It was a fault of Allister, this permitting of whiskey at all times and in all places, after a job was finished. And while it made the other men savage beasts, it turned Scottie Macdougal into a wily, smiling snake. He had bit the heel of more than one man in his drinking bouts.

Presently la Roche and Clune came in. They had been talking together again. Andrew could tell by the manner in which they separated as soon as they entered the room, and by their voices that they made loud and cheerful, and, also, by the fact that they avoided looking at each other. They were striving patently to prove that there was nothing between them, and if

Andrew had been on guard, now he became tinglingly so.

They arranged their bunks. Larry la Roche pulled off his boots and put on great, flapping slippers, which he always included in his pack. He took from his vest a pipe with a small bowl and a long stem and sat down cross-legged to smoke. Andrew suggested that Larry produce the contents of his saddlebag and share the spoils of war.

He brought it out willingly enough and spilled it out on the improvised table, a glittering mass of gold trinkets, watches, jewels. He picked out of the mass a chain of diamonds and spread it out on his snaky fingers so that the light could play on it. Andrew knew nothing about gems, but he knew that the chain must be worth a great deal of money.

"This," said Larry, "is my share. You gents can have the rest and split it up."

"A nice set of sparklers," Clune said, nodding, "but there's plenty left to satisfy me."

"What you think," declared Scottie, "ain't of any importance, Joe. It's what the chief thinks that counts. Is it square, Lanning?"

Andrew flushed at the appeal and the ugly looks that la Roche and Clune cast toward him. He could have stifled Scottie for that appeal, and yet Scottie was smiling in the greatest apparent good nature and belief in their leader. His face was flushed, but his lips were bloodless. Alcohol always affected him in that manner.

"I don't know the value of the stones," said Andrew.

"Don't you?" murmured Scottie. "I forgot. Thought maybe you would. That was something that Allister did know."

The new leader saw a flash of glances toward Scottie, but the latter continued to eye the captain with a steady and innocent look.

Scottie, decided Andrew instantly, *is my chief enemy.*

If he could detach one man to his side all would be well. Two against three would be a simple thing, as long as he was one of the two. But four against one—and such a four as these—were hopeless odds. There seemed little chance of getting Joe Clune. There remained only Jeff Rankin as his possible ally, and already he had stepped on Jeff's toes sorely, by making the tired giant stand guard. He thought of all these things, of course, in a flash. And then in answer to his thoughts Jeff Rankin appeared. His heavy footfall crashed inside the door. He stopped, panting, and, in spite of his news, paused to blink at the flash of jewels.

"It's comin'," said Jeff. "Larry, hop into your shoes. No, don't stop for that. Boys, get your guns and scatter out of the cabin. Douse that light. Hal Dozier is comin' up the valley."

There was not a single exclamation, but the lights went out as if by magic; there were a couple of light, hissing sounds, such as iron makes when it is whipped swiftly across leather.

"How'd you know him by this light?" asked Larry la Roche as they went out of the door.

Outside, they found everything brilliant with the white moonshine of the mountains.

"Nobody but Hal Dozier rides twistin' that way in the saddle. I'd tell him in a thousand. It's old wounds that makes him ride like that. We got ten minutes. He's takin' the long way up the cañon. And they ain't anybody with him."

"If he's come alone," said Andrew, "he's come for me and not for the rest of you."

No one spoke, until Larry la Roche said: "He wants to make it man to man. That's clear. That's why he pulled up his hoss and waited for Allister to make the first move for his gun. It's a clean challenge to some one of us."

Andrew saw his chance and used it mercilessly. "Which one of you is willing to take the challenge?" he asked. "Which one of you is willing to ride down the cañon and meet him alone? la

Roche, I've heard you curse Dozier."

But Larry la Roche answered: "What's this fool talk about takin' a challenge? I say, string out behind the hills and pot him with rifles."

"One man, and we're five," said Jeff Rankin. "It ain't sportin', Larry. I hate to hear you say that. We'd be despised all over the mountains if we done it. He's makin' his play with a lone hand, and we've got to meet him the same way. Eh, chief?"

It was sweet to Andrew to hear that appeal. And he saw them turn, one by one, toward him in the moonlight and wait. It was his first great tribute. He looked over those four wolfish figures and felt his heart swelling.

"Wish me luck, boys," he said, and without another word he turned and went down the hillside.

The others watched him with amazement. He felt it rather than saw it, and it kept a tingle in his blood. He felt, also, that they were spreading out to either side to get a clear view of the fight that was to follow, and it occurred to him that, even if Hal Dozier killed him, there would not be one chance in a thousand of Hal's getting away. Four deadly rifles would be covering him.

It must be that a sort of madness had come on Dozier, advancing in this manner, unsupported by a posse. Or, perhaps, he had no idea that the outlaws could be so close. He expected a daylight encounter high up the mountains.

But Andrew went swiftly down the ravine.

Broken cliffs, granite boulders jumped up on either side of him, and the rocks were pale and glimmering under the moon. This one valley seemed to receive the light; the loftier mountains rolling away on each side were black as jet, with sharp, ragged outlines against the sky. It was a cold light, and the chill of it went through Andrew. He was afraid, afraid as he had been when Buck Heath had faced him in Martindale, or when Bill Dozier had run him down, or when the famous Sandy had cornered him. His fingers felt brittle, and his breath came and went in short gasps, drawn into the upper part of his lungs only.

Behind him, like an electric force pushing him on, the outlaws watched his steps. They, also, were shuddering with fear, and he knew it. But stronger than the force behind was the desperate thrill, the old urge to cast himself away like a man on a cliff. A sort of terrible happiness was in Andrew, but a weakness in his legs made him walk slowly and more slowly. His knees were numb. A puma was crying among the mountains. He really did not hear the sound or recognize it; he only knew that something came to his ear like the moonlight on his eye, something that thrust a chill home to his heart.

Dozier was coming, fresh from another kill.

"Only one man I'd think twice about meeting," Allister had said in the old days, and he had been right. Yet there were thousands who had sworn that Allister was invincible—that he would never fall before a single man.

He thought, too, of the lean face and the peculiar, set eye of Dozier. The man had no fear, he had no nerves; he was a machine, and death was his business.

And was he, Andrew Lanning, unknown until the past few months, now going down to face destruction, as full of fear as a girl trembling at the dark? What was it that drew them together, so unfairly matched? A ghostly thought came to him that all this had been planned and arranged by some unearthly power, and now, against his will, he was dragged into the path of the destroyer.

He could still see only the white haze of the moonshine before him, but now there was the clicking of hoofs on the rock. Dozier was coming. Andrew walked squarely out into the middle of the ravine and waited. He had set his teeth. The nerves on the bottom of his feet were twitching. Something freezing cold was beginning at the tips of his fingers. And, unless he fought those beginnings down, a great trembling would sweep over him in a moment, and he would be helpless. How long would it take Dozier to come?

An interminable time. The hoof beats actually seemed to fade out and draw away at one time. Then they began again very near him, now they stopped. Had Dozier seen him around the elbow curve? That heartbreaking instant passed, and the clicking began again. Then the rider came slowly in view. First there was the nodding head of the cow pony, then the foot in the stirrup, then Hal Dozier riding a little twisted in the saddle—a famous characteristic of his. He came on closer and closer. He began to seem huge on the horse. Was he blind not to see the figure that waited for him?

A voice that was not his, that he did not recognize, leaped out from between Andrew's teeth and tore his throat: "Dozier!"

The cow pony halted with a start; the rider jerked straight in his saddle; the echo of the call barked back from some angling cliff face down the ravine. All that before Dozier made his move. He had dropped the reins, and Andrew, with a mad intention of proving that he himself did not make the first move toward his weapon, had folded his arms.

He did not move through the freezing instant that followed. Not until there was a convulsive jerk of Dozier's elbow did he stir his folded arms. Then his right arm loosened, and the hand flashed down to his holster.

Was Dozier moving with clogged slowness, or was it that he had ceased to be a body, that he was all brain and hair-trigger nerves making every thousandth part of a second seem a unit of time? It seemed to Andrew that the marshal's hand dragged through its work; to those who watched from the sides of the ravine, there was a flash of fire from his gun before they saw even the flash of the steel out of the holster. The gun spat in the hand of Dozier, and something jerked at the shirt of Andrew beside his neck. He himself had fired only once, and he knew that the shot had been too high and to the right of his central target, yet he did not fire again. Something strange was happening to Hal Dozier. His head had nodded forward as though in mockery of the bullet; his extended right hand fell slowly, slowly; his whole body began to sway and lean toward the right. Not until that moment did Andrew know that he had shot the marshal through the body.

He raced to the side of the cattle pony, and, as the horse veered away, Hal Dozier dropped limply into his arms. He lay with his arms sprawling at odd angles beside him. His muscles seemed paralyzed, but his eyes were bright and wide, and his face perfectly composed.

"There's luck for you," said Hal Dozier calmly. "I pulled it two inches to the right, or I would have broken your neck with the slug . . . anyway, I spoiled your shirt."

The cold was gone from Andrew, and he felt his heart thundering and shaking his body. He was repeating like a frightened child: "For God's sake, Hal, don't die . . . don't die."

The paralyzed body did not move, but the calm voice answered him: "You fool. Finish me before your gang comes and does it for you."

CHAPTER THIRTY-EIGHT

There was a rush of footsteps behind and around him, a jangle of voices, and there were the four huddled over Hal Dozier. Andrew had risen and stepped back, silently thanking God that it was not a death. He heard the voices of the four like voices in a dream.

"A clean one." "A nice bit of work." "Dozier, are you thinkin' of Allister, curse you?" "D'you remember Hugh Wiley now?" "D'you maybe recollect my pal, Bud Swain? Think about 'em, Dozier, while you're dyin'."

The calm eyes traveled without hurry from face to face. And curiosity came to Andrew, a cool, deadly curiosity. He stepped among the gang.

"He's not fatally hurt," he said. "What d'you intend to do with him?"

"You're all wrong, chief," said Larry la Roche, and he grinned at Andrew. His submission now was perfect and complete. There was even a sort of worship in the bright eyes that looked at the new leader. "I hate to say it, but right as you most gener'ly are, you're wrong this time. He's done. He don't need no more lookin' to. Leave him be for an hour and he'll be finished. Also, that'll give him a chance to think. He needs a chance. Old Curley had a chance to think . . . took him four hours to kick out after Dozier plugged him. I heard what he had to say, and it wasn't pretty. I think maybe it'd be sort of interestin' to hear what Dozier has to say. Long about the time he gets thirsty. Eh, boys?"

There was a snarl from the other three as they looked down at the wounded man, who did not speak a word. And Andrew knew that he was indeed alone with that crew, for the man whom he had just shot down was nearer to him than the members of Allister's gang.

He spoke suddenly: "Jeff, take his head . . . Clune, take his feet. Carry him up to the cabin."

They only stared at him.

"Look here, captain," said Scottie in a soft voice, just a trifle thickened by whiskey, "are you thinking of taking him up there and tying him up so that he'll live through this?"

And again the other three snarled softly.

"You murdering hounds," said Andrew.

That was all. They looked at each other; they looked at the new leader. And the sight of his white face and his nervous right hand was too much for them. They took up the marshal and carried him to the cabin, his pony following like a dog behind. They brought him, without asking for directions, straight into the little rear room—Andrew's room. It was a sufficiently intelligible way of saying that this was his work and none of theirs. And not a hand lifted to aid him while he went to work with the bandaging. He knew little about such work, but the marshal himself, in a rather faint, but perfectly steady voice, gave directions. And in the painful cleaning of the wound he did not murmur once. Neither did he express the slightest gratitude. He kept following Andrew about the room with coldly curious eyes.

In the next room the voices of the four were a steady, rumbling murmur. Now and then the glance of the marshal wandered to the door. When the bandaging was completed, he asked: "Do you know you've started a job you can't finish?"

"Ah?" murmured Andrew.

"Those four," said the marshal, "won't let you."

Andrew smiled. "Are you easier now?"

"Don't bother about me. I'll tell you what . . . I wish you'd get me a drink of water."

"I'll send one of the boys."

"No, get it yourself. I want to say something to them while you're gone."

Andrew had gotten up from his knees. He now studied the face of the marshal steadily.

"You want 'em to come in here and drill you, eh?" he said. "Why?"

The other nodded. "I've given up hope once . . . I've gone through the hardest part of dying . . . let them finish the job now."

"Tomorrow you'll feel differently."

"Will I? Not I."

Andrew stared at him.

"What have I got to live for?" asked the marshal. All at once his eyes went yellow with hate. "I go back to the desert . . . I go to Martindale . . . people I pass on the street whisper as I go by. They'll tell over and over how I went down. And a kid did it . . . a raw kid!" He closed his eyes in silent agony. Then he looked up more keenly than before. "How'll they know that it was luck . . . that my gun stuck in the holster . . . and that you jumped me on the draw?"

"You lie," said Andrew calmly. "Your gun came out clean as a whistle, and I waited for you, Dozier. You know I did."

The pain in the marshal's face became a ghastly thing to see. At last he could speak. "A sneak always lies well," he replied as he sneered at Lanning. He went on, while Andrew sat shivering with passion. "And any fool can get in a lucky shot now and then. But, when I'm out of this, I'll hunt you down again and

I'll plant you full of lead, my son. You can lay to that."

The hard breathing of Andrew gradually subsided. "It won't work, Dozier," he said quietly. "You can't make me mad enough to shoot a man who's down. You can't make me murder you."

The marshal closed his eyes again, while his breathing was beginning to grow fainter, and there was an unpleasant rattle in the hollow of his throat.

Andrew went into the next room. "Scottie," he said, "will you let me have your flask?"

Scottie smiled at him. "Not for what you'd use it for, Lanning," he said.

Andrew picked up a cup and shoved it across the table. "Pour a little whiskey in that, please," he said.

Scottie looked up and studied him. Then he tipped his flask and poured a thin stream into the cup until it was half full.

Andrew went back toward the door, the cup in his left hand. He backed up, keeping his face steadily toward the four, and kicked open the door behind him. War, he knew, had been declared. In the room he raised the marshal's head and gave him a sip of the fiery stuff. It cleared the face of the wounded man.

Then Andrew rolled down his blankets before the door, braced a small stick against it, so that the sound would be sure to waken him if any one tried to enter, and laid down for the night. He was almost asleep when the marshal said: "Are you really going to stick it out, Andy?"

"Yes."

"In spite of what I've said?"

"I suppose you meant it all? You'd hunt me down and kill me like a dog after you get back on your feet?"

"Like a dog."

"If you think it over and see things clearly," replied Andrew, "you'll see that what I've done, I've done for my own sake, and not for yours."

"How do you make that out . . . with four men in the next room ready to stick a knife in your back . . . if I know anything about 'em?"

"I'll tell you . . . I owe nothing to you, but a man owes a lot to himself, and I'm going to pay myself in full."

CHAPTER THIRTY-NINE

He closed his eyes and tried to sleep, but, although he came to the verge of oblivion, the voices from the other room finally waked him. They had been changing subtly during the past hours and now they rose and there was a ring to them that troubled Andrew.

He could make out their talk part of the time, and then again they lowered their voices to rumbling growls. At such times he knew that they were speaking of him, and the hum of the undertone was more ominous than open threats. When they talked aloud, there was a confused clamor; when they were more hushed, there was always the oily murmur of Scottie's voice, taking the lead and directing the current of the talk. More and more he felt that this man would be his stumbling block. One and all they hated the marshal and had no great love for their new leader, but the rest of them were rather dangerous mechanics in the world of crime. Scottie Macdougal was a thinking brain.

The liquor was going the rounds fast, now. Before they left for the Murchison Pass they had laid in a comfortable supply, but apparently Allister had cached a quantity of the stuff at the Twin Eagles shack. Of one thing Andrew was certain, that four such practiced whiskey drinkers would never let their party degenerate into a drunken rout, and another thing was even more sure—that Scottie Macdougal would keep his head better than the best of the others. But what the alcohol would do would be to cut the leash of constraint and dig up every strong passion among them. For instance, Jeff Rankin was by far the most equable of the lot, but, given a little whiskey, Jeff became a conscienceless devil.

He knew his own weakness, and Andrew, crawling to the door and putting his ear to the crack under it, found that the sounds of the voices became instantly clearer; the others were plying Jeff with the liquor, and Jeff, knowing that he had had enough, was persistently refusing, but with less and less energy.

There must be a very definite reason for this urging of Rankin toward the whiskey, and Andrew was not hard pressed to find out that reason. The big, rather good-natured giant was leaning toward the side of the new leader, just as steadily as the others were leaning away from him. Whiskey alone would stop his scruples. Larry la Roche, his voice a guarded, hissing whisper, was speaking to Jeff as Andrew began listening from his new position.

"What I ask you," said la Roche, "is this . . . have we had any luck since the kid joined us?"

"We've got a pile of the coin," said Jeff obstinately.

"D'you stack a little coin against the loss of Allister?" asked Larry la Roche.

"Easy," cautioned Scottie. "Not so loud, Larry."

"He's asleep," said Larry la Roche. "I heard him lie down after he'd put something ag'in' the door. No fear of him."

"Don't be so sure. He might make a noise lying down and make not a sound getting up. And, even when he's asleep, he's got one eye open like a wolf."

"Well," repeated Larry insistently, and now his voice was so faint that Andrew had to guess at half the syllables, "answer my question, Jeff . . . have we had good luck or bad luck, takin' it all in all, since he joined us?"

"How do I know it's his fault?" asked Jeff. "We all knew it

would be a close pinch if Allister ever jumped Hal Dozier. We thought Allister was a little bit faster than Dozier. Everybody else said that Dozier was the best man that ever pulled a gun out of leather. It wasn't luck that beat Allister . . . it was a better man."

There was a thud as his fist hit the rickety, squeaking table in the center of the room.

"I say, let's play fair and square. How do I know that the kid won't make a good leader?"

Scottie broke in smoothly. "Makes me grin when you say that, Jeff. Tell you what the trouble is with you, old man . . . you're too modest. A fellow that's done what you've done, following a kid that ain't twenty-five."

There was a bear-like grunt from Jeff. He was not altogether displeased by this gracious tribute. But he answered: "You're too slippery with your tongue, Scottie. I never know when you mean what you say."

It must have been a bitter pill for Scottie to swallow, but he was not particularly formidable with his weapons, compared with straight-eyed Jeff Rankin, and he answered: "Maybe there's some I jolly along a bit, but, when I talk to old Jeff Rankin, I talk straight. Look at me now, Jeff. Do I look as if I was joking with you?"

"I ain't any hand at readin' minds," grumbled Jeff. He added suddenly: "I say it was the finest thing I ever see, the way young Lanning stood out there in the valley. Did you watch? Did you see him let Allister get the jump on his gun? Pretty, pretty, pretty. And then his own gat was out like a flash . . . one wink, and there was Hal Dozier drilled clean. I tell you, boys, you got this young Lanning wrong. I sort of cotton to the kid. I always did. I liked him the first time I ever laid eyes on him. So did you all, except Larry, yonder. And it was Larry that turned you ag'in' him after he come and joined us. Who asked him to join us? We did."

"Who asked him to be captain?" said Scottie.

It seemed to stagger Jeff Rankin. "Allister used him for a sort of second man . . . seemed like he meant him to lead us in case anything happened to him."

"While Allister was living," said Scottie, "you know I would've followed him anywhere. Wasn't I his advance agent? Didn't I do his planning with him? But now Allister's dead . . . worse luck . . . but dead he is."

He paused here, cunningly, and no doubt during that pause each of the outlaws conjured up a picture of the scar-faced man with the bright, steady eyes, who had led them so long and quelled them so often and held them together through thick and thin.

"Allister's dead," repeated Scottie, "and what he did while he was alive don't hold us now. We chose him for captain out of our own free will. Now that he's dead we have the right to elect another captain. What's Lanning done that he has a right to fill Allister's place with us? What job did he have at the hold-up? When we stuck up the train didn't he have the easiest job? Did he give one good piece of advice while we were plannin' the job? Did he show any ability to lead us, then?"

The answer came unhesitatingly from Rankin: "It wasn't his place to lead while Allister was with us. And I'll tell you what he done after Allister died. When I seen Dozier comin', who was it that stepped out to meet him? Was it you, Scottie? No, it wasn't. It wasn't you, la Roche, neither, nor you, Clune, and it wasn't me. Made me sick inside, the thought of facin' Dozier. Why? Because I knew he'd never been beat. Because I knew he was a better man than Allister, and that Allister had been a better man than me. And it ain't no braggin' to say I'm a handier gent with my guns than any of you. Well, I was sick, and you all were sick. I seen your faces. But who steps out and takes the lead? It was the kid you grin at, Scottie . . . and I say it was a fine thing to do."

It was undoubtedly a facer, but Scottie came back in his usual calm manner.

"I know it was Lanning, and it was a fine thing. I don't deny, either, that he's a fine gent in lots of ways . . . and in his place . . . but is his place at the head of the gang? Are we going to be bullied into having him there?"

"Then let him follow, and somebody else lead."

"You make me laugh, Jeff. He's not the sort that will follow anybody."

Plainly Scottie was working on Jeff from a distance. He would bring him slowly around to the place where he would agree to the attack on Andrew for the sake of getting at the wounded marshal. And the big man did not have the mental endurance to hold out long against his more agile-minded comrade.

"Have another drink, Jeff, and then let's get back to the main point, and that has nothin' to do with Andy. It is . . . is Hal Dozier going to live or die?"

The time had come, Andrew saw, to make his final play. A little more of this talk and the big, good-hearted, strong-handed Rankin would be completely on the side of the others. And that meant the impossible odds of four to one. Andrew knew it. He would attack any two of them without fear. But three became a desperate, a grim battle, and four to one made the thing suicide.

He slipped silently to his feet from beside the door and picked up the canvas bag that represented his share of the robbery. Then he knocked at the door.

"Boys," he called, "there's been some hard thoughts between the lot of you and me! It looks like we're on opposite sides of a fence. I want to come in and talk to you."

Instantly Scottie answered: "Why, come on in, captain . . . not such hard words as you think . . . not on my side, anyways."

It was a cunning enough lure, no doubt, and Andrew had his hand on the latch of the door before a second thought reached him. If he exposed himself, would not the three of them pull their guns? They would be able to account for it to Jeff Rankin later on.

"I'll come in," said Andrew, "when I hear you give me surety that I'll be safe. I don't trust you, Scottie."

"Thanks for that. What surety do you want?"

"I want the word of Jeff Rankin that he'll see me through till I've made my talk to you and my proposition."

It was an excellent counter thrust, but Larry la Roche saw through the attempt to win Jeff immediately.

"You skunk," he said. "If you don't trust us, we don't trust you. Stay where you be. We don't want to hear your talk."

"Jeff, what do you say?" continued Andrew, imperturbable.

There was a clamor of three voices, and then the louder voice of Jeff, like a lion shaking itself clear of wolves: "Andy, come in, and I'll see you get a square deal . . . if you'll trust me."

Instantly Andrew threw open the door and stepped in, his revolver in one hand, the heavy sack over his other arm, a dragging weight and also a protection.

"I'll trust you, Jeff," he said. "Trust you? Why, man, with you at my back I'd laugh at twenty fellows like these. They simply don't count."

It was another well-placed shot, and he saw Rankin flush heavily with pleasure. Scottie tilted his box back against the wall and delivered his counterstroke: "He said the same thing to me earlier on in the evening," he remarked casually. "But I told him where to go. I told him that I was with the bunch first and last and all the time. That's why he hates me."

CHAPTER FORTY

While he searched desperately for an answer, Andrew found none. Then he saw the stupid, big eyes of Jeff wander from his face to the face of Scottie, and he knew that his previous advantage had been completely neutralized.

"Boys," he said, and he surveyed the restless, savage figures of Clune and la Roche, "I've come for a little plain talk. There's no more question about me leadin' the gang. None at all. I wouldn't lead you, la Roche, nor you, Clune, nor you, Scottie. There's only one man here that's clean . . . and he's Jeff Rankin."

He waited for that point to sink home; as Scottie opened his lips to strike back, he went ahead deliberately. By retaining his own calm he saw that he kept a great advantage. Rankin began fumbling at his cup; Scottie instantly filled it half full with whiskey.

"Don't drink that," said Andrew sharply. "Don't drink it, Jeff. Scottie's doin' that on purpose to get you sap-headed."

"Do what he says," said Scottie calmly. "Throw the dirty stuff away, Jeff. Do what your daddy tells you. You ain't old enough to know your own mind, are you?"

Big Jeff flushed, cast a glance of defiance that included both Andrew and Scottie, and tossed off the whiskey. It was a blow over the heart for Andrew; he had to finish his talking now, before Jeff Rankin was turned mad by the whiskey. And if he worked it well, Jeff would be on his side. The madness would fight for Andrew.

He said: "There's no more question about me being a leader for you. Personally, I'd like to have Jeff . . . not to follow me, but to be pals with me."

Jeff cleared his throat and looked about with foolish importance. Not an eye wavered to meet his glance; every look was fixed with a hungry hate upon Andrew.

"There's only one thing up between the lot of us. Do I keep Hal Dozier, or do you get him . . . to murder him? Do you fellows ride on your way free and easy, to do what you please, or do you tackle me in that room, eat my lead, and then, if you finish me, get a chance to kill a man that's nearly dead now. How does it look to you, boys? Think it over. Think sharp."

He knew while he spoke that there was one exquisitely simple way to end both his life and the life of Dozier—let them touch a match to the building and shoot him while he ran from the flames. But he could only pray that they would not see it.

"And besides, I'll do more. You think you have a claim on Dozier. I'll buy him from you. Here's half his weight in gold. Will you take the money and clear out? Or are you going to make the play at me? If you do, you'll buy whatever you get at a high price."

"You forget . . . ," put in Scottie, but Andrew interrupted.

"I don't want to hear from you, Scottie. I know you're a snake. I want to hear from Jeff Rankin. Speak up, Jeff. Everything's in your hands, and I trust you."

The giant rose from his chair. His face was white with the effect of the whiskey, and one spot of color burned in each cheek. He looked gloweringly upon his companions.

"Andy," he said, "I. . . ."

"Wait a minute," said Scottie swiftly, seeing that the scales were balancing toward a defeat.

"Let him talk. You don't have to tell him what to say," said Andrew.

"I've got a right to put our side up to him . . . for the sake of the things we've been through together. Jeff, have I?"

Jeff Rankin cleared his throat importantly. Scottie faced him; the others kept their unchanging eyes riveted upon Andrew, ready for the gun play, at the first flicker of an eyelid. The first sign of unwariness would begin and end the battle.

"Don't forget this," went on Scottie, having Jeff's attention, "Andy is workin' to keep Dozier alive. Why? Dozier's the law, isn't he? Then Andy wants to make up with the law. He wants to sneak out. He wants to turn state's evidence."

The deadly phrase shocked Jeff Rankin a pace back toward soberness. "I never thought . . . ," he began.

"You're too straight to think of it. Take another look at Lanning. Is he one of us? Has he ever been one of us? No! Look again. Dozier has hunted Lanning all over the mountain desert. Now he wants to save Dozier. Wants to risk his life for him. Wants to buy him from us. Why? Because he's turned crooked. He's turned soft. He wants to get under the wing of the law."

But Jeff Rankin swept all argument away with a movement of his big paws. "Too much talk," he said. "I want to think." His stupid, animal eyes went laboriously around the room. "I wish Allister was here," he said. "He always knew."

"For my part," said Scottie, "I can't be bought. Not me." He suddenly leaned to the big man, and, before Andrew could speak, he had said: "Jeff, you know why I want to get Dozier. Because he ran down my brother. Curse him, and curse him again. And are you going to let him go clear, Jeff? Are you going to have Allister haunt you?"

It was the decisive stroke. The big head of Jeff twitched back, he opened his lips to speak—and in that moment, knowing that the battle was over and lost to him, Andrew, who had moved back, made one leap and was through the door and into the little shed again. The gun had gleamed in the hand of Larry la

Roche as he sprang, but Andrew had been too quick for the outlaw to plant his shot.

He heard Jeff Rankin still speaking: "I dunno, quite. But I see you're right, Scottie. They ain't any reason for Lanning to be so chummy with Dozier. And so they must be somethin' crooked about it. Boys, I'm with you to the limit. Go as far as you like. I'm behind you."

No room for argument now, and the blind, animal hate that Scottie and la Roche and Clune felt for Dozier was sure to drive them to extremities. Andrew sat in the dark, hurriedly going over his rifle and his revolver. Once he was about to throw open the door and try the effect of a surprise attack. He might plant two shots before there was a return; he let the idea slip away from him. There would remain two more, and one of them was certain to kill him.

Moving across the room, he heard a whisper from the floor: "I've heard them, Lanning. Don't be a fool. Give me up to 'em."

He made no answer. In the other room the voices were no longer restrained; Jeff Rankin's in particular boomed and rang and filled the shed. Once bent on action he was all for the attack; whiskey had removed the last human scruple. And Andrew heard them openly cast their ballots for a new leader; heard Scottie acclaimed; heard the Scotsman say: "Boys, I'm going to show you a way to clean up on Dozier and Lanning without any man risking a single shot from him in return."

They clamored for the suggestion, but he told them that he was first going out into the open to think it over. In the meantime, they had nothing to fear. Sit fast and have another drink around. He had to be alone to figure it out.

It was very plain. The wily rascal would let them go one step farther toward an insanity of drink, and then, his own brain cold and collected, he would come back to turn the shack into a shambles. He had said he could do it without risk to them. There was only one possible meaning; he intended to use fire.

Andrew sat with the butt of his rifle ground into his forehead. It was still easy to escape; the insistent whisper from the floor was pointing out the way.

"Beat it out that back window, lad. Slope, Andy, they's no use. You can't help me. They mean fire . . . they'll pot you like a pig, from the dark. Give me up."

It was the advice to use the window that decided Andrew. It was a wild chance indeed, this leaving of Dozier helpless on the floor, but he risked it. He whispered to the marshal that he would return, and slipped through the window. He was not halfway around the house before he heard a voice that chilled him with horror. It was the marshal calling to them that Andrew was gone and inviting them in to finish him. But they suspected, naturally enough, that the invitation was a trap and they contented themselves with abusing him for thinking them such fools.

Andrew went on; fifty feet from the house and just aside from the shaft of light that fell from the open door stood Scottie. His head was bare, his face was turned up to catch the wind, and no doubt he was dreaming of the future that lay before him as the new captain of Allister's band. The whisper of Andrew behind him cut his dream short. He whirled to receive the muzzle of a revolver in his stomach. His hands went up, and he stood gasping faintly in the moonlight.

"I've got you, Scottie," he said, "and, so help me heaven, you're the first man that I've wanted to kill."

It would have taken a man of super-nerve to outface that situation. And the nerve of Scottie cracked.

He began to whisper with a horrible break and sob in his breath: "Andy . . . Andy, gimme a chance. I'm not fit to go . . . this way. Andy, remember. . . ."

"I'm going to give you a chance. You're pretty low, Scottie . . . I check what you've done, to the way you hate Dozier, and I won't hold a grudge. And I'll tell you the chance you've got. You see these rocks, here? I'm goin' to lie down behind them. I'm going to keep you covered with my rifle. Scottie, did you ever see me shoot with a rifle?"

Scottie shuddered—a very sufficient reply.

"I'm going to keep you covered. Then you'll turn around and walk straight back to the shack. You'll stand there . . . always in clean sight of the doorway . . . and you'll persuade that crowd of drunks to leave the house and ride away with you. Understand, when you get inside the house, there'll be a big temptation to jump to one side and get behind the wall . . . just one twitch of your muscles, and you'd be safe. But, fast as you could move, Scottie, powder drives lead a lot faster. And I'll have you centered every minute. You'll make a pretty little target against the light, besides. You understand? The moment you even start to move fast, I pull the trigger. Remember it, Scottie. For as sure as there's a hell, I'll send you into it head-first, if you don't."

"So help me," said Scottie, "I'll do what I can. I think I can talk 'em into it. But if I don't?"

"If you don't, you're dead. That's short, and that's sweet. Keep it in your head. Go back and tell them it would take too great a risk to try to fix me.

"And there's another thing to remember. If you should be able to get behind the wall without being shot, you're not safe. Not by a long way, Scottie. I'd still be alive. And, though you'd have Hal Dozier there to cut up as you please, I'd be here outside the cabin watching it . . . with my rifle. And I'd tag some of you when you tried to get out. And if I didn't get you all, I'd start on your trail. Scottie, you fellows, even when you had Allister to lead you, couldn't get off scotfree from Dozier.

Scottie, I give you my solemn word of honor, you'll find me a harder man to get free from than Hal Dozier.

"Here's the last thing. . . . If you do what I tell you . . . if you get that crowd of drunken brutes out of the cabin and away without harming Dozier, I'll wipe out the score between us. No matter what you told the rest of them, you know I've never broken a promise, and that I never shall."

He stopped and, stepping back to the rocks, sank slowly down behind them. Only the muzzle of his rifle showed no more than the glint of a tiny bit of quartz; his left hand was raised, and, at its gesture, Scottie turned and walked slowly toward the cabin doorway. Once, stumbling over something, he reeled almost out of the shaft of light, but stopped on the edge of safety with a terrible trembling. There he stood for a moment, and Andrew knew that he was gathering his nerve. He went on; he stood in the doorway, leaning with one arm against it.

What followed Andrew could not hear, except an occasional roar from Rankin. Once Larry la Roche came and stood before the new leader, gesturing frantically, and the ring of his voice came clearly to Andrew. The Scotsman negligently stood to one side; the way between Andrew and Larry was cleared, and Andrew could not help smiling at the fiendish malevolence of Scottie. But he was apparently able to convince even Larry la Roche by means of words. At length there was a bustling in the cabin, a loud confusion, and finally the whole troop went out. Somebody brought Scottie his saddle; Jeff Rankin came out reeling.

But Scottie stirred last from the doorway; there he stood in the shaft of light until someone, cursing, brought him his horse. He mounted it in full view. Then the cavalcade started down the ravine.

Certainly it was not an auspicious beginning for Scottie Macdougal.

CHAPTER FORTY-ONE

The first ten days of the following time were the hardest; it was during that period that Scottie and the rest were most apt to return and make a backstroke at Dozier and Andrew. For Andrew knew well enough that this was the argument—the promise of a surprise attack—with which Scottie had lured his men away from the shack.

During that ten days, and later, he adopted a systematic plan of work. During the nights he paid two visits to the sick man. On one occasion he dressed the wound; on the next he did the cooking and put food and water beside the marshal, to last him through the day.

After that he went out and took up his post. As a rule he waited on the top of the hill in the clump of pines. From this position he commanded with his rifle the sweep of hillside all around the cabin. The greatest time of danger for Dozier was when Andrew had to scout through the adjacent hills for food— their supply of meat ran out on the fourth day.

But the ten days passed, and, after that, in spite of the poor care he had received—or perhaps aided by the absolute quiet— the marshal's iron constitution asserted itself more and more strongly. He began to mend rapidly. Eventually he could sit up, and, when that time came, the great period of anxiety was over. For Dozier could sit with his rifle across his knees, or, leaning against the chair that Andrew had improvised, command a fairly good look-out.

Only once—it was at the close of the fourth week—did Andrew find suspicious signs in the vicinity of the cabin—the telltale trampling on a place where four horses had milled in an impatient circle. But no doubt the gang had thought caution to be the better part of hate. They remembered the rifle of Andrew and had gone on without making a sign. Afterward Andrew learned why they had not returned sooner. Three hours after they left the shack a posse had picked them up in the moonlight, and there had followed a forty-mile chase.

But all through the time until the marshal could actually stand and walk, and finally sit his saddle with little danger of injuring the wound, Andrew, knowing nothing of what took place outside, was ceaselessly on the watch. Literally, during all that period, he never closed his eyes for more than a few minutes of solid sleep. And, before the danger line had been crossed, he was worn to a shadow. When he turned his head, the cords leaped out on his neck. His eyes were buried in his head by the long vigil, and his mouth had that look, at once savage and nervous, that goes always with the hunted man.

And it was not until he was himself convinced that Dozier could take care of himself, that he wrapped himself in his blankets and fell into a twenty-hour sleep. He awoke finally with a start, out of a dream in which he had found himself, in imagination, wakened by Scottie stooping over him. He had reached for his revolver at his side, in the dream, and had found nothing. Now, waking, his hand was working nervously across the floor of the shack. That part of the dream was come true, but, instead of Scottie leaning over him, it was the marshal, who sat in his chair with his rifle across his knees. Andrew sat up. His weapons had been indeed removed, and the marshal was looking at him with beady eyes.

"Have you seen 'em?" asked Andrew. "Have the boys shown themselves?"

He started to get up, but the marshal's crisp voice cut in on him. "Sit down there."

There had been—was it possible to believe it—a motion of the gun in the hands of the marshal to point this last remark.

"Partner," said Andrew, stunned, "what are you drivin' at?"

"I've been thinking," said Hal Dozier. "You sit tight till I tell you what about."

"It's just driftin' into my head, sort of misty," murmured Andrew, "that you've been thinkin' about double-crossin' me."

"Suppose," said the marshal, "I was to ride into Martindale with you in front of me. That'd make a pretty good picture, Andy. Allister dead, and you taken alive. Not to speak of ten thousand dollars as a background. That would sort of round off my work. I could retire and live happy ever after, eh?"

Andrew peered into the grim face of the older man; there was not a flicker of a smile in it. "Go on," he said, "but think twice, Hal. If I was you, I'd think ten times."

The marshal met those terrible, blazing eyes without a quiver of his own. "I began with thinking about that picture," he said. "Later on I had some other thoughts . . . about you. Andy, d'you see that you don't fit around here? You're neither a man-killer nor a law-abidin' citizen. You wouldn't fit in Martindale any more, and you certainly won't fit with any gang of crooks that ever wore guns. Look at the way you split with Allister's outfit. Same thing would happen again. So, as far as I can see, it doesn't make much difference whether I trot you into town and collect the ten thousand, or whether some of the crooks who hate you run you down . . . or some posse corners you one of these days and does its job. How do you see it?"

Andrew said nothing, but his face spoke for him.

"How d'you see the future yourself?" said the marshal. His voice changed suddenly: "Talk to me, Andy."

Andrew looked carefully at him, then he spoke. "I'll tell you short and quick, Hal. I want action. That's all. I want something to keep my mind and my hands busy. Doing nothing is the thing I'm afraid of."

"I gather you're not very happy, Andy?"

Lanning smiled, and it was not a pleasant smile to see. "I'm empty, Hal," he answered. "Does that answer you? The crooks are against me, the law is against me. Well, they'll work together to keep me busy. I don't want any man's help. I'm a bad man, Hal. I know it. I don't deny it. I don't ask any quarter."

It was rather a desperate speech—rather a boyish one. At any rate the marshal smiled, and a curious flush came in Andrew's face.

"Will you let me tell you a story, Andrew? It's a story about yourself." He went on: "You were a kid in Martindale. Husky, good-natured, a little sleepy, with touchy nerves, not very confident in yourself. I've known other kids like you, but none just the same type. You weren't waked up. You see? The pinch was bound to come in a town where every man wore his gun. You were bound to face a showdown. There were equal chances. Either you'd back down and take water from somebody, or else you'd give the man a beating. If the first thing happened, you'd have been a coward the rest of your life. But the other thing was what happened, and it gave you a touch of the iron that a man needs in his blood. Iron dust, Andy, iron dust.

"You had bad luck, you think. I tell you that you were bound to fall out with the law, because you were too strong, too touchy . . . and too quick with a gun. You had too much of the stuff that explodes. Also, you had a lot of imagination. You thought you'd killed a man . . . it made you think you were a born murderer. You began to look back to the old stories about the Lannings . . . a wild crew of men. You thought that blood was what was a-showing in you. Partly you were right, partly you were wrong. There was a new strength in you. You thought it was the strength of a desperado. Do you know what the change was? It was the change from boyhood to manhood. That was all . . . a sort of chemical change, Andy.

"See what happened. You had your first fight and you saw your first girl, all about the same time. But here's what puzzles me . . . according to the way I figure it, you must have seen the girl first. But it seems that you didn't. Will you tell me?"

"We won't talk about the girl," said Andrew in a heavy voice.

"Tut, tut. Won't we? Boy, we're going to do more talking about her than about anything else. Well, anyway, you saw the girl, fell in love with her, went away. Met up with a posse that my brother happened to lead. Killed your man. Went on. Rode like the wind. Went through about a hundred adventures in as many days. And little by little you were fixing in your ways. You were changing from boyhood into manhood, and you were changing without any authority over you. Most youngsters have their fathers over them when that change comes. All of 'em have the law. But you didn't have either. And the result was that you changed from a boy into a man, and a free man. You hear me? You found that you could do what you wanted to do . . . nothing could hold you back except one thing . . . the girl."

Andrew caught his breath, but the marshal would not let him speak.

"I've seen other free men . . . most people called them desperadoes. What's a desperado in the real sense? A man who won't submit to the law. That's all he is. But because he won't submit, he usually runs foul of other men. He kills one. Then he kills another. Finally he gets the blood lust. Well, Andy, that's what you never got. You killed one man . . . he brought it on himself. But look back over the rest of your career. Most people think you've killed twenty. That's because they've heard a pack of lies. You're a desperado . . . a free man . . . but you're not a man-killer. And there's the whole point.

"And this was what turned you loose as a criminal . . . you thought the girl had cut loose from you. Otherwise to this day you'd have been trying to get away across the mountains and be a good quiet member of society. But you thought the girl had cut loose from you, and it hurt you. Man-killer? *Bah!* You're simply lovesick, my boy."

"Talk slow," whispered Andrew. "My . . . my head's whirling."

"It'll whirl more, pretty soon. Andy, do you know that the girl never married Charles Merchant?"

There was a wild yell; Andrew was stopped in mid-air by a rifle thrust into his stomach.

"She broke off her engagement. She came to me because she knew I was running the manhunt. She begged me to let you have a chance. She tried to buy me. She told me everything that had gone between you. Andy, she put her head on my desk and cried while she was begging for you."

"Stop," whispered Andrew.

"But I wouldn't lay off your trail, Andy. Why? Because I'm as proud as a devil. I'd started to get you and I'd lost Gray Peter trying. And even after you saved me from Allister's men, I was still figuring how I could get you. And then, little by little, I saw that the girl had seen the truth. You weren't really a crook. You weren't really a man-killer. You were simply a kid that turned into a man in a day . . . and turned into a free man. You were too strong for the law.

"Now, Andrew, here's my point. As long as you stay here in the mountain desert you've no chance. You'll be among men who know you. Even if the governor pardons you . . . as he might do if a certain deputy marshal were to start pulling strings . . . you'd run someday into a man who had an old grudge against you, and there'd be another explosion. Because there's nitroglycerin inside you, son.

"Well, the thing for you to do is to get where men don't wear guns. The thing for you to do is to find a girl you love a lot more than you do your freedom, even. If that's possible. . . ."

"Where is she?" broke in Andy. "Hal, for pity's sake, tell me where she is."

"I've got her address all written out. She forgot nothing. She left it with me, she said, so she could keep in touch with me."

"It's no good," said Andy suddenly. "I could never get through the mountains. People know me too well. They know Sally too well."

"Of course they do. So you're not going to go with Sally. You're not going to ride a horse. You're going in another way. Everybody's seen your picture. But who'd recognize the dashing young man-killer, the original wild Andrew Lanning in the shape of a greasy, dirty tramp, with a ten-days'-old beard on his face . . . with a dirty felt hat pulled over one eye . . . and riding the brake beams on the way East? And before you got off the beams, Andrew, the governor of this state will have signed a pardon for you. Well, lad, what do you say?"

But Andrew, walking like one dazed, had crossed the room slowly. The marshal saw him go across to the place where Sally stood; she met him halfway, and, in her impudent way, tipped his hat half off his head with a toss of her nose. He put his arm around her neck and they walked slowly off together.

"Well," said Hal Dozier faintly, "what can you do with a man who don't know how to choose between a horse and a girl?"

ACKNOWLEDGMENTS

"Iron Dust" by George Owen Baxter first appeared as an eight-part serial in Street & Smith's *Western Story Magazine* (1/29/21–3/19/21). Copyright © 1921 by Street & Smith Publications, Inc. Copyright © renewed 1948 by Dorothy Faust. Copyright © 2010 by Golden West Literary Agency for restored material. Acknowledgment is made to Condé Nast Publications, Inc., for their co-operation.

ABOUT THE AUTHOR

Max Brand is the best-known pen name of Frederick Faust, creator of Dr. Kildare, Destry, and many other fictional characters popular with readers and viewers worldwide. Faust wrote for a variety of audiences in many genres. His enormous output, totaling approximately thirty million words or the equivalent of five hundred thirty ordinary books, covered nearly every field: crime, fantasy, historical romance, espionage, Westerns, science fiction, adventure, animal stories, love, war, and fashionable society, big business and big medicine. Eighty motion pictures have been based on his work along with many radio and television programs. For good measure he also published four volumes of poetry. Perhaps no other author has reached more people in more different ways.

Born in Seattle in 1892, orphaned early, Faust grew up in the rural San Joaquin Valley of California. At Berkeley he became a student rebel and one-man literary movement, contributing prodigiously to all campus publications. Denied a degree because of unconventional conduct, he embarked on a series of adventures culminating in New York City where, after a period of near starvation, he received simultaneous recognition as a serious poet and successful author of fiction. Later, he traveled widely, making his home in New York, then in Florence, and finally in Los Angeles.

Once the United States entered the Second World War, Faust abandoned his lucrative writing career and his work as a screenwriter to serve as a war correspondent with the infantry in Italy, despite his fifty-one years and a bad heart. He was killed during a night attack on a hilltop village held by the German army. New books based on magazine serials or unpublished manuscripts or restored versions continue to appear so that, alive or dead, he has averaged a new book every four months for seventy-five years. Beyond this, some work by him is newly reprinted every week of every year in one or another format somewhere in the world. A great deal more about this author and his work can be found in *The Max Brand Companion* (Greenwood Press, 1997) edited by Jon Tuska and Vicki Piekarski. His Website is www.MaxBrandOnline.com. His next Five Star Western will be *The Black Muldoon*.